To
Chris
Hope you
My book.

Carl P. Welborn
6 - 7 - 97

MW00723318

The Loves of Ivy

The Loves of Ivy

Carl R. Williams

Rutledge Books, Inc. Bethel, CT

Copyright© 1996 by Carl R. Williams

ALL RIGHTS RESERVED
Rutledge Books, Inc.
8 F.J. Clarke Circle, Bethel, CT 06801

Manufactured in the United States of America

Cataloging in Publication Data
    Williams, Carl R.
        The loves of Ivy/ Carl R. Williams.
          p. cm.
        ISBN 1-887750-27-4
        1. United States--History--Civil War, 1861-
1865--Fiction. 2. Missouri--History--Fiction.
I. Title.
813.54--dc20   96-69981
                              CIP

∾ *Dedication* ∾

A special thanks to Josh French, Eddie Pierce,
and Amy Wright for all their help.
To my dear mother who tried to teach me right from wrong.
To my loving daughter, Vickie who said she would never
stop sitting on my lap.

~ Preface ~

As I tried to cover the inevitable life through death of the Paty family, their ups and downs made me really feel a kinship. Their first home in Missouri was less than three miles from where I was born and raised. I knew all of them well with the exception of Buck.

There are many truths in the book and many falsehoods. It was based on fact, and most things could very easily have happened the way I depicted them. Either way, it would be nearly impossible to prove or disprove.

This real-life scenario was very interesting to me. The excitement, suspense, love, and the lifestyles—from the beginning, through the difficult times, to the exhilarating end—were unique and could probably never happen again.

∽ ONE ∽

I t was October and the mornings of North Louisiana were
beginning to become a little cool.
     Buck Paty owned a small farm, or plantation, some called it.
He had eighty acres, all of which was good, cultivatable soil.

It was all that he and his two slaves, Bill Coleman and John
French could do to care for it. They could plant the crops—
which consisted mostly of cotton—but in the fall, if they had had
enough rain, they would need help picking the cotton, gathering
the corn, and canning the vegetables and fruit from the garden.

Buck's wife, Ethel, died in the spring in an emaciated condition. She left Buck with a twelve-year-old daughter, Lucy,
and a fourteen-year-old son, Clay. Ethel had been a hard worker, a good wife, and a loving mother. She kept their two-story
colonial home spotless and delightfully decorated. She simply
worked too hard and allowed her own welfare to go without
care. She had been losing weight for some time. In addition to
the work, she worried about Bill and John whom she treated
like her own. She taught them both to read and tried to spend
time with them after their bath and supper, along with Lucy
and Clay. While she taught Lucy social graces, she supplied
Clay with books about photography. She explained work
ethics and how to manage a farm and home, along with personal business and hygiene to Bill and John.

After Ethel died, Buck lost all interest in the plantation and
life in general.

Bill and John saw to it that the crops were harvested and

sold. Lucy and Clay tried to cheer up their father but nothing seemed to help. Buck only sat on the front porch with his feet propped upon the rails smoking cigars and sipping cold drinks. He always had a faraway look on his face and sometimes had to be shaken to get his attention. It was becoming a major effort for him to get out of bed and get dressed each day. His condition deteriorated all winter. Clay and Lucy had to help Bill and John with the chores in addition to caring for their father.

The Civil War was raging by now and this was constantly on all of their minds, especially Bill and John.

Lucy, Clay, Bill, and John sat in the big family room in front of the fireplace each night and talked. They all knew that something had to be done but no one made a suggestion.

Buck was still spending most of his time on the front porch, weather permitting. He only came in when it became too dark, when it was too cold, or when rain was blowing on him. His only conversation to the four was very matter-of-fact, pertaining to the day's business, or a polite "good night" as he made his way up the stairs to his bed. His behavior was the same all fall and winter. When winter began to give way to spring, they all knew that something had to be done before crop-planting time. When they sat in front of the fire each night, they longed to hear his usual, "time to go to bed kids," but no orders had been heard in a long time.

One evening in late March Clay said, "Something's got to be done, and soon. We must talk to Dad and see what we can work out." They all agreed and decided that Clay should be the one to bring up the subject. They planned a big meal one night, and prepared all of the things Buck liked. Lucy explained their situation as best she knew how to their nearest neighbor, Mrs. Sarah, as she called her.

Sarah, as well as the whole community, was aware of the situation. In fact, it was the gossip of all the women whose husbands had volunteered to fight for their way of life.

Sarah volunteered to help prepare the meal and slipped in the back door so Buck would not suspect anything and would think Lucy and Clay had prepared it.

That night, the table was spread with the finest linens. The silver was polished. Everything looked elegant and delicious. Extra candles were placed in the room.

Clay went to the front porch when everything was ready and insisted that Buck come to dinner.

Clay had shaken his father three times before he roused him. He rubbed his eyes with the knuckles of both hands, stretched his legs, pointed his toes, and rolled his ankles before he stretched both arms upward. He then turned to Clay and said, "I think I have slept long enough, don't you? Spring is here and we must do something."

Clay could hardly believe his ears, and he was further shocked when Buck stood up and placed his arms around his neck as he said, "Come on, son, it's time to get with it."

Clay leaned on his father with his left arm around his waist while taking a skip step to be in rhythm with his father as they walked to the dining room. When they entered the room, Buck stopped as he noticed all the extra candles on the table as well as around the wall. He also noticed all of the food.

Clay released his hold on his father and pulled back the big arm chair with all the fancy needle work. Buck took his usual place at the head of the table as he nodded to Lucy, Bill, and John, gesturing for them to be seated.

Everything was already on the table including the drinks and desserts. As soon as everyone was seated, Buck reached his hands to opposite sides of the table so they could all join to make a big circle. The circle being complete, Buck just sat and stared at the four of them for a few moments before he closed his eyes and said, "Ethel trained you well, I feel her presence here now. Forgive me for taking so long to say good-bye to her and to realize life must go on. I miss her so very much. God grant me the wisdom to make the decisions that will be the best for all of us. Lucy, Clay, Bill, and John, I love each of you. Bless this food and be our guide as we decide the course we must take. Amen."

When they dropped hands, the four came with tears in their eyes to the head of the table to give Buck a big hug to let him know how happy they were that he was back. When they had each returned to their respective places, Buck said, "After the table has been cleared and the baths have been taken, I would like to see all of you in the family room. Lucy will clear the table; Bill, you wash the dishes. John, dry them and Clay, you will sweep and clean up. Thanks for being patient with me. Now start the chicken to your left followed by the potatoes, gravy, bread, and then the vegetables. Lucy, did you make the apple pie? It sure looks good."

Buck had lost twenty pounds since Ethel had died. This was the first time that he had showed a sincere interest in food. Tonight he ate with gusto and these were the first orders he had given since her death. Needless to say, this made all four of them very happy.

After everyone had eaten their fill and chores were finished, Buck strolled through the dining room and kitchen to inspect—to see if his orders were carried out.

Buck then went to the family room, built a large fire in the fireplace, and arranged five chairs in a horseshoe shape with himself at the toe, Bill and John on his left, and Clay and Lucy at his right.

It wasn't long before baths were finished and all four appeared in their night clothes, each taking the seat Buck assigned.

Many things were going through their heads but they were all very happy to have a leader again.

Buck took his seat and asked them to bow their heads. "Now each of you take a few moments of silent communion with your soul. Ask Ethel what we should do, then consult God. When you think you have a decision, raise your head."

It wasn't long before all heads were raised and they were all staring at Buck.

"Now, one at a time I will ask you for your decision. Ladies first. Lucy, did you reach a decision as to what we should do?"

"Yes, Father. Mother and God both said I should follow you. Whatever you decide, I should do, and that's good enough for me. She also said it was time for you to quit grieving."

Bill spoke up without being asked and said, "They both

told me the same thing."

"Clay, what about you?"

"Mother said she would like for me to continue studying photography, but that I should do whatever you ask."

"How about you, John?" Buck asked.

"They both told me to listen to you; that you would know best. I am now twenty-three years old and I haven't seen my parents in ten years. I would like to see them as soon as possible, but I don't know where they are."

"I never told you, John, but before we leave Louisiana, I'll tell your parents where to find you when it is safe for them to come. Right will prevail in this war and it is right that no man should be a slave. Bill just nodded his head in agreement.

"I really don't know how long the South can hold out. The North has the most factories, railroads, money, and men. All that the South has is a will to fight and they are fighting on home soil. I just wish that it could be settled by a more peaceful means.

"All of you have had a chance to express your opinions and it looks like it is my decision to make. I have given this a lot of serious thought and here is what I plan for us to do.

"First, I will make it known in the community that I am back in charge of my faculties. I will join the Confederate Army with plans to report for duty in two months. In the meantime, we will sell most everything we own, including the house, its contents, and the plantation. We will keep a team of mules and our best wagon. We will also keep our best buggy and two horses, one to ride and one to pull the buggy. We will build a false bottom in both the wagon and the buggy. You will see the reason later. This is to be our secret.

"I want to travel north to Missouri where we will be on the border of the North and South. I'll try to find a place for Bill and John where they will be safe until after the war. My biggest concern is what to do with Lucy and Clay."

Lucy quickly spoke up saying, "We want to go with you, Father."

"I don't like the idea of taking you into the war with me,"

Buck Paty before the War with the same pistol that he carried during the War.

Buck said. "I wish it was possible but see no way."

"I'm twelve now and I know how to handle a rifle. I could help feed and care for the wounded," Lucy chimed in.

"We'll have to talk about this later," Buck said, "We have a few months to pack and decide what to take with us."

The two months passed in a hurry. Buck enlisted and received his uniform and sword. They all thought that he looked handsome in his uniform. Both Clay and Lucy were proud of their dad.

The farm and all possessions were sold at a public auction. All, that is, except for what they decided to keep and take with them.

They rebuilt both the wagon and the buggy. Both had false bottoms with a six-inch storage space between the two. In a secret spot in the buggy, they sealed all the money they had along with the family silver and jewelry. A six by six inch box the width of the buggy was built in front between the floors, to hide their money. Behind the box they stored all of the food staples they had.

Between the false floors in the wagon, they stored more food and tools, along with special quilts and fancy needlework that Ethel had made. Having completed the hidden compartments and filling them with their valuables and necessities, they were ready. They planned to start north on the second of June.

Bill and John would drive the team of mules that was pulling the wagon loaded with furniture and the food for both them and the animals. Buck would drive the buggy which held some food but contained mostly bedding. They also brought a fairly large canvas tent to pitch if the weather was bad and demanded they stop for a while.

The morning of the second arrived too soon. No one was completely ready. They all thought of something to stick in a cranny that was not yet filled. Buck found his compass which he hung on a string around his neck.

They all gathered at Ethel's grave with a flower for her and to say good-bye. Buck turned back as they walked away and said, "We'll be back for you as soon as we are settled."

The day began cloudy and threatening rain but soon gave way to sunshine—a beautiful spring day.

They never thought that this would be the last time they would ever see Ethel's grave.

With mixed emotions and eager anticipation, they were anxious to move on to the next phase of their lives.

Tears were streaming down both of Lucy's cheeks. Clay placed his right arm around her neck as he pulled a big red handkerchief from his pocket and began wiping them away without saying a word.

As they rounded the corner of the house removing the grave from view, Lucy turned and said, "Mother, I love you and I'll be good."

She grabbed Clay's red handkerchief and cleaned her face while sucking hard through her nose.

∽ TWO ∽

Buck mounted the big sorrel mare and gave them the "head 'em out" sign while Clay drove the buggy and John slapped the mules with the long, heavy leather reins and yelled, "Gitty up you lazy old farts!"

They headed north out of Winnsboro up a trail along the bank of Bayou Macon. The second day, they left Louisiana and crossed the border into Arkansas. There was no one on the trail and everything was peaceful and pleasant. The foliage was a lush green and the bayou was becoming smaller the further north they went. They could hear the Mississippi late at night when everything was quiet.

The next morning, Buck decided to veer northwest away from the big river which was used for transportation of troops and supplies.

It wasn't long before they came to the Arkansas River which was flowing from the direction they wanted to travel. The third day they came to a small settlement called Little Rock. There, they took a ferry across the river and headed north through the Ozark hills where there were many clean streams among the big rocks and beautiful pine trees. This was the first time they saw all this. It was very different from where they had come. There the streams were muddy and the trees were hanging full of Spanish Moss.

Buck was very impressed with the valleys on both sides of the clear streams. The fields were much smaller but they were fertile. He would have liked to find a place to settle but no one lived here. Besides, he wanted to settle in Missouri. So far there had been no scarcity of food or water for the horses and mules. Each night they would water them, then tie them together on a long rope so they could graze on wild grass. Thus far they had no major problems. Only once had they heard gunfire.

Buck prayed that they would make it to Missouri without any conflicts, however, the following morning, they did see fresh tracks of both horse and man along the trail they were following.

They had only traveled a few hours that morning when two Confederate soldiers jumped from behind the trees with their rifles pointed at them. They yelled, "Halt, and identify yourself!"

Buck was in his new uniform and explained to them how he was looking for a place to settle his family before he was to report for duty.

While one soldier held a gun on them, the other began to look through boxes, raise the canvas, and jerk the lids from containers.

Bill and John jumped down from the wagon and ran to where Buck was still sitting astride his horse.

Buck said to them, "Get your black asses back where they belong! Who told you to come up here?"

They looked at each other with an astonished expression but soon realized that Buck was under pressure.

The soldier holding the gun on them asked, "Who are they and where are you taking them?"

"They belong to me and I am taking them to work for my family in Missouri while I am in the Confederate Army." Buck pulled his enlistment papers from his coat pocket and extended them toward his captor who took them and looked at them for a while before he asked, "What do they say?"

The soldier who had been inspecting the wagon and buggy returned with an open can of peaches from which he had been eating. He took one more peach and handed the remaining to his buddy. "They sure got a lot of good things to eat," he commented.

His buddy took the peaches and handed him the papers. "Here," he said, "can you read this?"

"Sure, I can read. My mamma didn't raise any fools. It says, 'Buck Paty is to report for duty in the Confederate Army in two months.' It is dated May tenth."

"What day is today?" asked the other soldier.

Both shrugged their shoulders and looked at Buck for an answer.

Buck replied, "Today is June fourteenth. I have a little less than a month before I have to report. Now, may we go?"

"Hold on. We are here to protect the rear of an advancing regiment. We don't have any food but it looks like you have plenty. Would you rather share it with us or a whole regiment? I know we may slow you down, but think about it."

"Looks like you have us between a rock and a hard place. What time do you want your meals?" Buck asked disgustedly but could see their point.

"We want one now! Them peaches was the first food we had in two days except for some berries and some of them made us sick," one of the soldiers said. "By the way, my name is Seth and his is Leonard," he offered in a much more docile voice.

"I can read," Leonard broke in.

Leonard was the shorter of the two. He had long, blond hair and a spark of intelligence in his eyes. It was obvious that he came from a decent family. Both his clothes and his skin looked fairly clean.

Seth, on the other hand, had dark, black hair with pock marked, dirty skin. His eyebrows joined in the middle with a brush pile look. He was tall and thin. His shoes were badly in need of some oil and some new heels and soles. The heels were twice as thick on the outside as on the inside, indicating that he was probably pigeon-toed. His front teeth were black and badly rotted. The only attractive thing about him were his pale blue eyes, but even they lacked luster.

His only pride seemed to be his rifle which was clean and still pointed at Buck. This gave him a feeling of power and importance.

Leonard finally noticed the rifle and told him, "Lower your gun, Seth, they ain't the enemy. The enemy will be wearing blue."

Seth lowered his gun and Buck introduced himself, Clay, and Lucy. He yelled, "You black asses take care of the animals and fix a meal. We will be staying here the rest of the day and also tonight. Pitch the tent too, it could rain. Get a move on unless you want to feel the leather.

"Lucy, you supervise the cooking. Fix a big meal, something good. Peel some potatoes and slice some of that smoked ham. Make plenty of coffee. You could even bake a fruit pie in the old Dutch kettle. Be sure to put lots of coals on the top. Make sure Bill and John wash and keep things clean. I had better not even suspect that they spit in the food. Watch close."

While they were preparing the food, Buck and Leonard sat on an old dead log and discussed the events of the time. Leonard came from Louisiana also. He was from the southern part of the state near New Orleans on the bank of Lake Poncetuan where alligators sometimes grew to a length of ten feet.

Leonard thought that there would be a big battle about the time they reached the Missouri border. Missouri had sided with the South but their biggest concern were the bushwhackers and the Kansas Jayhawks. They were both taking advantage of the situation with their main objective being to line their own pockets. Many of them were becoming very rich, sometimes robbing several farms and people each day while burning and hanging all resisters.

The next morning, they could hear guns firing to the north. Buck told Leonard to take all the food they could carry because they would be veering to the west. He wasn't yet ready to begin active duty. He must get his family settled first, he kept thinking.

Leonard understood. After filing bags with food and tying them to the saddle horn, he and Seth bid them good-bye and they parted ways.

Three days later, Buck arrived at a small settlement called Thomasville. He liked what he saw very much. There were two small, clear streams running through the edge of town. On both sides of the streams were large, level fields of rich, sandy loam soil. It looked like the ideal place to settle. The names of the streams were the Middle Fork and the Eleven Point.

That night they camped between the streams. Buck didn't sleep much. His mind was buzzing with what he was going to do. He had come to the place where he must make big decisions.

At dawn, he was up and walking into the town while Bill and John were preparing breakfast.

The company store was open and serving hot coffee. Buck went in and found a vacant seat in the rear, close to the old potbellied wood burning stove that had kept the loafers warm the past winter. The benches hadn't yet been moved to a cooler spot near the front door.

Buck introduced himself and told the complete story. He told about Bill and John. He said, "They were both good, young men. They are educated and hard workers. I would like to find one or two families that would treat them right. As soon as the war is over, either their parents or I will be back to care for them." Buck looked the group over with a pitiful and desperate expression.

One man on the opposite side of the stove stood up and said, "Alpha Roberts would be a good one. He has three girls and could sure use the help."

"I'll go get him" an old man said as he pushed his chair back and drained the last drop of coffee from his cup. He slowly rose to his feet with a cane in one hand and the other hand on his back.

In practically no time, the old man was back with Alpha, both showing excitement.

Buck had never seen a man so tall. He estimated him to be seven feet tall as he moved his eyes from two enormous shoes to the top of a black collapsed hat.

The old man introduced Buck to Alpha and poured Alpha a cup of coffee while he refilled his own.

"How tall are you?" Buck asked as he stuck his right hand

out and upward to test his grip which didn't disappoint him.

Before he could answer, the old man butted in, "You should see his daughters. They all three are over six feet tall and beautiful. Why, the Queen of England sent somebody over to offer him a job as her personal body guard, but Julie, his wife, wouldn't give up her citizenship. I don't think Alpha would have left Thomasville anyway, but it was a great honor to have been asked."

The Company Store was owned by ten of the most affluent families in Thomasville. The store was the Wal-mart of its day. You could buy over three hundred items, groceries, soap, salt, produce, and all kinds of hardware, building, and cleaning items.

"Is that so?" Buck asked.

"Sure as hell is," the old man answered.

Alpha hung his head and shook it a little in disgust and embarrassment.

Alpha finally spoke. "I would like to meet the men but I couldn't possibly take but one of them."

"Come on, we are camped between the rivers. They should have breakfast ready by now."

Alpha didn't take long to make up his mind. He had never seen such handsome and intelligent young men. He quickly told them that he wished he could take them both but only had room for one. "I'll try to find a suitable place close by for the other," he offered. "I know old Jeff Griffith could use some help and he would treat you good. He only lives about a quarter mile from town. You would be close to each other and could visit often."

While Bill and John served breakfast, Buck asked many questions about the town.

Clay and Lucy came strolling over from their tent when they heard conversation. They were wiping sleep from their eyes as they glanced around for a place to sit while they had breakfast.

"These are my children, Clay and Lucy," Buck offered, as they both nodded their heads not having noticed how tall their guest was.

When Alpha stood up to say he would go see old Jeff about taking one of the boys, Clay almost swallowed his fork when he looked up at him. "My God!" Clay said. "How big are you?"

"I'm six foot seven inches in my sock feet. These boots make me look taller. Sometimes my feet drag the ground when I ride a short horse. I'll see you later," he said as he started to leave.

Buck stood and followed him out of hearing range of the kids. "I need to find a place for Lucy and Clay also. I have to report to the army next week. I would like to buy a farm here and settle when the war is over," Buck announced. "For some reason, I feel like I can trust you. Keep your eyes open for me." Buck stuck out his hand and gave Alpha a firm sincere handshake as he turned to go back to camp.

Alpha soon returned with old Jeff in his buggy. Jeff said "he would be happy to have a young man around the house to help him and his wife, Roushe." They were both getting old and really needed the help.

Buck explained to both Bill and John what was going to happen. Both of them wanted to go with Alpha. Buck broke straws and held two between his forefinger and his thumb. The tops were even, but you couldn't see the bottom. Buck stuck his hand out to the two and said, "The one who draws the long straw gets to go live with Alpha."

Bill drew the long straw, but John didn't seem too disappointed.

Buck gave each of them a big hug and told them to gather their belongings. He also said that he would check on them before he left for the army.

As soon as Bill and John were gone, Buck called Clay and Lucy to his side to talk to them about their situation and what he was going to do.

Clay in no uncertain terms announced to his father that he was going with him. "I'll get a camera and follow you, taking pictures to record history."

Buck looked shocked, but knew how Clay loved photography. "I really don't know what to say. We'll go down to the court house where they are enlisting and see what they say. We also need to find a place for Lucy to stay. We need to deposit some of our money and I would like to find some land to file on before I have to leave."

Lucy spoke up too. "I want to go with you, too, Papa."

"Now that is out of the question," Buck said, "That request gets a flat NO! War is no place for a young lady.

"Let's get in the money box and get out eight thousand dollars. It wouldn't do for us to let people know that we have over fifty thousand. That is a lot of money. When we find a suitable place to file a claim, we'll bury the rest of it. But nothing must be written down. We will have to remember where it is buried."

As soon as Buck had the money he wanted to deposit, he headed straight for the bank. A tall, well dressed man was behind the cage. He said, "My name is Weaver. I don't remember seeing you around here before. How may I help you?"

"We just arrived yesterday. My name is Buck Paty and these are my children, Clay and Lucy. We would like to open an account."

"I'll be glad to accommodate you," Mr. Weaver answered. "How much?"

"We would like to deposit all we have. A total of eight thousand dollars. We sold everything when we left Louisiana."

Mr. Weaver's eyes bugged out as he asked, "How do you want to deposit it?"

"I'd like two thousand in a checking account and the rest in a savings account. What does your savings account pay? We'll deposit it for one year."

"For a year we can pay you two and one half percent."

"That will be fine. May I have some checks? Also, I need to find someone to keep Lucy while I am gone to the war. I am willing to pay whatever need be for the best person."

Mr. Weaver stroked his long beard with his left hand as he made out the deposit slip.

Lucy had to tug at her father's coat to get his attention. When he finally turned to acknowledge her, she said, "I want to help you in the war. I saw the big tents on the river bank and was told that it was a field hospital for the South. I could help there. I'm twelve years old and Mama taught me a lot. I can carry them food and water, and help with their laundry."

Mr. Weaver overheard. "I'll tell you what, young lady, I bet Miss Thomas over at the hospital could use you. We have three doctors, Dr. Davis, Dr. Plummer, and Dr. Pace, but there is a shortage of gray ladies. Most of the women around here have children and jobs at home. Why don't you check with her?"

"Sounds like a good idea," Buck said as he picked up his deposit slip and some blank checks. "We'll head right on over there. Miss Thomas, you say. She'll be easy to find, you say." Buck turned and left the bank.

"I'm really big for my age and strong, too. I did a lot of work after mom died and while you were in mourning. Just look at me," Lucy said as she dropped his hand and stood as tall as possible.

This was the first time that Buck didn't see his little girl but saw a developing young lady. "I guess you are growing," he said. Clay started to laugh. Lucy picked up a handful of gravel and hurled it at him. He only turned his back and trotted on ahead.

When they reached the tents, Buck asked the first person he saw if he could see Miss Thomas.

"No telling where she is," was the reply. "She is the only nurse here today. You'll just have to look for her."

They started walking through the tents where several soldiers lay on cots. Some were missing arms and legs. Some were moaning and groaning in real pain. Some were asking for a drink or for help to go to the toilet. Soon Lucy was stopping to talk to them asking where she could get them a drink. "From the creek!" one yelled. "Didn't you see it?"

Lucy saw an old metal pitcher sitting on the floor by a cot. She picked it up and found it empty. She quickly ran to the creek and dipped it full of cool, clear water. Back in the tent she found a gourd dipper which she poured full and started making the rounds to the eight men in the tent. The bloody sheets and missing limbs, eyes, and wounds didn't seem to bother her. When she had almost made the round, a tall, black headed, middle-aged lady dressed in a gray dress covered with a white apron came into the tent.

"Who are you, and where did you come from?" she asked.

"I'm Lucy Paty and these men said they were thirsty. You would be Miss Thomas. My dad is looking for you."

"I am Miss Thomas. What does your dad want?" she answered.

"He wants to give me to you."

Miss Thomas stepped back raising the back of her right hand to her forehead and said, "Would you care to explain? I sure could use some help but can't see a father giving away such a beautiful and healthy looking little girl."

"Oh, I should explain. My mother died and my dad has to go into the army. He wants someone to keep me until he returns."

"I see," Miss Thomas said as she turned to see who was entering the tent.

"You found her first," Buck said to Lucy. "Have you been introduced?"

"I told her, Dad," Lucy said as she poured another dipper of water for the last soldier in the tent. Lucy couldn't help but notice how young he was and that one leg was missing just below the knee. She also felt the boy's eyes on her. She thought that he was quite handsome. She moved over close to his cot and placed her hand on his forehead. "My name is Lucy," she said.

Buck again explained the situation to Miss Thomas and for the first time since his wife died, he had some feelings for a woman. "My, she is beautiful," he thought.

Clay spoke up to remind his father that they still had to go to the court house to talk to the army recruiter about him.

"I know, son," Buck said, as he introduced his family again and told Miss Thomas about Bill and John and how they hoped to settle in the area when he returned. Seeing Miss Thomas made him more sure that he would like to return here.

Buck asked, "Is the town Thomasville named after you?"

"No! My father John gave ten acres to start the town. I still live at home with him and my mother Mitalda," she added. "They are getting old and need what little time I can give them. I spend most of my time here at the hospital. We have four other gray ladies who help when they can, and about Lucy, they all have families and small children so their free time is very limited. Right now, I really need help," Miss Thomas said. "I could certainly use Lucy's help and we have plenty of room at home for her. When will you be leaving?"

"Probably in about five days. I need to look for a piece of land. I hear that most around here has already been claimed."

Miss Thomas replied that her father was one of the first settlers here and if there was any available land, he would know. She lowered her chin and glanced sheepishly at Buck and asked, "Would your family like to have dinner with us tomorrow? I want you to meet the people you are leaving your daughter with."

Buck, without hesitation, said, "That is very considerate of you. Yes, we would love to come. What time would be best?" Buck asked. "They usually eat at six, but Dad would enjoy visiting with you anytime. We live in the northwest corner of town. A two-story white house is not hard to find. I hope I can be there to dine with you. You may leave Lucy here if you wish," Miss Thomas said as she turned to continue her rounds.

"May I, Dad? Please let me stay. They need me," she commented as she ran to squeeze his hand. Lucy really felt excited as she looked up smiling at her father.

Buck glanced at Miss Thomas. She was nodding her head yes and reaching her hand out to Lucy, which Lucy took, kissed, and grasped with both her hands. Looking up into her beautiful, dark eyes, Lucy said, "I just know that we are going to be great friends."

"We have work to do," Miss Thomas said as they left the tent followed by Buck and Clay.

Lucy turned to her father and said, "I'll come up and get my clothes tonight if we have time. Don't wait on me, I may be very busy," she added as an afterthought.

Buck and Clay both smiled as they headed back across the two streams toward the court house. At the court house, they asked where the recruiter was.

The court house was made out of large, white oak logs. It was a square, two-story building approximately thirty by thirty feet. There were no doors or windows on the ground floor.

After walking around the building to make sure there was no door, they climbed the stairs to the second floor and opened the door. The room was divided into four parts with a desk in the center of the room with a large braided rug under it.

At the desk was a big man, bulging in the middle, and wearing a shiny star. He looked up from his work and asked, "Can we help you?"

Buck gave a brief introduction but had already noticed the recruiter sitting in the corner straight ahead and to his left.

They walked to the corner desk where the recruiter sat. "Hello, I'm Buck Paty. I have already enlisted and will be reporting for service soon. This is my son Clay. He has been studying photography for some time. I know he is young, but he is tough. He wants to go to the front with me as a photographer. Just wondering if this would be possible?"

The recruiter leaned back in his chair and ran his fingers through his hair, scrutinizing Clay. He looked him over from head to toe before he pulled a note pad and pencil from his desk.

Clay was becoming nervous when the recruiter said, "Pull up a chair here beside my desk, young man. Anyone can learn to take pictures, but how well can you describe what you see? Here is a pencil and a pad of paper. See the picture behind me? I want you to describe what you see in it."

Clay pulled the chair up close and picked up the pencil and paper. He looked at the picture and began to write. He described it in such detail that anyone who read what he wrote could see a very vivid picture in his mind.

When the recruiter read what Clay wrote, he said in no uncertain terms, "We have a need for you, young man. We have a camera that we will furnish you and the newspaper will pay you for each picture and article they use. You, naturally, will stay behind the lines."

Clay stood up and shook the recruiter's hand before turning his attention to his father. Looking up into Buck's face, he asked, "What do you think, Dad?"

"Sounds good to me," Buck answered.

The recruiter removed the cloth cover in the corner and revealed a new camera. "All the film, fluids, paper, and the such are here—it came as a kit. It has been just sitting here, waiting for you."

Clay thanked the recruiter again as he picked up all he could carry and handed the rest to his dad. He couldn't believe he could be so lucky. His heart was beating fast with eager anticipation.

"Guess I'll have to use the buggy," Clay commented as they made their way down the stairs and back toward their camp. Clay could hardly wait to try the camera. "Can we take it to the Thomases tomorrow night and take some pictures?" Clay asked.

"I don't see any reason why not," Buck answered. Clay could hardly restrain himself, he was so happy. It seemed that all his dreams were coming true. His mind was whirling ninety miles an hour. He could hardly wait to get started.

The next day, Clay checked every minute detail. He asked his dad to pose for him. After a few shots, he developed the film, and much to his surprise, they all came out very good.

He could hardly wait to show his skills to the Thomases. The day was spent making plans about how he was going to arrange the camera in the buggy. He knew that his father would make the buggy as comfortable and handy as possible. The buggy would have a large canvas cover and a shock absorbing place for the camera. He would also have to carry food for himself and the mare that would pull it. The day passed very quickly. Soon they were ready to go to the Thomas' for dinner.

When they arrived in their buggy, Old John Thomas was outside waiting. He grabbed the mare by the halter and led her to a hitching place where there was some grass that needed mowing.

Buck introduced himself as he stepped down. He then introduced Clay and asked if it would be all right if Clay took some pictures. "Sure would," Mr. Thomas replied. "We never have enough pictures. Come on in and make yourself at home. Matilda is inside, she will help you."

Buck continued to tell the whole story as Mr. Thomas led the way to the front porch. The sun was setting behind Rich Hill, upstream from where Mr. Thomas built his house. The sun set beautifully among a few cumulus clouds. The frogs, birds, katydids, and many other minor sounding insects were all members of the loud orchestra playing their final good night to Old Sol as he showed his gratitude with long, bright spikes reaching upward through the clouds.

"Care for a glass of wine before dinner?" Mr. Thomas asked.

"That would be great," Buck answered, as he sat and looked around at the scenery. He was thinking how good it would be if there was no war.

John's wife, Matilda, came to the porch and introduced herself to Buck just as Clay was coming up to the steps carrying the camera tripod.

"This is Clay, Dear," John offered. "He will be taking pictures this evening."

"Oh, great," Matilda said as she led Clay through the front

door and into the large dining room.

The table was already set and the meal prepared. "Set up your camera wherever you like. The head of the table is next to the kitchen and your father will be to John's right. Move anything that is in the way."

"Thank you, Mrs. Thomas," Clay said as he was deciding where best to place the camera. He finally decided on the foot of the table facing Mr. Thomas and his father. He assumed that Mrs. Thomas, her daughter, and Lucy would also be seated near the head of the table.

It wasn't long before Mrs. Thomas announced that they must eat. Delia and Lucy suddenly came through the front door in a big hurry to wash and join them. The meal looked really good—fried chicken, mashed potatoes, and gravy with a lot of chicken crispies in it. The pan of hot rolls also looked good. The thought of the hot rolls with butter and strawberry jam made the saliva start to flow in all of their mouths. This brought fond memories to Clay of how it was before his mother died.

When Mrs. Thomas brought in a tray of glasses with ice and tea, it really made Clay take notice. Ice this time of the year was unheard of in Louisiana.

When everyone was seated and their linen napkins folded neatly in their laps, Mrs. Thomas asked, "Papa, will you ask the blessing?"

After the blessing, Clay had forgotten about the picture taking. He was too anxious to begin eating. He had hardly finished filling his plate when Buck asked, "When are you going to take pictures?"

"I'm sorry," Clay said as he took another big bite of chicken and a mouthful of potatoes and gravy. He wiped his mouth, pushed back his chair and said, "Excuse me please. The food was so good, I forgot all else."

He quickly focused the camera so everyone but himself would be in the picture. He took two shots and then asked Lucy to come and press the button so he could be in one picture.

After everyone had eaten about all they could hold, Mrs.

Thomas went to the kitchen and returned with a hot apple pie and whipped cream to go on top. It was truly a feast fit for a king.

After dinner, Buck and John retired to the front porch where John filled his pipe and offered tobacco and papers to Buck. John told Buck that most of the good land around Thomasville was taken, but about six or seven miles to the northeast was Spring Creek with some good land. None of it had been settled. John also said that he would be glad to show him some of it if he would bring the buggy by tomorrow morning. Buck said that would be kind of him and he would be there whatever time he thought best.

John said, "Come around about seven. We'll go before it gets too hot. The heat didn't use to bother me, but it does now."

Buck and Clay thanked them for the delicious dinner and said they would see them in the morning. Lucy came running out of the house and down the steps to give Buck a big hug and to tell Clay she hoped that he would enjoy his work as much as she was liking hers.

As they started to leave, Buck commented to Clay, "Your little sister is growing up fast."

"I know," Clay said, "I hope Miss Thomas explains a few facts of life to her."

"Who explained them to you?" Buck asked.

"Dad, I watched the animals and Bill and John told me a few things. Besides, I'm older than Lucy."

"Come on, son, we have to get up early tomorrow. Do you realize that we only have three more days until we have to report for duty?"

Neither one slept very well that night, even though it was cool in the valley between the two streams. There were no mosquitoes and the only sounds in the star-lit night were those made by the two streams running around, over and through many rocks. Every once in a while, the bullfrogs, with their deep, gruff voices would give their opinions.

Buck commented, "Those bullfrogs are big ones. We should go catch them and have them for breakfast."

"I'm too tired," Clay said, "Besides, I hear there are big cottonmouth snakes in those streams. Good night, Dad. I am anxious to see Spring Creek."

In no time, they were both sound asleep, adding soft snores to the other night sounds. All of them together was beautiful music. They were both dreaming of what they hoped they would find tomorrow.

The next morning was a beautiful, clear summer day. The sun was trying to burn the morning fog from the streams when Buck awoke. He reached over and gave Clay a gentle nudge. Clay kept right on sleeping, even after a pretty stiff shake. Buck then yelled, "Snake!"

Clay stood straight up in bed throwing his cover high in the air while looking down in every direction. When he saw his dad laughing, he knew what had happened. He quickly picked up his cover and threw it over Buck's head while tackling him and flattening him on the ground. He quickly locked his legs around him and started pinching him while yelling, "Snake! Snake!"

Buck didn't realize how strong his son had become. They hadn't wrestled for many years. It used to always make Ethel nervous. She would yell at them to stop it before they broke something. She was really afraid someone would get hurt.

Buck finally freed himself from the blanket and Clay staggered to his feet. "Who taught you that leg hold?" Buck asked. "I thought you were going to squeeze the shit out of me."

"Bill, John, and me used to wrestle in the hayloft of the barn a lot. They are both real strong. They would let me loose anytime I yelled 'calf rope', and I yelled it a lot."

"You get Pet and hitch her to the buggy while I hustle us up something to eat," Buck said while he relieved himself.

In no time, Clay had Pet harnessed and hitched up. He brought her over close to where Buck was removing a skillet of bacon and scrambled eggs from the fire.

∽ THREE ∽

John Thomas was sitting on the front porch with a cigar in his mouth and some plat papers in his right hand when Buck and Clay pulled up alongside the yard's picket fence.

"Let's hurry," John said as he handed Buck the papers and pulled himself up onto the front seat beside him. "Good morning, Clay," John said turning to look up at him. "And how did the pictures turn out?" John asked.

"I haven't had no time to develop them yet. This buggy is my lab you know. Maybe tomorrow."

"Let's turn right at the next street, then head north at the next intersection," John offered as he exhaled big clouds of white smoke. "I'll take those plats now. They just finished surveying the area and I have copied some of the plats where I want to show you land. The marked trees should be easy to find."

Pet seemed to sense the excitement and picked up her pace. She was probably traveling at twenty miles an hour down the dirt road.

After flushing up an old mother turkey hen and what looked like at least two dozen young ones and watching both fox and gray squirrels cross their trail over logs and up trees, Buck was becoming very pleased with Thomasville. There were few trees and practically none on the plains to the west but to the east there were large oak trees and both white and yellow pines. He had noticed several springs running from beneath rocks and ledges on the hillsides. They passed through an opening where two large and high

27

hills tapered to the ground. It was almost like going through a gate into a new world.

As soon as they passed through the opening, there were probably a hundred level acres of rich loam soil with only a few small trees growing in it.

Buck pulled back on the reins and yelled, "Whoa" to Pet. "This is it!" he said with much excitement in his voice. "Now we must find a bench mark or a surveyors' tree so we can know where to stake our claim. Check the plats to see if this place is available," Buck said with much excitement.

"Hold on, Buck," Mr. Thomas said, "This is the first big field you have seen. You haven't even seen Spring Creek yet."

"This is good enough for me," Buck said.

Mr. Thomas reached over, took the reins and said, "Get up, Pet!"

Pet started up in a slow walk as Buck looked in every direction. They soon passed a large spring that came down from the hills and crossed their trail. The water was crystal clear, with a cool fog rising from it.

"Whoa, Pet," Mr. Thomas said as he stopped her and gave her some slack in the reins so she could lower her head for a drink. Buck and Clay jumped out of the buggy and went upstream from Pet where they cupped their hands and dipped a drink.

"This is the best water I ever drank," Buck said. "Nothing like this in Louisiana. It's cold and full of minerals. God, it is good," he said as he dipped another drink.

Mr. Thomas reached into his jacket pocket and retrieved a collapsible metal cup. Tossing it to Clay, he asked, "Care to go get me a drink?"

Clay filled it and handed it up to John. "Man, that is good water. I don't think I ever tasted better. I bet it would make excellent whiskey. Here, get me another," he asked after draining that cup. John finished his second cup before collapsing it and replacing it in his pocket.

"This has got to be it!" Buck yelled as he walked over to Clay and gave him a big bear hug while lifting him off the ground and shaking him. "This is home, Son. I just wish your mother could have seen it."

"Come, get in!" John yelled. "There is more to see."

They had only gone a few yards around another hill when they saw Spring Creek. John pulled back on the reins and spoke softly to Pet, "Whoa, girl."

Buck jumped from the wagon again and walked the few steps to the creek. He leaned over to test the coolness of the water.

The sun was about half way to its zenith and beams coming through the slightly moving leaves were sparkling in the water.

Buck then turned his back to the sun to look westward in the direction from which they came. He could see the clearing and the hill that tapered down like a foot to Spring Creek. While pointing to the arch of the foot with his mind whirling he said, "We'll build our house there with the morning sun shining on our front porch and the house shaded in the evening by the hill and all of the trees. This is perfect."

"I'll agree that this is a beautiful spot and I saw a marked tree not far back. We can check our map and step off approximately where your one hundred sixty acres will lie."

Back at the tree the little square of tin nailed to it gave them explicit directions as to where their claim was located.

John pulled out an old compass from his bib pocket and handed it to Buck. "Now," he said, "Give me the grid coordinate on the tree and I will tell you how many feet in each direction you will go."

Buck gave him the information he needed. After checking John said, "Walk four hundred forty, one-yard steps due east. That will be your southeast corner. Pile up a bunch of rocks, then walk the same due north; then west; then south and it should bring you back to this tree."

Buck and Clay struck out walking and counting while John leaned back in the buggy for a nap. He had hardly gone to sleep when Pet nickered in excitement. John roused to see a big buck deer drinking in the creek, a short distance from them.

This was probably the first deer Pet had ever seen. She started backing up. John picked up the reins and spoke softly to her to settle her down. The buck then noticed her and snorted loudly while pawing the water with one foot. Pet, knowing Mr. Thomas was awake and aware, relaxed and enjoyed the show. The buck soon decided that he wasn't scaring anyone and hopped across the stream, up the hill, and among the trees.

He had hardly left when John heard a noise coming from the north. He listened as it grew closer and soon decided that it was Buck and Clay. He yelled, "Here I am!" and they answered as they made their way to the marked tree.

"How did you do?" John asked, as soon as he saw them.

"Great," Buck said. "We were almost directly on target as we came toward the tree. I couldn't be happier. A big valley surrounded by hills with lots of trees, a good creek, and several springs. I wish I didn't have to go to this damn war. I don't like it at all or what they are fighting for. Never mind. Let's go," he said as his eyes turned red and tears began to run down both cheeks. He reached skyward and asked, "Please let it end soon, dear Lord."

"Tomorrow, Clay and I will file on this one hundred sixty acres and come back to put up signs showing where the corners are. Did you see that big buck deer? It came right by us."

"Yeah. Pet and I watched it for some time," John replied.

They made it back to Thomasville before the court house closed, and decided to take John with them to file their claim that evening. Buck was very anxious to get his name on the proper papers to insure the land was his.

Filling was no problem. John showed them the spot on the newly surveyed plat map. The clerk outlined one hundred sixty acres in red and wrote Buck, Clay, and Lucy Paty's name on the plat along with the date of June 28, 1862 showing they filed on this piece of land. Everything was fine but Buck still had to go to Cape Girardeau to the National Land Office to complete the paper work and finalize the claim.

Buck told Mr. Thomas that he wanted to take Lucy with them tomorrow so she could see the place and that he would pick her up around eight A.M.

Again, Buck didn't sleep very well. Everything was going through his mind; the kind of house he would build, what kind of cattle and hogs he would raise. He really didn't want to go into the service. Although the fighting was for a cause he really didn't believe in, there was no alternative.

It seemed like he had just gone to sleep when the morning birds and the bright sunshine in his face woke him.

Clay was still asleep after Buck dressed and finished preparing some breakfast. Buck first called, then shook Clay lightly and pulled the covers over his head and fell on top of him. Buck decided that it was time to stop wrestling with his son unless he wanted to be embarrassed. Clay was becoming extremely strong and growing quickly into a young man.

When they finished their routine of getting up, they had their breakfast of bacon, eggs, and biscuits that were probably three days old. They had to soak them in their coffee in order to eat them.

Clay harnessed Pet and gave her a drink out of the Middle Fork Creek. He had her hitched to the buggy by the time Buck had the bedding and breakfast pans cleaned and stored away in the wagon.

They were ready to go pick up Lucy when they heard her yell, "Wait for me!" as she came running toward them. "I can't wait. I want to see our new home," she said as soon as she got her breath.

They all sat in the buggy seat while Pet moved along at a fast trot, seeming to sense where they were headed.

In no time, they were at their destination. Lucy thought the spring coming out of the rocks and cascading down the hill among moss was beautiful. She insisted they stop for a few moments so she could have a good look.

They drove down to Spring Creek where Buck showed her where they would build their house as soon as he returned from the war.

Again, Lucy was excited about the clear, cool water and the spot he had selected for their new home.

Buck said, "Now we need to bury the rest of our money until its time to build. Everyone look around for a good spot. We will have to remember. I don't want to draw a map. The only map must be in our minds.

They were all looking in every direction when suddenly Lucy exclaimed, "Look, look!" as she pointed to an outcrop of rocks on the hill behind where they planned to build their home. "There is a big rock that looks like a woodchuck."

They all recognized the resemblance and hopped from the buggy to have a closer look. The spot was almost barren of trees and brush but the ground was covered with Virginia Creeper. Buck looked around and saw that the shadow of the woodchuck rock reached some forty steps west and downhill at 9:40 A.M.

He said, "This will be the spot, June fourth at 9:40 A.M., forty steps to the edge of his shadow. We will remember all three fours.

"Let's part the Virginia Creeper without killing it. We'll bury all the rest of the money here. Most of it is silver and gold and the box is metal and sealed good so it should be free of moisture for a long time. Let's get it and something to dig with."

In no time, they dug a big hole and were ready to place the box in it.

"How much money is in it?" Lucy asked.

"A lot," Buck said, "There is a little over forty thousand."

They carefully replaced most of the dirt and scattered the remainder so not to leave a hump. They then replaced the Virginia Creeper vines over it. From a few feet away, you couldn't tell anything had been disturbed.

"This is our big secret," Buck advised them. "No mention is ever made to anyone besides us three. Do you understand?" Buck asked looking at both of them.

They both nodded their heads yes. "We won't mention it to anyone," Lucy commented.

"There are lots of bushwhackers that would kill to get their hands on this money. I hope you understand."

After sitting on the creek bank and tossing a few stones, they decided that they must get back to town. They still had to find a place to store their wagon and what they brought with them. They also had to do something with the team of mules and mother's old pump organ that Lucy was learning to play.

Back in Thomasville, they went to the company store where they found something to eat. They shared summer sausage, some cheese, a can of peaches, and had a banana each.

Lucy was in a hurry to finish eating so she could get back to the field hospital to see if there were any new patients and to make her rounds with water, a kind word, and a gentle touch. She was the favorite among all the wounded. She brought smiles to their faces when she came into their tent.

∽ FOUR ∾

*T*he next morning, Buck and Clay were awakened by gunfire. They both sat up and looked at each other. It wasn't just a few shots from hunters, but volleys of fire coming from up the river. It wasn't long until they heard cannons also.

Buck told Clay, "We better find out what's going on. Quick, hitch the mules to the wagon and I'll harness Pet to the buggy."

Buck drove the buggy and Clay drove the wagon as they made their way to the courthouse. Buck went up the steps two at a time to the sheriff's office. There were three other men already there reporting to the sheriff. Buck found that it wasn't Yankees that they were fighting. It was a bunch of bushwhackers that called themselves the "Sons of Liberty." They planned on pillaging Thomasville but a company of Confederates were camped outside of town and were taking care of them.

The Sons of Liberty had taken an oath that "No damn Yankee would ever be allowed to settle in their home town." The gang of bandits was made up of thugs from all the surrounding towns, that didn't go into the army but stayed home to rob and pillage while most men were away.

The gang from Thomasville was mostly made up of the Jamison brothers and a few more undesirables who were a little wanting mentally and easily led astray.

One day, there were two young men who drifted into town and made the mistake of saying they were from the North.

The Jamisons heard of them and quickly escorted them up Birch Tree hollow, north of Thomasville, where they used them for target practice.

They removed their bullet riddled clothes and threw them on the stairs leading up to the sheriff's office.

Everyone in Thomasville was afraid of them after this and took extra precautions by locking doors and keeping a loaded gun close by. The sheriff finally wrote the state governor for help.

The governor sent Colonel Monk and an army of thirty well-armed men to restore order and to rid the community of the Sons of Liberty.

One short shoot-out left three Jamisons dead and convinced the rest of the gang that they had better leave. The town thought they were rid of them but there were still some around.

The sheriff commented, "I know some of them and they won't fight fair. They are a bunch of yellow-bellied thugs looking for some easy money."

Buck talked to the recruiter again and showed him his enlistment papers. He only had two days before he had to report.

The recruiter told him that he could report to Captain Donivan since he already had his uniform and equipment. They were bivouacked about a mile up the river.

Buck then turned to the sheriff and asked if he knew of anyone who would store his wagon load of furniture for the use of his mules while he was gone.

The sheriff answered that there were probably many around who would go for that deal. "What are you going to do with your two mares?" the sheriff asked.

"Clay will take Pet to pull the buggy and camera and I will take the big sorrel if the army will allow it. If not, I will sell her to the army. I hear they are always in the need of good saddle stock."

"Take your mules and team over to the Lasley farm. I'm sure they will be happy to deal with you. They are located up the river; the first house you see."

Buck thanked him and went back down the stairs where Clay anxiously awaited him. Clay wanted to know when he was to report.

"You can go with me the day after tomorrow," Buck answered. "In the meantime, we have to get squared away. You must develop the pictures you took at the Thomases and I have to store the furniture and do something with the mules."

It was only a short distance to the Lasley farm, where he found Mr. Lasley in the big field plowing corn. He waited at the end of the row in which he was plowing.

"You must be Buck Paty," he said as he halted his team and wrapped the reins around a plow handle. "I'm Adam Lasley," the man said as he extended his hand. "I heard about you. Yes, I'll be glad to store your belongings for the use of your team and wagon. I assume that's what you are here for. Mr. Roberts and Mr. Griffith both told me about you."

Buck hesitated before he answered. "Yes, that's why I'm here. I'm Buck Paty and this is my son, Clay. We have to report to the army tomorrow. Sure ain't looking forward to it."

"How old is your boy?" Adam asked.

"He's only twelve. He's going on a special assignment. He's a photographer."

"I see. There's an empty stall," Mr. Lesley said as he pointed toward the barn. "Pull your wagon all the way to the end of the hall. Might take the tongue off and stand it in the corner so as not to take up extra room. Do you have any idea how long you will be gone?"

"No idea. Just wish I didn't have to go. I really don't believe in slavery and I don't know if I could shoot another man."

"I know what you are saying. I don't like it either. I'm sixty-four and glad that I don't have to make that decision. Well, I got to get back to work. Don't worry about your things. There are about ten cats that live in the barn. A mouse or a rat don't have a chance. I'll see you when you get back," Adam said as he unwrapped the reins and yelled, "Gitty up you lazy jackasses; we got to finish this field before night."

Buck and Clay placed the wagon close to the left side and all the way to the end of the hall. They had to open the hall doors in order to get the mules out. They removed the tongue and stood it in the corner. They found the empty stall, unharnessed the mules, and hung the harnesses on the wall. They ran the mules out of the barn and into the lots where there was some grass and a pond full of water.

They walked back to town and began preparing to leave the next day. There was no longer any shooting in hearing distance.

Clay soon developed the pictures for the Thomases. The picture of the dining room with the table full of food looked the best to Clay. When he gave them to John and Matilda, they were pleased and thanked him with a big sack full of food to take with him. Clay couldn't have been more pleased.

No sooner did he get back to the camp than he began to look through the sack. He found summer sausage, jerky, hard tack, canned peaches, apples, and cherry pies. He tried one of each and found them much to his liking.

He then packed all of his photography supplies and clothing into the buggy. He also packed a good sleeping bag with extra covers. He thought of his mother as he carefully folded two of the quilts she had pieced by hand. Tears came to his eyes as he placed them in the secret compartment they had fixed to hide their money in.

Buck rolled a good sleeping bag and tied it behind the cantle of his saddle. He packed one saddle bag with extra socks, underwear, and a change of clothes. The army gave him one uniform. Neither Buck nor Clay slept very well that night. They were up and dressed at the break of dawn. They both had a hard tack with a slice of summer sausage. They had never tasted anything like it before. They decided it must have been made from venison. It wasn't as tasty as beef but was still very good.

As soon as they were ready, they rode over to the Thomases to catch Lucy before she went to the hospital. Matilda met them on the front porch with a cup of coffee and two fried pies. She saw them coming and knew that they were in a hurry.

"Lucy didn't come home last night," she informed them. "They probably got in a new bunch of patients. It happens pretty often now. That sure is a fine girl you got there, Mr. Paty. You can leave the cups at the hospital. Delia and Lucy will bring them home."

As they started to leave, Buck turned to Matilda and said, "Please take good care of my little girl."

"Don't worry. She'll be fine. Between Delia and me, we'll see about her."

"Thanks," Buck said, as he turned back to Matilda who offered her hand. Buck and Clay took turns kissing it and then went on their way.

When they arrived at the field hospital there was no one in sight but they could hear sounds of pain and agony coming from one tent. When they pulled back the flap to see what was going on, they saw Doctor Plummer standing to one side of a table in the center of the room with his right hand moving back and forth in a sawing motion. Delia was across from him with gauze and clamps trying to stop bleeding while the doctor was cutting through the bone just above the knee.

Lucy was standing by the patient's head holding a cotton soaked in something dabbing at his nose, and bathing his forehead with a wet washcloth.

As soon as the doctor was finished amputating the leg, Delia looked up, picked up the shattered part that was removed, and handed it to Buck saying, "Put it in the grave out back with the rest, We'll cover it up when we are finished. Only two more to go."

When Buck returned to the tent, Clay had his camera set up in the corner and was taking his first pictures of the war.

The doctor had left a big flap of skin on the lower part of the leg which he had pulled over the stub and was sewing it over the exposed bone and muscle. Buck was fascinated at the good job the doctor was doing sewing the skin together.

Buck looked at the soldier's face and couldn't believe how

Buck Paty soon after he enlisted in the Confederate Army in 1862. After his wife's death, he wore her wedding band on his little finger.

young he looked. His light brown hair and his fine features made him a very handsome young man. There was no sign that a razor ever touched his face. He had some very fine, short hair on his upper lip and a little on the side of his face.

"How old is he?" Buck asked Lucy.

"I don't know, Dad, but his name on his tag says Pete Amonette and he is from Louisiana. That's about all I know."

"Too bad," Buck commented as the doctor finished stitching the flap of skin in place.

"Will he live?" Buck asked as the doctor looked his way.

"Some do, some don't. If we can keep infection out, he'll probably make it," he commented and then yelled, "Bring me another!" while two young men were carrying the patient on a stretcher to another tent.

Lucy looked up at her dad and said, "I'm going to take real good care of this one, he's from Louisiana. I won't let him get an infection. He looks special to me. When do you have to go?" she asked as she followed Pete to the next tent.

Buck followed her while Clay placed his camera back in its proper place in the buggy.

"We must leave soon, I mean, we have to report tomorrow. I guess this is good-bye," he said as he picked her up in his arms and gave her a big squeeze while tears rolled from both eyes.

Lucy, using the gauze in her hand, wiped the tears as she said, "Don't worry about me, Dad, you be careful and make Clay stay back where he belongs."

Buck lowered Lucy to the ground as Miss Delia Thomas came from the tent with a big wad of blood-stained cloth. Buck walked over to her and said, "Please take good care of Lucy."

"Oh! I will," Delia said as she stuck her cheek up to Buck and said, "My hands ain't suitable for kissing. I hope to see you again soon, but not as a patient."

Buck's heart was doing double time as Miss Delia walked away. His mind was whirling. He had to come back soon. She was the most beautiful female he had seen since his wife had died. He couldn't understand why she wasn't already married.

He walked away with his mind still spinning, turning back to see her just one more time.

Clay noticed Buck's anxiety as they walked back to their horses. Clay asked, "Do you like Miss Delia, Dad?"

"How would you like for her to be your new mama?" Buck asked.

"I'd rather she be my girlfriend," Clay replied.

Buck looked at Clay with a surprised look. Clay began to grin as Buck slapped playfully at the top of his head. Clay dodged the blow and broke into a fast run for his buggy. Buck caught him in only a few steps with one arm around his neck he rubbed his head with the knuckles of the other hand.

"You are growing up too fast," Buck commented as he released the arm lock and placed his hand on Clay's shoulder. They walked the rest of the way to their horses with Clay's arm around his dad's waist.

~ FIVE ~

Morning came too quickly for Clay. He was sound asleep when his father shook him and told him it was time to get up and get started.

In a few minutes, they both got dressed, saddled the horses, and ate a hard tack with some summer sausage. Buck also brewed a pot of coffee that he set in the buggy.

Buck tied Pet behind the buggy and they both climbed in the buggy seat with the blue granite coffee pot at their feet. The pot looked more black than blue now as the result of much use in an open fire and only a few scrubbings. They both thought the coffee tasted better from an unclean pot.

Clay picked up the reins and yelled, "Gitty up you lazy old B——," which he cut short not wanting his father to hear him use such language. He looked up at his father with a slight flush on his face as he pulled the right rein and said, "Ge-Ge" to head her in the direction from which they heard the gunfire two days earlier.

After only about an hour, they came to the spot where the army had been camped. They had brushed the area and cleared away all rubbish, but it was plain to see that several had spent some time there. It was also clear the direction which they had gone. It looked like most of them were on horseback but a few were walking.

Clay stopped the buggy. He and his father both listened intently but could hear nothing.

"We better see if we can catch up with them," Buck said as he picked up the reins and slapped the mare on the back. He then shouted, "Gitty up, you old bitch!"

The mare moved in a trot the rest of the morning. The trail was fresh but they still could hear nothing when they stopped for lunch.

"They must have left early yesterday or we would be catching up by now," Buck commented.

Again they asked the mare to go at a trot. It was almost dark when two soldiers suddenly stepped from behind the trees in front of them with their rifles leveled in their direction.

Buck pulled back hard on the reins as he yelled, "Whoa! Whoa! Don't shoot! We are on your side!"

"Advance and be recognized," one of the soldiers said still holding them in the sights of his rifle.

When they recognized Buck's uniform, they both lowered their guns. One said, "We thought you was one of them bushwhackers. We lose more men to guerrillas than we do to damn Yankees."

"I'm supposed to report to Captain Donivan today," Buck said, "Is he here?"

"Captain Donivan and the rest of the company are only a short distance ahead. You'll see him. He is on the big black stallion. He tries to look the part of a great leader, but when there is a fight, you can always find him in the rear; guess he don't want to get his horse shot," one of the rear guards said sarcastically.

"Guess we had better hurry," Buck said not wanting to encourage any more insubordination.

In only a shore time, they caught up with the company just as they were setting up camp for the night. The rear guard soldier was right. Captain Donivan was easy to recognize even off the big black stallion. He was very tall and his uniform was extra clean with lots of gold braid trim.

Buck stepped out of the buggy and walked over to the Captain and giving him a half-hearted salute he said, "Recruit Buck Paty reporting for duty, Sir!"

"And who is that in the buggy?" the Captain asked.

Buck yelled for Clay to come forward as he explained to the Captain that this was his son and what his assignment was.

"Come here, son," the Captain said. "Let me have a good look at you. I suppose you will want a picture of me."

"Yes Sir," was Clay's reply, "and I will try to stay out of the way. Here are my orders," Clay offered as he handed the papers to Captain Donivan.

"This will be a new experience for me. I never had a twelve-year-old photographer under my command before. I assume you are potty trained," the Captain said with a snicker.

"I can take care of myself," Clay bristled. "I am supposed to make regular reports to General Walker who will relay my reports along with pictures to his commander-in-chief. I hope I can have something good to report about you and your command," Clay answered.

"I can see I misjudged you, Son," Captain Donivan said while removing his glove and extending his hand to Clay. "I'll try to make your stay with us as comfortable as possible."

"I'll sleep in my buggy but will take my meals with you when it is convenient," Clay answered while shaking the Captain's hand.

Buck was assigned a tent and was introduced to the other three who would occupy it with him. He was told that meals would be served when possible at six, twelve, and six o'clock, and there would be no late snacks.

That night, Buck and Clay sat together on a log as they ate their fill of brown beans, poke salad, and corn pone. They had a choice of water or coffee to wash it down.

Soon after their evening meal, the captain fell them in formation to inform them of what would be happening the next day as soon as all twenty-eight of them were accounted for. The captain then told them that they could be at ease.

"Tomorrow morning soon after six A.M. we will start an all day march toward Batesville, Arkansas, on the White River. There's a company of Yankees headed down the river with a supply of ammunition. We are supposed to intercept and either sink their boats or capture them. Keep your powder dry and your guns loaded. We should reach the river tomorrow afternoon. Are there any questions?" he asked. "If not, you are excused until six A.M."

By six A.M. everyone had struck their tents and stashed them on the supply wagon. With the supplies on the food wagon, and Clay in his buggy bringing up the rear, they all headed south soon after breakfast.

Buck was allowed to keep Pet, but had to share her with another soldier. They both tied their bed rolls across the back of the cantel and took turns riding.

They moved fast all day trying to reach the river near Batesville before dark. It was almost dark before they heard the sounds of the river as it cascaded over and around large rocks. As soon as they reached the river, they pitched camp back out of sight from the river with instructions that there would be no fires. The captain called two of his better men with good horses and instructed them to ride upstream until they found the boats and to return as quickly as possible so they could get ready to ambush them.

It was becoming too dark to travel, so the two scouts stopped and had a few bites while they waited for the moon to rise and to furnish enough light to move on. It was almost midnight when they first saw some small fires on the bank of the river.

Dismounting and tying their horses, they walked and crawled close enough to count five boats and probably twenty Yankees seated around the fires enjoying fish and potatoes with something stronger than water to drink, judging by the noise they were making.

The two scouts spent the remainder of the night finding their way back to camp.

The moon had gone down but the east sky was showing morning gray when they arrived back at camp. They immediately reported their finding to Captain Donivan, and estimated that it would take at least six hours for them to float down the river to the place where they were camped.

Captain Donivan gave orders for everyone to fall in. He

then informed the food wagon to fix a good breakfast and told half of the men to cross the river at the first shoal. They were ordered to attack and try to drive the boats to the opposite side of the river where the remaining half would capture them when they tried to dock their boats and take cover.

It was about two o'clock when Captain Donivan and his crew heard the first volley of fire with very little return fire. The sound of the guns echoed up and down the river bouncing and echoing from across and upstream. Captain Donivan peeped out from behind a tree and saw two boats headed for the sand and gravel bar directly in front of them.

They reached the beach and four men jumped from the boats and started running for the woods directly in front of Captain Donivan and the hidden troop. Only two of the Yankees were carrying guns and they looked wet.

The other three boats were beginning to sink as they were floating down the river. There was no sign of life in either of them.

Captain Donivan stepped from behind his tree with both pistols drawn and yelled, "Halt! Lay down your arms or die!"

The Yankees looked up in complete surprise and quickly dropped their guns. "Don't shoot! Please don't shoot!" one cried as he saw the rest of the company step from behind trees.

"Leave your guns and lace your fingers behind your head," Captain Donivan ordered. "Four men, advance forward and take the prisoners. Tie their hands behind their backs and lead them back to camp," he ordered.

The remainder of the company walked down the opposite bank toward the other boats that became lodged on rocks near the shoal. Their sides were full of bullet holes and they were quickly filling with water.

The confederate soldiers found ten dead Yankees and two that were badly wounded. They took the two wounded and floated the dead to shore. The two wounded were bleeding badly and were both dead before supper. Neither regained consciousness before he died.

Each of the four captured Yankees was assigned a

Confederate to watch and look after them twenty-four hours a day. Their hands were to remain tied to each other even as they slept. They had no idea how long they would have to keep the Yankees.

The next morning they headed east toward the Mississippi River, hoping to unite with more Confederates and find a place to leave the prisoners.

Buck and his charge, whose name was Bob Arnot, became good friends. Bob was a farmer in Illinois and was the father of two children. He didn't like the war either but felt strongly against slavery. While they made their march toward the Mississippi, Buck and Bob became closer friends and they soon began to explore possible methods of leaving the army. They even discussed self-inflicted wounds, but they never decided where or how.

One night while they were discussing their situation, Bob asked, "How about me taking you prisoner and delivering you to the Yankees?"

"They would probably hold me until the end of the war. Besides, what would I do with Clay?" Buck replied.

"You could tell Clay to go back to where your daughter is and wait for you," Bob answered.

They discussed the pros and cons of Bob's suggestion. Clay thought that if they did hold him, at least he would come out of the war alive. But how would they make it believable? How do the Yankees treat prisoners? Many things went through Buck's mind. The only thing that he was certain of was that he had no stomach for this war and couldn't see dying for something that he didn't believe in.

Finally, Buck said, "Let's make plans for you to capture me. I'll tell Clay to go back to Thomasville if anything happens to me."

"What do you suggest?"

They decided to sleep on it and discuss it again the next day. They saw others look at them suspiciously, and they were scared that people were thinking that they were up to something. Buck and Bob were too friendly, other soldiers were saying.

The company had already reached the Mississippi River,

and having not seen any other soldiers, started marching south.

Buck and Bob decided that the next night they would pitch their tent near the edge of the camp and they would leave as soon as the guard passed the tent while making his circle. They then realized that the moon was in its last quarter and would not rise until almost three A.M.

Their plans were changed to a more suitable time when the moon would give some light to travel by. They started saving some of their non-perishable food along with other necessities like coffee, soap, salt, clean socks, and the like.

They traveled three more days toward the south and they still met no other Confederate soldiers.

The fourth day, Captain Donivan called the company together and told them that they would continue down the river until they met up with some more Confederate soldiers. They were all weary and their food supply was almost gone.

"Tomorrow we will not march. We will stay in camp and rest. Any of you hunters who think you can find us something to eat will be excused at nine and must return before five."

Captain Donivan noticed that several of the soldiers seemed more restless than usual. Realizing that something was wrong, he asked, "Is there a problem, men?"

One young man stood up and said, "Sir, wild animals stir early and late. In the middle of the day, they sleep and are hard to find."

"I beg your pardon. You may leave when you like, but return before dark. You are excused until tomorrow. Let me know between now and tomorrow morning if you plan to hunt. Oh, by the way, no one guarding a prisoner will be allowed to go."

Buck noticed a lot of traffic to the Captain's tent but didn't realize until the next morning that all the men that weren't guarding prisoners went hunting.

Buck found a large log near the perimeter of the camp. The log was large enough that they could sit on the ground and lean back with their head and arms resting on top of it.

Buck sat about six feet away from his prisoner who had his

feet tied together and a rope from them around Buck's neck. The prisoner was to his right and a loaded musket was leaning on the log at arm's length to his left.

Buck had dozed off when the Captain came by and kicked him on the bottom of his left foot. Buck quickly reached for his gun before he realized that it was the Captain.

"Relax, soldier, I'm sure that if your prisoner had moved his feet, you would have been ready for him. I sure hope we have some good hunters in this company, don't you?" the Captain commented.

Buck saluted and said, "I could sure go for a good venison steak or some breast of a turkey, sir."

"Go ahead with your rest," the Captain said as he nodded to Buck's prisoner. "I'll see how the rest are making it."

"We can and must talk," Bob whispered out the corner of his mouth. "The moon is about right. How about tomorrow night? We sure could use a compass."

"That's no problem," Buck answered. "Clay has one in the buggy. I haven't seen him today. I'll ask the Captain if I can check on him."

With all the planning and the comfortable place they had found to relax, the morning flew by. Before noon, the hunters began returning with a bountiful supply of food. The first two who returned had a large male deer hanging from a pole on their shoulders. They had field dressed the deer, removing all the excess weight they could but it still was a heavy load.

The next to return had a large turkey gobbler. It almost made the saliva start flowing just to see the abundance of fresh meat. Buck and Bob saw deer, turkeys, squirrels, woodchucks, opossums, and other small varmints as the hunters returned to camp. One soldier found a turkey's nest and the eggs had not yet started to form young turkeys. They would sure taste good fried or scrambled. One soldier brought back a large sack of watercress. One soldier even killed two wild pigs.

When everyone had returned from the hunt, the Captain came out with his pen and paper to take inventory. He had everyone bring their kill to the center circle and stand by it.

Captain Donivan diligently made note of each soldier's name and the food he returned with. There were two deer, three turkeys, two wild pigs, ten squirrels, three woodchucks, one opossum, ten turkey eggs, and a large mess of watercress that had been found in a very cold spring near the camp.

He then turned to the hunters and congratulated them. He said, "I don't want any wasted. Tonight, we will dine on venison steak, baked potatoes, and a nice watercress salad. Now listen to what I have to say: We will cut one deer into steaks. Anything that won't make a steak, cut it up for stew meat. The remainder and the other one we will cut into strips and make jerky. Roast one of the pigs and pickle the other one in salt. Fry the squirrels, roast the opossum. It might not be recognized in stew.

"Oh, by the way, we will stay here another day and night. This will give us time to care for all the meat and rest. Now, get to work. The weather could turn hot any day and we don't want to let anything spoil. Dinner tonight will be at six-thirty. You may ask all the prisoners and their guards to help. Any questions?"

One soldier stood up and asked, "What did you say to do with the opossum?"

The Captain stood still for a moment before turning to face the soldier and said, "It would make you a good jockey strap. Be sure and turn the tail to the rear. I'll see you at six-thirty. Now get busy."

Everyone was soon at work. Some gathered firewood. Some built a spit with two forked poles and a crooked one to string the venison and the pig on. Some built racks to hang the jerky on. They built them close enough to the fire to keep flies and insects off. A hole was dug under one side of the fire to bake the potatoes in. The steaks were stuck on forked sticks and draped over rocks and above a bed of coals so they could turn them whenever necessary. The drippings on the fire hissed and gave off a very good smell, starting saliva to flow.

At six-thirty, all the work was finished and all the food was ready except for the steaks.

Everyone could choose the one they wanted and finish

cooking it the way they liked. The cook had made a big pot of tea with the cool water from the nearby spring. It was truly a feast to remember. The turkeys hanging by wires at the ends of the spit were sure smelling good.

The Captain emerged from his tent and asked if the men thought it would be proper to ask a blessing over the meal. "Is there anyone who would like to do the honor?" he asked.

Buck stood up and said, "Dear God, make us ever mindful of your presence. We thank You for this blessing and all Your blessings. Guide and protect us from harm. Help us to realize that we are all Your children and make us aware of the needs of others. Forgive us when we fail to do what pleases You."

There were a few coughs, and a few men had to clear their throats. One man had to clear his head by blowing first one nostril and then the other. Buck looked up but caught no eyes looking at him.

"Be with those in need and be merciful to the wanting. These favors we ask in Jesus' name and for his sake, Amen."

"Amen," several said as they picked up their plates and started filling them. No one finished cooking his steak, but they ate them at whatever stage they were at. Some were done, but most needed a few more minutes over the fire.

The cold tea and the watercress were also a treat. Someone heated grease, vinegar, and salt in a pan to pour over the watercress. This made it very tasty. The baked potatoes were just right. They washed the ashes off, split them, doused them with a little salt and pepper, and poured some of the meat drippings on them. It was the best meal they had had since they came into the army.

Clay had his camera equipment set up at one corner and really caught some good shots. He couldn't decide on an appropriate story to go with the picture, but several ideas were coming to mind.

The Captain wasn't sure they were the kind of pictures he should be sending back home. He thought it looked more like a picnic than any army bivouac. In fact, the Captain asked to censor all the pictures and stories before they were sent back home to the paper.

This really killed Clay's enthusiasm. From that day on, he left his camera in the buggy and spent all his time either reading or visiting with his father. If he couldn't write what he wanted, he decided he wouldn't write at all.

The next day they all stayed in camp and finished taking care of their assigned duties, making sure all the meat was either dried, cooked, or salted down.

Buck and Bob found it easy to stash a good supply for their getaway.

This was the night they had planned to leave. Buck made sure that his horse and another one were tethered near the outer fringe of where the horses were tied. Buck again told Clay that if anything happened to him, he was to go to Lucy, and not to let the Captain know that he was told this.

It was a little after nine P.M. when they slipped out of camp with their knapsacks. They untied two horses and quietly led them into the woods where they had stashed two saddles and a few other supplies.

The moon was beginning to show red in the eastern sky. It would soon be light enough to ride and move faster. At every stream, they traveled upstream as far as it allowed. They were headed north, parallel to the Mississippi River. After a long trip upstream, they used brush to wipe away their tracks when they were forced by deep water to leave the stream. They had traveled many miles, possibly thirty-five or forty when moonlight gave way to a rising sun. They kept up a hard and fairly fast pace, and wondered when it would be discovered that they were gone and what the Captain would think and do.

It was after eight A.M. when someone asked why Buck and Bob weren't at breakfast. One soldier said with a snicker, "They sure seem awful friendly."

The Captain, pointing a finger at the soldier who made the comment, said, "You go and check on them."

He returned, soon saying, "There is no one there. They have taken their belongings and bugged," he reported to the Captain.

The Captain stood up, and walked to Buck's tent. "Go check the horses," he said to a soldier on his way to their tent.

He soon discovered that two horses, along with saddles and gear, were gone.

"What are you going to do?" the soldier asked Captain Donivan.

"We're not in much of a position to do much of anything," the Captain answered. "We need to keep moving and try to find some more troops to find out where we are needed. We will head down river until we find a place where we can cross and move east where I imagine there is more action. I bet you Buck went to sleep and his prisoner took advantage of him. Buck is probably the prisoner now."

Clay walked up to Captain Donivan and asked, "What should I do? I wanted to stay with my dad."

"Did he say anything to you about deserting?" the Captain asked.

"My dad would never do that," Clay replied.

"What would you like to do?" the Captain asked.

"I would like to go see about my sister at Thomasville if I can't be with my dad."

"Good. I was thinking about sending someone back to see if he returned there."

"I'll guarantee you that he didn't desert, but I'd be happy for someone to go with me. When can I leave?"

"We're pulling out early tomorrow to the south. You are free to leave when we do. Take enough food for the trip."

"Thank you, Captain, I really appreciate you letting me go and sending someone with me. Good luck to you and your men. Who will you be sending with me?" Clay asked.

"I'll send Don Walker. We don't have a rifle for him anyway. He doesn't have a wife or family."

"Thanks again, Captain. I'll try to have something good to say about you in the paper."

"Thank you. Be sure to take some food. You may need it before you reach Thomasville."

∽ *SIX* ∽

*B*ack in Thomasville, the only thing that was growing was the cemetery. Lucy was spending long hours at the hospital. She was taking special care of Pete Amonette. His leg was healing and there was no sign of infection. Each day, Lucy was at work early, and each night, she worked late. There was always water to carry, cleaning to do and washing to be done. She really made a change since she started helping. Each time she entered a tent, she made a difference. She always smiled and called the men by name and said, "Good Morning," and "How are you today?" She washed their faces and hands. She even cut Pete's hair. She was spending more time with him each day. She allowed him to lean on her while he learned to use one crutch since there weren't enough crutches for each amputee to have two. They either had to borrow one or find someone to lean on.

Their walks were becoming longer each day. They would walk over to the company store and have some candy or something to drink.

Pete and Lucy were becoming very fond of each other. They talked about their families and what they planned to do after the war. Lucy could hardly believe she had been working at the hospital for almost a year. Time really passed quickly.

Lucy was more or less on her own at the hospital. She carved out her own niche. Miss Thomas only called on her when there was a bunch of new wounded soldiers. Nothing seemed to shake Lucy. She could carry an amputated limb without grimacing or showing any negative expression.

They had just left Pete's tent to start their evening walk when Clay pulled up in his buggy. Lucy broke loose and ran to Clay with outstretched arms not knowing what to expect. "Where's Dad?" she yelled when she came close to Clay.

"I really don't know. He and a Yankee he was guarding disappeared one night and we haven't seen them since. We thought maybe they had come here."

Clay and Lucy embraced, holding each other close. Lucy had her head on his shoulder and Clay kissed her on the side of her head. "It's so good to see you," Clay said.

"You too," replied Lucy. "What do you think happened to Dad?" Lucy asked.

"God, I hope they don't come here if a Yankee is with him."

She told Clay about the group of men in Thomasville that called themselves the Sons of Liberty. They were mostly Jamisons. Some people called them the Jamison Gang. Just recently, again two young men wandered into town and the Jamisons took them up the hollow and used them for target practice. They brought their bullet-riddled clothes back and threw them on the stairs of the sheriff's office with a note that said, "No damn Yankee will ever be allowed to live in Thomasville."

"They say that they have taken an oath to that effect. The sheriff is afraid of them. Mrs. Thomas wrote a note to the governor, asking him to send help to restore order here. I sure hope they don't find out she wrote it. The gang was run off once but they are back," Lucy said excitedly.

"What are you going to do now?" Lucy asked. "And who is this with you?"

"Just someone Captain Donivan sent with me to see if Dad was here."

Pete hopped over close to where Clay and Lucy were and parked himself on a big tree stump.

"Who is this following you?" Clay asked.

Lucy didn't see Pete but immediately went to him and

called to Clay to come over.

"This is my best friend, Pete Amonette. Pete, this is my brother Clay. I'm so glad you are getting to meet him."

Clay stuck out his hand and gave a firm handshake and told him how glad he was to meet him.

"Are you hungry?" Lucy asked. "We just finished eating."

Clay's friend stepped forward and said, "I don't know about Clay, but I sure as hell am. We have been traveling six days and I sure could use a warm meal and a bath."

"Come on," Lucy answered as she placed her arm around Pete's waist and his around her shoulders. "I'll show you where the mess tent is and where you can get some soap. Everyone bathes in the creek. About a hundred yards downstream, there is a good spot where you are hidden by a high bank and some brush. There is a good gravel bar where you can dry your clothes if you have laundry to do."

The cooks at the mess tent filled their plates and the group just sat down when Lucy and Pete came in and introduced Clay and his friend.

One cook stood up and pointed to a stack of trays and instructed them to fill their own. "It's all still on the stove and warm. If you need anything, just ask," he said as he sat down and began eating.

Lucy and Pete sat at a table near the edge of the tent away from the heat of the cookstove. Lucy poured each of them a glass of tea to which one of the cooks added a few mint leaves. It gave it a little different flavor.

Clay and his friend rounded their trays up and took an extra piece of cornbread and a large hunk of butter. They even had a big glass of milk which neither had seen for a long time. Clay crumbled one piece of cornbread in his milk and smeared butter and applesauce on the other piece. This, along with a big tray full of thick stew with chunks of meat and potatoes, tasted good to them.

"Where are you going to stay?" Lucy asked.

"I'll stay in the buggy for the time being. I'm sure glad Dad put my name on the checking account. I think I'll get started on the house," Clay said, then turned to his escort and asked,

"When do you go back? By the way, what would you like for me to call you?"

"My name is Donald Walker, but you can call me Don," he answered.

"What are you planning to do?" Clay asked.

"I really don't know," Don replied. "I think I'll stay here a while. There is no telling where my company is by now."

"I would like to see our claim," Clay announced. "Anyone want to come with me?"

Lucy said, "Wait a few minutes. I'll see if Pete can go with us." She came back quickly and announced that it would be fine.

Clay drove Pet down to the creek from the spot he tethered her to graze. After a long drink she was ready to go again. Clay and Don sat on the front seat while Pete and Lucy sat on a bed roll in the back.

As soon as they arrived at Spring Creek, Clay pulled back on the reins and stopped the buggy at the spot where they decided to build their house. Clay asked Don to go with him. He wanted to walk around the perimeter to check and see if all their markers were still there.

Clay and Don struck out to the east and left Pete and Lucy in the back of the buggy.

Pete placed both arms around Lucy and pulled her close to him and kissed her hard on the mouth. Lucy liked the feel of him holding her but when he pushed her backward and moved on top of her she felt smothered and also felt like she was being taken advantage of. This advance took her by surprise.

Lucy placed both of her hands on his chest and shoved him as she slid from under him and hopped out of the buggy. Pete jumped out of the back and landed on his good foot but pushed too hard and was unbalanced. He tried to hop to regain his balance but caught his toe on a rock and fell on his face.

Lucy ran to the side to help him up but ended up lying beside him. She asked, "Are you hurt?" really being concerned.

Pete pulled her closer to him and began stroking her hair

and upper body while kissing her gently.

Lucy finally allowed Pete to have his way with her which first hurt then felt good. They laid in the shade of the big white oak tree among what Lucy thought was Virginia Creeper. She later found out it was poison ivy.

They had hardly gotten up and straightened their clothes when they heard Clay and Don coming.

They sat on the ground at the base of the big oak tree and were tossing pebbles in Spring Creek when Clay and Don walked up to them from the direction of the back of the buggy.

They couldn't help notice all the vines that had been disturbed. It really looked like something had been wallowing on the ground behind the buggy.

Clay looked at Lucy and asked, "What happened at the back of the buggy?"

Pete and Lucy looked at each other, each waiting for the other to answer. Finally Lucy said, "Pete tried to jump out of the buggy and fell. He hurt his leg and rolled with pain until I helped him get up. It started bleeding and I had to tear off a piece of my slip to bandage it after it finally stopped."

"I guess you know that is poison ivy that you were wallowing in," Clay told them. "It can cause serious skin rash."

Pete and Lucy looked at each other both knowing that they had used the leaves to clean themselves with.

"I thought that was Virginia Creeper," Lucy said.

"I'm afraid not. You should go down to the creek and wash anywhere it touched you," Clay suggested in an almost demanding tone of voice.

Again they looked at each other with sorrowful faces as they got up and walked down to the creek.

Lucy helped Pete, who left his crutch in the buggy. Pete stopped at the nearest spot but Lucy walked downstream to be out of sight of Clay and Don.

They both stripped to the skin and completely submerged themselves in the freezing cold water of Spring Creek. They wished for some soap as they washed all over, rubbing their privates and rinsing with lots of cold, clear water.

Clay had noticed Pete's crutch and picked it up to take to him. He discovered Pete completely nude, sitting in the Creek with his back to him. He was scrubbing his front side hard in his crotch area.

Pete was shocked when he heard Clay yell, "Here's your crutch, thought you might need it!"

Pete didn't answer but turned on his stomach and started making his way on his hands and knee toward the bank where his clothes were.

It wasn't long before Lucy and Pete, both red-faced, made their way back to the buggy. They realized that Clay must have known what happened but didn't want to believe it.

Hardly a word was spoken all the way back to Thomasville. Clay didn't know if he should confront Pete or not. He could hardly stand the idea that his only sister was growing up too fast. He just hoped that nothing came of this episode. What would Buck think if something did happen? It would be hard to explain. "You should be looking after your sister," Buck would say.

The next morning when Clay went to breakfast, Lucy wasn't there. He found Miss Thomas and asked about her.

Miss Thomas said, "She has the worst case of poison ivy I have ever seen. She is lying on a clean sheet in the nude with baking soda all over her, trying to stop the itching. I don't think she wants to see you."

"Where is Pete Amonette?" Clay asked.

Miss Thomas walked to the front of the tent, pushed back a flap, and pointed, "He is in the third tent down. The one with both front and back flaps tied back."

Clay quickly walked to the tent, not knowing what to say. When he entered the tent, he saw one cot in the middle of the tent so it would catch a breeze from both ends. Pete was lying so he would feel the breeze. Pete was also on a cot completely nude, covered with poison ivy. His eyes were swollen shut and his genitals looked awful. He didn't realize that Clay entered the tent. Clay just stood there for a while, looking at him. The longer he stood there, the more he felt sorry for him.

Finally, Clay shook his head and left the tent, and thought, "What a penalty to pay."

Pete didn't know anyone had been in the tent and didn't really care. He was hurting to bad both physically and mentally. His entire body itched and ached. It hurt when he made water, and when he had a bowel movement it felt like he was tearing tissue.

His mind was working overtime trying to cope with the physical pain, not to mention the agony of wondering what else might happen. He knew Lucy was too young. What if she accused him of rape? What would he do if she was pregnant? He started praying to God, asking both for forgiveness, and that Lucy was not pregnant.

⌒ SEVEN ⌒

C lay and Don were still asleep in the buggy. It was barely long enough for Don. He was a good six feet tall. They rolled out the beds so that their heads were where you put your feet when driving. The canopy over the seat kept rain off their upper half and Clay had a tarpaulin over the back half. It was really a pretty comfortable bed since there was about four inches of straw under their bed roll. Many things were going through Clay's mind. He didn't like sleeping with Don, and he was anxious about Lucy.

Clay had a hard time getting some sleep. He wanted to start their new home and all kinds of plans were running through his head. He needed tools. He needed to find a stone mason. He needed someone to make the shingles. He needed many things. He kept tossing and turning, keeping Don awake.

Don finally turned on his back and asked, "What the hell is wrong with you? I'd like to get some sleep if you don't mind."

Clay told him what was on his mind and asked, "What did you do before the war?"

"I was a carpenter," Don replied. "I can do it all. Now get to sleep. We'll talk tomorrow."

"How old are you?" Clay asked.

"Thirty-eight," Don replied. "What does that have to do with anything?"

"Do you have a family?" Clay asked.

"No. As ugly as I am, no one would want me."

"I see a lot of Indians around here. They ain't too good looking. Maybe you are too particular."

"Would you shut up, boy? Anybody who would look at me, I probably wouldn't want them. Now get to sleep, we'll talk tomorrow."

It must have been past midnight before Clay went to sleep. He dreamed of a nice house with a photo shop in it with people coming from miles around to get their pictures taken. Then he dreamed of putting their pictures on cards so they could write and mail the pictures. He thought this was a novel idea and still remembered it when he woke up the next morning.

"We need to do some serious talking," Clay told Don as he shook him until he was sure that he was wide awake.

"I'm going to start our house on Spring Creek and I'd like to hire you to help me. I'll pay you twenty cents an hour plus room and board. Now what do you say?"

Don scooted from under the buggy seat and sat up. He leaned back against the seat and rubbed his eyes and ran his fingers through his hair. Clay began to see what he was talking about when he said, "A woman who would look at me, I wouldn't have her." He really did look like a scarecrow. He was tall and thin with one big ear and one small one. His eyebrows came to a peak right above his eyes. His hands hung almost to his knees. He had very dark, leathery looking skin with wrinkles far beyond his age. If he had beauty spots, they didn't show.

Don scratched his head a few more times, stuck out his hand and said, "You just hired the best carpenter in town. When do we start?"

"I want you to make a list of things we need and we will start the day after tomorrow. I'll talk to Mr. Hass down at the company store about letting you charge. Mr. Weaver at the bank will let him know about our account, I'm sure. I want a three bedroom house with a long front porch facing east. The north end will be two stories with my photo studio on ground level with the three bedrooms above it.

"There will be two fireplaces on the south end. A big one in the library and parlor and a smaller one in the kitchen and dining room. I want large rooms with lots of windows.

"Can you read and write?" Clay asked.

"Sure can. I can figure, too."

"Good," Clay said. "Spend the day deciding what we need and get plenty. I'll see if the store will deliver. Make a list."

Don spent most of the day trying to think of everything they would need. As soon as he decided that he thought of everything, he went over to the store and handed the bill to Mr. Hass. Mr. Hass looked at the bill and asked, "What kind of roof are you going to put on the house?"

"Shake shingles," Don answered. "I didn't think you'd have any."

"Yeah, we got them. Old Man Wilcox makes them and brings in a square at a time. I give him a buck and sell them for a buck and a half. How many squares do you need?"

"I need about twenty-five squares," Don answered.

"I'll have to bring the shakes and the cement to you later. You won't need them now anyway. I'll bring out the rest as soon as I can have someone to haul it," Mr. Hass said.

"The entire bill will come to seven hundred eighty-four dollars. Can you cover that?"

"This order is for Clay Paty. I thought he asked you. Talk to Mr. Weaver at the bank," Don answered as he turned to leave the store.

Mr. Hass yelled, "Have a soda and some candy on me."

Don kept on walking and only answered, "Later, after you have checked the bank."

"No need to get huffy, Don. That's a lot of money. Come on back and try one of my new Coca-Colas. They say they are real good."

Don turned around and came back to a bench beside the old heating stove. Mr. Hass opened a Coke and handed it to him.

"How long are you going to be in town?" Mr. Hass asked.

"Really don't know."

"How is the Coke?"

"Good."

"Are you married?"

"Nope. Thanks for the Coke. I'll probably think of more material later. I'm building Buck Paty's new house," Don said as he finished his Coke and left the store.

∽ EIGHT ∽

Buck and Bob kept moving north up the Mississippi River. They had been traveling twelve days when they came to a small settlement called St. Genevieve.

Buck and Bob thought they would surely find some Yankee soldiers before now. Buck seriously thought about switching sides, but they finally decided to turn Buck over as a prisoner of war. At St. Genevieve, they found out that many prisoners were being sent from St. Louis on the Illinois Central Railroad to Camp Douglas in Chicago.

Bob and Buck again had a hard time deciding what to do. They finally decided to catch a boat up the Mississippi to St. Louis, then catch the Illinois Central on to Chicago. At St. Louis, they soon found the railroad station and were surprised to find a trainload of Confederate prisoners headed for Camp Douglas. Bob was assigned to the car in which Buck was riding.

The car was overcrowded with barely enough room for the men to sit, let alone lie down. They traveled the remainder of the day and all night, and arrived in Chicago a little before noon.

When they were ordered off the car, they were given time to go to the bathroom and to get a drink of water. They were each handed a small, hard piece of bread that was hard to chew or swallow without more water.

The haggard and war-torn soldiers were ordered to fall in.

There were twelve boxcars and each of them held between thirty and fifty men. Bob was in charge of a car containing forty-two men.

It was the end of July now but it was nice and cool compared to the heat and humidity Buck was accustomed to. Buck looked around and soon decided that he was in good condition compared to the rest of the Confederates.

In Buck's group was the commander of over six hundred whom had surrendered. His romantic name was Simon Bolivar Buckner. Buck was told that he asked for terms from General Grant and was told that the term would be "Unconditional surrender" to which Buckner replied, "This is ungenerous and unchivalrous." The prisoners laughed and had nothing good to say about their leader. Many of them thought that he had a faulty mind and was more than a little wanting mentally.

They marched around Lake Michigan to the southeast. Buck thought it was a very pleasant stroll on a cool summer afternoon, but for most of the men, it was torture. Some had no shoes and many were sick. All were very thin, many with their bones showing through their skin. They all were very dirty and hungry. Most had not had a decent meal in many days.

Bob happened to be in charge of a group near the head of the march. As they walked along the shore, Buck asked Bob if they could take a bath in the lake.

"That sounds like a good idea," Bob said. "I'll have to check with the Colonel. Dovell!" Bob yelled, but to no avail. The breakers were too noisy along with the talk and the men marching. Finally, Bob walked ahead of his group and told the soldier in the rear of the first group to pass the word to the Colonel that the guard in the group behind him would like to speak to him.

Colonel Dovell stepped aside and waited for Bob's group to catch up.

When he saw Bob, he asked as he returned Bob's salute, "What is it, soldier?"

"Beg your pardon, Sir, but would it be possible for these prisoners to take a bath and wash their clothes? Some of them smell pretty bad."

Without saying a word, the Colonel trotted back to the head of the first group and told their guard to halt the prisoners. "I want to talk to them."

The colonel walked back to the middle of the group and said, "Men, I know you are tired. I want you to take a bath here first with your clothes on, and then with them off. You can wring the water out of your clothes and lay them on the rocks to dry. Guard, tell the guard behind you to pass the word on. The groups will not be allowed to intermingle. Now get to it. I'll stay with your group."

Almost in unison, the group very humbly said, "Thank you, Sir."

"Never mind," Dovell replied. "I just wanted to see if you Southern boys were any different than us."

It was now three-thirty P.M. and they were within a mile of Camp Douglas. They could spend at least two hours swimming, washing, and resting. Some of the men needed rest badly. They didn't spend much time in the water since it was Lake Michigan and always cold. They were encouraged to at least wash off and rinse their clothes. Some were too weak to wring the water out, but the rocks were hot and with the convection air currents near the lake, their clothes dried quickly.

Some of the men were shaking from the chilly water and from their weakened condition. As soon as they warmed up on the beach, they were soon stretched out and asleep. It really bothered Colonel Dovell to see these sharp shooters who were pale and so thin. He wondered what they thought of the war and the dashing Dixie Greys now. Colonel Dovell did previously realize the sad condition of some of the prisoners. It never occurred to him that some of the shaking might be attacks of ague chills, which came with Malaria. He knew that they were all sallow-faced and most had sunken eyes with extended stomachs.

Colonel Dovell also didn't know the structure of Camp Douglas. He had never been there before. He only had orders to deliver these prisoners.

When they arrived at the gate, a guard instructed them to march around the perimeter to the back gate. The prison was a separate part of the camp. The front was a Yankee training camp.

When the gate of the prison was opened, Colonel Dovell could not believe his eyes. He saw prisoners scantily dressed in rotten and ragged clothes. Their hair was matted and filthy. No doubt they were covered with lice. The prison was in a swampy area that was an extension of Camp Douglas. It was completely separate from the camp. The ground was one big quagmire! Not a dry spot was in sight. All the prisoners had ash-colored faces and all were in an emaciated condition. He could plainly see the dejected look on their faces as they squatted, barefooted in the mud. The internal pain plainly showed on their faces as some raised their heads from their knees to see who was coming.

When Buck saw the conditions, he turned to the soldier next to him and said, "I wonder which is worse, summer or winter. God, I hope we make it out of here. By the way, what is your name?"

"I'm Henry Morgan Stanley. If we stick together, maybe we can figure something out. We both have good shoes and I can tell by the look in your eye that you're no fool."

Buck looked at him with a blank expression while they waited for Colonel Dovell to find out what to do with them.

Little did Buck know that nine years later it would be this man who in Africa would say, "Dr. Livingston, I presume?"

Buck stuck out his hand and introduced himself. "I guess we could take turns carrying each other so as not to wear out our shoes."

Colonel Dovell finally returned and announced with a dejected look on his face, shaking his head slowly from side to side, "Drop off ten at each of the already crowded barracks."

Bob started his group toward the barracks while he apologized to Buck.

"It's O.K.," Buck said. "You didn't know."

Bob said, "I'll try to do something, but now I don't know what."

Buck and some of his fellow prisoners at Camp Douglas in Chicago. The youngest was thirteen and the oldest was fifty-three. As you can see, they were in bad need of clothing.

"I want you to meet my friend, Henry Morgan Stanley," Buck said as Henry stuck out his hand.

"We'll make it," Henry said, as he reached the first barracks.

Bob counted off ten as he made sure Henry and Buck were together. "I'll be in touch," Bob said as he marched the remaining distance.

Neither Buck nor Stanley had any gear. They sat on the floor in the middle aisle between the two double-decked cots.

"Do you have any suggestions?" Henry asked.

Buck thought for a moment, then said, "Let's pick the two that don't look like they are going to make it long and sleep on the floor close to their bed."

"Good thinking," Henry said. "I studied to be a doctor before I came into the army. We'll have to make sure they don't have something contagious. If they have chills or cough a lot, don't sleep too close. I have never seen such filth. We'll see if we can clean this place up some while we still have our strength."

A bell began to ring and those who were able picked up their mess cup and began plodding through the muck toward a larger building near the center of the camp.

Neither Buck nor Henry had a cup. "If they don't give us one, what are we going to do?" Henry asked.

"Find a healthy looking one and borrow his after he has finished eating," Buck offered.

When they reached the area where they were serving almost clear soup and a piece of bread, there were stacks of metal cups for the new prisoners.

Buck noticed that there were some prisoners in the serving line which gave him an idea.

The soup did have some cabbage and some salt and pepper. It was warm and didn't taste too bad. It tasted more like tea than soup and the hard bread tasted good soaked in it. Henry and Buck were both hungry and were lucky enough to get another cup full before they ran out.

When Bob and Colonel Dovell left the prison, they went to see the post Commandant.

He treated them well and was very aware of everything they were saying.

He realized that something had to be done. A civilian watchdog organization had already been on his back to do something about the deplorable latrines. They reeked with unspeakable odors and filth.

There were over seven thousand men in an area that was designed for two hundred. There were over ten deaths each day in the camp and even more in the hospital.

The president of the Chicago Board of Trade had no sympathy for the prisoners at Camp Douglas. He had read about the horrors of Andersonville in Georgia.

Those who died of small pox were buried in a small plot near Camp Douglas. The rest were buried en masse at the city cemetery located in south Chicago, sometimes called Oak

Woods. Those buried there had their graves marked with their names and home addresses.

Bob and Colonel Dovell suggested that they bathe the soldiers in Lake Michigan. They also suggested that they do a one-on-one trade for Yankee Soldiers. They also suggested that the prisoners be offered a chance to sign a statement that they would not participate in the war if they were set free.

The Commandant thanked them for their suggestions and said that he would consider them.

Bob volunteered to stay and be a guard.

The Commandant thanked him and said, "We need more of everything. We have no money—we're understaffed. We do not have enough food—we are at the mercy of the local churches. We do better in the summer than in the fall but neither are good. Tomorrow I understand we will have our first beans and potatoes this summer. Very seldom do we have fruit. Almost every prisoner has scurvy. I have my hands full trying to run Camp Douglas; let alone the prison." Turning to Colonel Dovell, he asked, "How would you like to be in charge of the prison?"

Colonel Dovell looked shocked as he swallowed hard and squirmed first to the right, then to the left in his chair. Finally the colonel asked, "Could I have my friend Bob as my adjunct? I know we would have to give him a promotion but I believe we could make a difference."

"You've got it," the Commandment said as he stood up and shook both of their hands. "I'll do the paperwork to make you an officer, Bob, and also to place the two of you in charge of the prisoners."

⌒ NINE ⌒

The word soon spread through the prison. All prisoners were asked to assemble near the center of the camp. When everyone who was able to walk was there, Captain Bob introduced Colonel Dovell telling them that from now on, he would be in charge of the camp.

Colonel Dovell gave a salute with the riding crop. "Men, I don't like what I see here and together we will do something about it.

"First, every day we will bathe in Lake Michigan. If you have a buddy unable to walk the few yards there, carry him.

"Second, while at the shore, pick up all boards and pieces of wood you can find. We'll place them around the latrines in the southeast corner of the campground.

"Third, no pissing anywhere else but there.

"Fourth, wash your clothes and your body while at the lake. Help your weak buddy to do the same.

"Fifth, eat everything that is offered to you and feed your weak or sick buddies.

"Now, you'll be interested in this. I'm trying to work out a one for one prisoner exchange. I will try to get you out of here before winter. With your clothes, you'll never survive this winter.

"Something else I'd like to ask you. How many of you would sign an affidavit that you would never take part in this war again if we let you go free?"

No hands went up but the colonel could see the expressions on their faces and hear them mumbling.

"This is a serious decision and I'm sure you would like to keep your thoughts private. Everyone, lower your heads and close your eyes. Now, raise your hand if you would be interested."

Colonel Dovell noticed how carefully the hands began to go up. Nobody wanted to reveal the show of a hand to his neighbor. The Colonel estimated that well over half would sign and leave. For some reason, he thought that he could believe them.

"Thank you. You may lower your hands and open your eyes. That will be all for now," Colonel Dovell yelled. "Just remember which latrine you are to use. We will leave for the lake at eleven A.M. tomorrow and return in time for your evening meal. You should take your cups with you to the lake to clean and drink from. I'll see you then. Do you have anything more to add, Captain Bob?"

"Not at this time," he answered.

While Colonel Dovell made the rounds of churches, social organizations, and companies willing to furnish some soap, shoes, clothing, and the like, Captain Bob escorted the prisoners on their daily trip to the beach and Lake Michigan. In no time, the prisoners carried back enough wood to cover the entire south third of the campground enabling them to walk on a dry surface. The horrible smell around the barracks and eating area was gone in only a few weeks.

The prisoners began carrying their cups full of water and washing the steps and floor of the barracks. The food was getting better and there was more of it. The death toll was becoming much smaller. Some of the prisoners even began to smile.

Buck and Captain Bob became very good friends and spent most of their time at the beach just sitting and talking. Often Bob would give Buck an apple or some kind of fresh fruit.

Buck asked Bob what he thought about just walking away. Bob advised against it, pointing out all the hazards, but told him that if he did decide to leave, he would loan him some money.

It was now the end of August and there was very little rain. The ground in the prison yard was completely dry. No one was being carried to the beach, even though many were still very sick.

Even though the camp population continued to grow, conditions were much better than when Buck arrived. Now there was estimated to be over ten thousand prisoners in camp. It was the second day of September when Colonel Dovell again called the prisoners together in the center of the campground. He previously arranged to have a high platform constructed from which they could have mail call or make important speeches.

As soon as everyone gathered around, he yelled, "Men, I have good news for you. There will be a one for one exchange September the tenth. The South has almost eight thousand men that they want to exchange. Almost everyone that is not in the hospital will be exchanged. Those who make trouble will not be exchanged and those who wish to sign the papers that they will no longer participate in the war will be allowed to remain in Chicago or go home.

"The Yankees will arrive on the Illinois Central and report to Camp Douglas. As soon as they are in camp, we will board the train back south. I understand it will go to St. Louis where you can catch another train or a boat to points further south."

The prisoners could hardly contain their elation. "Thank you, Colonel Dovell and Captain Bob. God bless you." They were yelling in unison, and their thanks to both men were obvious.

They then broke into their favorite song, "Dixie," with emphasis on the line about dying in Dixie.

There was much hugging and many tear-stained faces as they started filing by the platform to shake Colonel Dovell and Captain Bob's hands.

It was time for their evening meal before they all had a chance to thank the two Yankee officers. The bell was ringing but no one broke line to get to their cup until they had a chance to shake their hands.

The time could not pass fast enough. It seemed like the tenth would never arrive.

Buck wrote to Lucy and Clay and told them that he was getting out. He hadn't written before because he didn't want them to know he was in a P.O.W. camp. He was hopeful that he would be allowed to leave the service and get on with his life. He asked them to say hello to Miss Thomas for him.

The tenth of September finally arrived and the exchange went well. The two groups never saw each other. The Yankees were inside Camp Douglas compound before the Confederates started their march to the train depot.

Buck rode the train to St. Louis where he caught a boat to Cape Girardeau where Thomasville men went once each year for supplies. He was hoping he could catch a ride home. Cape Girardeau was the nearest place where the company store could purchase salt and other staples.

Buck reached the cape on the seventeenth and rested a few days before he started his trek to Thomasville. He tried to buy a horse but no one would sell him one on credit.

It took him until the middle of October to reach Thomasville. The trip had taken a toll on Buck. His shoes would barely stay on his feet and he lost several pounds and became very weary before he reached home.

Buck reached Thomasville early in the morning of October the twenty-first eighteen hundred and sixty-three. He made his way directly to the hospital to see Lucy.

Lucy happened to look toward town as she went to get a bucket of water. She could hardly believe her eyes. Dropping the bucket, she ran. With tears running down both cheeks, she threw both arms around Buck's neck and kissed him several times on both cheeks. Buck finally grasped both upper arms and held her at arm's length.

"Here, let me have a look at you. I can't believe you have grown up so fast. You're no longer my little girl. You're a young lady." Buck never suspected that she was pregnant. "Where is Clay?"

"Oh, Dad, I have so much to tell you, but come, let's get

you something to eat."

As they walked back to the creek, Lucy filled the bucket to carry water back to the sick. She set it down outside a tent and led her dad by the hand to the cook tent. Inside the tent, she introduced her father and told the cooks that he was very hungry.

Buck was served a bountiful meal with fresh milk and bread. All the gardens in Thomasville produced an abundant amount this summer and they gave much to the hospital. Lucy said she would go water the troops while he enjoyed his food. Before Buck finished his meal, Lucy was back with Pete. She walked around the end of the table and helped Pete sit opposite her father. She sat beside him and held his hand. "Dad, this is a very good friend, Pete Amonette. Pete, this is my dad, Buck Paty."

Buck wiped his hand and reached across the table and said, "Any friend of Lucy's is a friend of mine. How did you lose your leg?"

"I guess you could say I lost it to a hand saw. I was wounded and it got infected. Gangrene set up and the doctor said the saw was the only medicine."

"Where is Clay?" Buck asked.

"Oh, Dad, you won't believe this. Clay already started building our house. He made the most beautiful plans." Lucy was so excited to get to tell him about the house first. "It has a big dining room and a kitchen. The family room is plenty big to party and dance in. I know you will be pleased."

"Where did he get the money and who is helping him?"

Lucy told the whole story. She told him about the man named Don Walker who brought Clay home and how he was a carpenter. She told him that Clay wrote checks to pay for everything.

She leaned over and whispered in his ear, "The other money hasn't been touched.

"I have also learned that Virginia Creeper has five leaves and poison ivy has three. I'll have something to tell you some day."

"When can we go see Clay and what he is doing?" Buck asked.

"I can be off most any time now, we don't have many patients. We can rent a horse and buggy at the livery stable behind the store. Give me twenty minutes and I'll be ready to go. Oh, is it O.K. if Pete comes with us?" Lucy asked.

"Don't you think it will be a little crowded?" Buck asked, looking at Pete and his crutch.

"I like to sit close to Pete," Lucy answered, as she left in a hurry.

Buck asked Pete about his family and where his home was, but Pete seemed pretty evasive about everything. He never gave a definite answer. Not only did he seem very detached from all the questions that were asked of him, but he never asked any of his own.

Lucy soon returned and they made their way to the livery stable where they rented a horse and buggy.

On the way to Spring Creek, Lucy and Pete held hands, but very few words were spoken. Buck asked about the man that was helping Clay.

"His name is Don Walker and I think he is the ugliest man I ever saw," Lucy replied. "He is tall, thin, has one big ear and one small one. His hands hang almost to his knees. He is probably forty years old and never been married. He says he would like to have a wife, but not many would give him a second look. When you see him, you'll see what I'm talking about."

When they finally arrived at Spring Creek, Buck could hardly believe what he saw.

Clay didn't even stop working when the buggy pulled up. He thought it was more supplies from the store.

Lucy yelled, "Clay, look who is here!"

Clay looked and saw his dad. He wasted no time getting down from his ladder to run and greet him.

Clay was almost as tall as his dad. He stuck out his hand but that wasn't enough for Buck. He pulled Clay to him and gave him a bear hug as he lifted him off the ground and shook him vigorously, giving him a kiss on the head.

Buck couldn't get over how his children had grown both physically and mentally.

"Come, Dad. Let me show you what we are doing."

They stopped on the north end of the house where Clay's enormous studio was almost finished. It had a dark room, two places for backdrops, and a lounge area large enough for a big bedroom where he and Don lived while they worked on the house.

Above Clay's studio there were three bedrooms. To the south of them, on ground level, was the remainder of the large house with two fireplaces and a long porch on the eastern side. The sub-floor for the entire house was complete and they were ready to put up the walls.

The entire structure met with Buck's approval. He turned to Clay and gave him another big hug and said, "I couldn't have done it better myself."

Clay called Don over to introduce him to his father. "Here is the man you can thank. Dad, this is Don Walker; without him, I'd be lost."

Don stuck out his hand and Buck gave him a firm shake and a pat on the back. "How can I ever thank you?" Buck asked.

"Find me a wife," was Don's reply.

"I'll see what I can do," Buck answered.

They spent that whole afternoon visiting and working. Buck expressed concern about getting the roof on and the fireplaces finished before the fall rains got any worse. He thought about hiring extra help. He wanted to check the buried money but didn't dare with so many people around. This, however, didn't keep him from looking at the rock shaped like a woodchuck. And the "fours" were going through his mind. He really didn't need to remember them. He felt that he could walk directly to the exact spot.

Time flew by and it was important that they headed back to Thomasville before the sun went down.

Buck asked Clay if he was going to need Pet and the buggy before tomorrow. He would like to use his own buggy so he wouldn't have to rent one. Clay had no need, so Pete drove the rented buggy and Buck drove his own back to town.

Buck forgot to get a bedroll but Lucy told him that there were plenty of empty beds in the hospital.

The next morning, as soon as Buck finished breakfast, he led Pet from the spot he staked her to the water where she drank like a camel. He then harnessed and hooked her to the buggy.

He hadn't seen Miss Thomas yet and he was anxious. She either hadn't been at the hospital or he just hadn't seen her. He headed for John and Matilda Thomas' home to see if she was there. Buck pulled up in front of their house and tied Pet to the hitching rail. He made his way through the picket gate and up the steps to the front door. He gently knocked but there was no response. He then knocked much harder. Matilda came to the door with her finger to her lips.

"Oh, how good to see you, Mr. Paty. I'm sorry you can't come in. Delia is sleeping and I am afraid that she is very ill."

"Is there anything I can do?" Buck asked.

The door opened wider and John pushed past his wife, came to the front porch with an outstretched hand, and said, "Good to see you again. Say, that boy and girl of yours are something else. You must be proud of them."

Matilda eased the door closed. John found a chair on the front porch and motioned to Buck to pull one up beside him. As soon as they were seated, John offered Buck a cigar. They barely lit up when Matilda gently opened the door with two cups of coffee in her hands.

Buck stood and thanked her. "What seems to be wrong with Delia?" Buck asked.

"We really don't know. She has been losing weight and running a fever for some time. Her cough is getting worse. It doesn't look good. We can only hope and pray and take good care of her. One of the doctors comes by each day. They don't speak very encouragingly."

"I'm so sorry," Buck replied with a most sorrowful look on his face.

"I imagine it is something she has caught from one of the soldiers. She really worked too hard. She cared for everyone's welfare except her own. There were many times that she worked all night long. I don't know what the doctors would do without her. Lucy has been like an angel sent from Heaven. Just hope she doesn't come down with something. I imagine it is consumption. That is such a wasting disease, especially if it gets in the lungs. Very few people ever recover from tuberculosis. We just hope and pray for Delia."

"I saw a lot of that in the army. It is really an awful disease, but I have seen some get over it. Lots of fresh fruits and vegetables along with fresh air seems to help."

"Delia has almost given up. Maybe you coming home will help. We'll tell her you are home from the army and try to get her up more often. She is so weak."

"I'd be glad to come by and help get her up if you think it would help," Buck said.

"We'll talk to her doctor and let you know. I don't see how it could hurt anything."

"There are things I need to work on. Clay made a lot of progress on the house but he needs my help. I was looking forward to spending time with Delia. I do hope she recovers."

"What do you have on your mind?" John asked.

"Oh, many things," Buck answered. "I'm concerned about Lucy and her friend Pete. I want to hire some help for the building of my house. I also need a stone mason. I'm also concerned about this man Don Walker who is helping Clay. He is almost forty years old and he has never been married. He is very plain looking and hasn't been able to find a wife. I'm afraid that he will leave if we don't find him someone."

"Well, I can help you some," John answered. "There are two sisters who stayed here when the rest of the Osage Indian women moved to Oklahoma. Many of the men stayed but none will have anything to do with the sisters. When you see them, you will understand why.

"About the extra help and the stone masons, you ask Mr. Hass at the store. He can fix you up."

"Where can I find the two sisters?" Buck asked.

"They live in Shantytown along with most all the other

wanting people in Thomasville. It's about five blocks north of here. There are probably fifty people who live in shacks on one small parcel of land. Like I say, they aren't very desirable. They are poor and most are lazy and have a drinking problem.

"About Lucy and Pete, I'll have a talk with her the next time I see her. She doesn't come around here since Delia has been ill."

Buck finished his coffee and sat his cup on the porch rail as he stood up and thanked John gratefully.

"I think I'll go see the two sisters. What are their names?"

"Their real names or what they are called down at the store?" John asked.

"Maybe I had better have their real names."

"They like to be called the Crow Sisters; Jean with the bun on top and Jane with the part down the middle."

Buck again thanked John and headed for Shantytown which wasn't hard to recognize. All of the shacks were built together and shared outside walls. There were few windows and everything was built with cull lumber.

Buck saw a young boy playing in the street out front and asked if he knew where the Crow sisters lived.

The young boy laughed and replied, "I thought all men knew where they lived."

"Well, I'm afraid I don't," Buck answered. "Will you show me?"

"What's it worth to you?" the young boy asked.

"Do you work for them?" Buck asked.

"Sometimes," he answered, as he dug his big toe into the mud. He lowered his face and glanced sideways at Buck.

"Here," Buck said as he tossed him a penny.

The boy caught it in one hand and stuck it into his mouth to check the metal before pointing his finger at the house directly behind him.

Buck got down from the buggy and handed the boy the reins saying, "Hold her, I won't be gone long."

Buck walked over the boards through the mud to the door where the homeliest creatures that he ever saw were peering from parted rags over the windows.

The first knock on the door was answered quickly.

Both sisters stood directly in front of him as if to give him a choice. "Are you the Crow Sisters?" Buck asked.

"Sure are. I'm Jean," one said stepping forward, "and she is Jane," indicated her sister.

"I'm not here for your services. I'm here to offer you a marriage." Their eyes opened wide but their mouths opened even wider. "Are you interested in marrying a man about your age who will take care of you and move you out of this muck?"

Without even asking any questions, they both said, "Yes." They both thought Buck was asking for himself.

Buck saw the expression and quickly added, "I'm not asking for myself but what I've told you is true."

"When?" was Jane's next question.

"Soon," Buck replied, "but first I have some things I want you to do. Go to the river and take a good bath using much soap."

"The river is cold," Jane replied.

"Hell, I'd break the ice for a man of my own," Jean chimed in.

"After you bathe, go by the store and pick out for each of you a complete new outfit of clothes."

Again, their mouths fell open, unable to believe their ears.

"Each of you may take one bag of belongings. If there is anything else, we'll get it later. Also, pick out a suit of clothes for a six-foot, very thin man with big feet.

"I'll tell Mr. Hass to allow you to put your clothes on my account. Now hurry. I'll pick you up here in two hours."

"We don't have a timepiece," Jane said.

"Here," Buck said, as he pulled his watch from his pocket and handed it to Jane. "You do know how to tell time, don't you?"

They both dropped their chins and shook their heads no.

"Never mind," Jane said. "We'll be ready."

"Be clean, too," Buck said as he headed back to the buggy.

At the buggy, the young boy stuck out one hand while he held the reins tight in the other. Buck asked, "Do you still have your penny?"

The boy shook his head yes and reached in his ragged pants with his filthy little hand. He pulled it out and showed it to Buck who reached and took it. Buck rubbed it and handed it back to him and said, "For being a good boy, I'm going to allow you to keep it. Are either of the Crow girls your mother?" Buck asked.

The young boy made a horrible face as he turned and spat. "Hell, No! I'm glad you ain't my old man either. Take your damn reins," he said as he plodded barefooted through the mud down the street.

Buck, feeling a little sorry for him, yelled, "Hey, what's your name?"

The boy stopped and turned back and said, "Bullshit, what's yours?"

Buck, shaking his head, climbed into the buggy with the reins in his hands. He turned Pet around and headed back to town and the company store.

At the store, he told Mr. Hass about his needs. A carpenter and two stone masons were at the head of his list. Mr. Hass looked toward the back of the store where several men were loafing and playing checkers. He yelled, "I need a carpenter's helper and two stone masons."

Four men immediately came to the front of the store. "I only need three men," Buck said.

"We are stone masons," two said, "and you can have your pick of the other two."

Buck made his selection. They agreed on the wages and the time they were to report to work the next day.

The men walked back to their games and talked excitedly over their chance to make some money.

"Oh, yes, I told two ladies that they could charge some clothes to me," Buck said to Mr. Hass.

This statement really created some excitement. Everyone wondered who the ladies were. No one was about to leave the store until they saw who they were.

"Is there a preacher or a justice of the peace in town?" Buck asked.

"Yes, there are both," Mr. Hass replied. "Mr. Edwards is the justice of the peace and Mr. Howell is the preacher."

"Can you tell one of them to come to my place tomorrow at twelve noon and I'll give him three dollars to perform a wedding. Maybe you better send the preacher," Buck said. "It sounds better to be married by a preacher."

This really created some excitement. A wedding in Thomasville had always been a well-planned and very special occasion.

"Have you seen my niggers?" Buck asked.

"They seldom come to town but Mr. Roberts and Mr. Griffith both speak very highly of them."

"Give them the word that I'll be seeing them soon, will you?"

"No problem," Mr. Hass answered.

Buck picked up a soda and walked back to where the action was. Two checker games were in progress and men were waiting for someone to leave so they could play.

Buck pulled up a chair and sat down among them. Some he met on his earlier visit to Thomasville, and some he hadn't. Nobody bothered to make the introductions but everybody wanted to ask about the young ladies. Games were won and lost but nobody got up to leave.

"They will be here soon," Buck told them.

Everyone kept one eye on the front door anxious to see who the two ladies were.

It wasn't long before the door opened and everyone stretched their necks to see who it was.

When they saw the Crow Sisters, they returned to their games. But, when the sisters walked back to the clothing section and started making selections to try on, everyone gave Buck some side glances. No one said anything and Buck didn't offer any explanation.

After they completed their selection, including shoes, hats, and a shawl, they placed them on the counter for Mr. Hass to check the prices. Buck slowly strolled to the front of the store where he leaned over and whispered to them, "Go put them on."

They went back to the dressing room and donned their new outfits. When they returned, everyone admitted that they looked better, but one person said, "They need something to cover their faces."

Buck walked out of the store to the buggy as Jane and Jean sauntered along behind him, carrying the suit they selected for Don.

After they were out the door, Mr. Hass told about the preacher or justice of the peace who was to go out tomorrow. The people still shook their heads and wondered. They thought that it must be someone else besides Buck that would marry these sisters. Their curiosity was really aroused.

Buck helped them into the buggy. They had to hold their long dresses up with one hand. Evidently they hadn't been in a buggy before. Buck looked at them and wished they purchased a droopy hat instead of the ones that showed their faces.

All the way to Spring Creek, they sat like two statues with their hands folded in their laps. Buck looked over at both of them and asked, "Are you having second thoughts?"

They both shook their heads and said, "No."

"How much further is it?" Jane asked, still looking terribly forlorn.

"Not far. We are almost there."

Don had no idea what Buck had in mind when he promised him a wife. He kept working until Clay bumped him with a two-by-four and said, "Look at the new help Dad brought."

When Don looked, he almost went into shock. He laid his saw down and walked briskly to the buggy to assist the ladies down. If he noticed their faces, he never showed it. He was grinning from ear to ear. "Hello ladies," he said with a slight bow. "Welcome to Spring Creek."

"Well, what do you think?" Buck asked.

Don looked at Buck, still smiling as he asked, "Are they for me?"

"This is Jane," he said with his arm on her shoulder, "and

her sister, Jean Crow. Which one do you want to marry?"

Don could hardly believe his ears. "Do I have to choose?" he asked. "I think I will take both of them."

"Tomorrow, someone will be here to marry you. You'll need to decide before then. You can have the rest of the day off and the studio is yours for tonight."

Don placed his arms around both of them and started walking toward the creek. Buck and Clay continued cutting studs for the walls as they talked excitedly. Both were happy for Don.

It was almost dark when Don, Jean, and Jane returned from the creek. Buck yelled to them, "Supper is almost ready!"

"We're going to skip this evening's meal," Don yelled back as they opened the door to the studio.

Buck and Clay looked at each other and smiled. They laid down their tools and went to the creek before dinner. Their meal was ham hock with beans along with some leftover corn pone. The beans were hanging in a pot over an open fire all day, so they were well done.

"I'll be glad when the women take over the cooking and the cleaning," Clay said, "It has been a long time since Mom died. Just hope they cook better than they look."

"That would be nice," Buck replied.

After their meal, they took their pans to the river and gave them a good rinsing before they poured boiling water over them. Buck and Clay made their bed in the buggy that night. They were both very tired and Buck was snoring before it got dark.

The next morning, Buck and Clay were up early, but there was no sign of Don or the girls. Clay walked over to the studio and eased the door open. They were all three in his bed. Don was flat on his back and one was on each arm. All of them were sound asleep. He gently closed the door and reported to his dad.

"We won't bother them this early," Buck answered. "No one should have to work on his wedding day."

Buck and Clay had another bowl of beans but there wasn't

any ham left. They gathered their tools and began cutting more studs for the walls. It was almost ten o'clock when Buck decided it was time to wake them. They carried the cut two-by-fours above where Don and the girls were sleeping and noisily dropped them on the floor. They placed the base two-by-four on the floor and with hammer and nails began anchoring it to the floor. Don came out of the door and looked up at them with a sheepish expression on his face.

"Time to get up," Buck said. "You got to clean up and put on that new suit before the preacher gets here. Take the girls down to the river with you. We left you some beans in the pot if you and the ladies are hungry. Be ready a little before twelve. I'm not paying the preacher overtime."

Don went back into the studio and soon he and the two women came out, each with a sheet or blanket wrapped around them. Jane never bothered to look up at either Buck or Clay, but Jean gave them a Mona Lisa smile.

"I have never seen such expressionless women," Buck said. "Go down and get your camera set up where you want it. We need some pictures."

"How about one at the creek?" Clay asked before he broke into a laugh. He ducked quickly to avoid a chunk of wood that Buck threw at him.

Buck continued working after he walked to the back of the house to relieve himself over the edge. He just began working again when he heard a noise coming from Thomasville. He immediately turned toward the creek and yelled, "Here comes the preacher!"

Looking toward the creek, they all ran to the house like scared deer. Their sheets were flapping in the wind exposing their nudity. One of the girls' sheets got caught on a thorn bush where it remained while she picked up speed toward the studio. "Talk about running," Buck thought. "All I saw was a streak." He turned to Clay where he was setting up his camera to use the trees for a background. "Did you get a shot of that?" Buck asked.

"My shutter speed isn't fast enough to catch that. Did you

ever see any woman move that fast? Their mother must have been scared by a cheetah when she was carrying them."

They hardly made it inside the cabin when the preacher rode out of the forest and up to the cabin. Buck looked behind him and saw other buggies and people hiding in the brush. He looked at his watch and saw that it was after eleven. He climbed down and walked around to where the preacher parked his buggy and tied his horse.

"Glad to see you," Buck said, "I'm Buck Paty and this will be my home some day," he said while gesturing toward the house under construction.

"I'm the Reverend Howell. I preach at the Community Building every Sunday. We'd be glad to have you. Will this be your first marriage?" the reverend asked.

"Oh, it's not me getting married, but it will be their first marriage. Why don't you ask your friends to come out of the bushes so they can see better?"

"Well, I don't know," the reverend said as he pawed the ground with his right foot and looked down. "I didn't ask them to come. Some I don't even know. I think they are the Checkers, and the Spit, and Whittle Clubs from down at the company store. I never go back there. Their talk is too rough for me," the reverend said with an embarrassed look on his face.

Buck started walking toward the brush where they were hiding. He got within good hearing distance and yelled, "Come on to the house so you can witness the wedding. Everyone is welcome." He gave a big "come on" sign with his right arm, making several big circular motions from the trees to the house.

One by one, they came forward. None were bearing gifts and all really felt out of place. When they reached the house, Buck recognized them as the ones from the store.

"So glad you could take time out of your busy day to help us celebrate this special occasion. Where I came from, not only are weddings a special occasion, but the building of a new home is also special. Come, we have a few minutes before the wedding. I'll show you the house." He walked around the east where the long porch floor was completed and overlooked Spring Creek. Across the porch and into the house, all the sub-floor was down. "This will be the family room and library," he said, pointing to where the walls would be. "We plan to have a big dance here with plenty to drink and good music for every-one who helped as soon as it is finished. Buck hoped they had taken the bait.

He turned to the north and said, "There will be three bed-rooms there and a kitchen and dining room to the west. There will be two big fireplaces on the south. We sure are trying to get it finished before winter." He could tell from their expressions that they had swallowed the bait, hook, line, and sinker.

As he turned and started to leave the house, one of the men asked, "Who's getting married? We got some bets on."

"Don Walker is his name. He brought my son Clay home from his army assignment. He's the one helping Clay build the house."

All the men were silent and walked back to the big oak tree where they assumed the wedding was going to take place. The same man who asked about the wedding asked, "Ain't there two women?"

"Sure are," Buck replied. "Damned if I know which one he will marry. Any of you want the other one? I'll pay the preach-er."

No one answered. There were nine unexpected guests sit-ting on the ground facing the same direction. Clay aimed the camera at them.

"Sorry I don't have anything to offer you," Buck said. "But if you tell Mr. Hass to give each of you a cool one on me, I'm sure it will be all right."

The men began to grudgingly say thank you, but were interrupted by Don as he led both girls by the hand to a spot pointed to by Clay.

"Don, Jane, and Jean, may I introduce the Reverend Howell, and these men are your admirers," Buck said, pointing toward the congregation. "Are you ready, Reverend?"

"I'm ready, but who is to be the bride?" he asked.

"I am," both Jane and Jean answered.

The reverend looked completely befuddled as he turned to Buck and said, "This can't be."

"Which one will it be?" Buck asked Don.

"I'll take them both," Don answered. "I've been saving for forty years."

"You can't be married to both of them at once," the Reverend scolded among the laughs and snickers of the uninvited guests.

"I'll marry Jane for Monday, Wednesday, and Friday, and Jean for the other four days."

The nine men, including Buck and Clay, were laughing so hard that the Reverend couldn't make himself heard as he tried to explain that it wouldn't work.

One man stood up and shouted, "Is it against the law, Preach?"

"I, I never heard of it, but it don't look right to me."

"Come on, Preach, we'll stay for both ceremonies."

That Mona Lisa smile appeared again on Jean as she looked at her savior and muttered, "Thank you, sir."

The preacher started squirming and looking for an exit but the nine guests stood and surrounded him.

"We're ready, Preach," their spokesperson leaned over and whispered to him.

The preacher slowly opened his Bible, too afraid not to perform the weddings. There was no way he could beat them back to town. He looked up, and thought, "I wonder if this is part of the Jamison Gang or The Sons of Liberty." He then reached both hands toward heaven and said, "Forgive me God."

"Which one of you, (He couldn't continue without clearing his throat with much gusto.) ladies want to be first?"

"I'd like to be first," Jane said with her head bowed. "I'm the oldest."

The preacher cut the ceremony short, wanting to hurry to the part where he said, "I now pronounce you man and wife." Before he said it, he hesitated and said, "I now pronounce you

Don Walker, Jane, and Jean Crow, looking the way they were expected to in 1863. If you look closely, you can see Jane's "Mona Lisa" smile. Jane is on the side with Don's small ear. It is hard to believe that this is a wedding picture.

wife number one for Monday, Wednesday, and Friday, and the same goes for you, Jean, except you are wife number two for the other four days. Don, you may now kiss your wives. So may the rest of you," the Reverend said sarcastically looking at the crowd as he headed for his buggy in a hurry.

"You may get your two dollars from Mr. Hass at the store!" Buck yelled as the reverend slapped his horse on the rear with the reins only to change his mind and yell "Whoa!" as he pulled back on the rains. "How about four dollars since there were two weddings."

"Two dollars and a bottle of Sarsaparilla," Buck yelled, barely being heard above the laughter.

"Gitty up you old fart," the Reverend yelled, slapping the horse on the rear with the reins.

Everyone except the newly married trio was almost hysterical. "Come on," Clay yelled to Don. "Come over here where the light is right. I want some pictures."

Before the crowd of men left, one asked Buck if they could bring their women when they came to work on the house.

Buck tried to look shocked but answered, "They would be very welcome. We want to meet the people so we can invite them to the first dance. Thanks very much," Buck said, giving the stranger a firm handshake.

"I can't remember when I ever had so much fun," Buck heard them say. "Can't wait to get back to Thomasville and tell everyone."

"I'm sure the women will want to come and help them get into the house before winter."

⌒ TEN ⌒

S oon after the wedding, Buck informed Jane and Jean what their responsibilities would be. Breakfast would be at seven, lunch at twelve, and dinner at seven. They would also be responsible for the laundry and the cleaning. In exchange, they could use the studio until a bedroom was completed.

The next morning, soon after sunrise, the wagons and buggies began to arrive. Men pilled out with hammers and saws in their hands. The women carried picnic baskets and large containers of tea, lemonade, and coffee. The cool drinks were placed in the creek and the coffee was placed near the fire. They all walked up to Buck with one question: "What do you want us to do?"

After a few questions and a few conferences with Don, Buck divided the men up with specific instructions.

By noon, all the studs were up and the dropsiding was going on the outside. Both chimneys were half-completed. They had to wait for the mortar to dry before they could go any higher.

Don cut pattern rafters and they were going up fast, along with decking ready for the shakes. The posts were set for the front porch, and were ready to be tied together on top.

The noon meal was spread on the front porch. What a feast! Fried chicken, roast pork, venison, and every kind of vegetable mentionable was there. Pies, pies, pies; chocolate, custard, raisin, apple, and even lemon were there. The meal alone was enough to make everyone want to come back again the next day.

After everyone had eaten their fill, there was lots of food left. One man said, "Guess we will eat leftovers tomorrow. I think we can finish her up in one more day."

Buck looked surprised, but was elated to know they were coming back and that they would be in the house before winter.

The next day many returned to help. They finished the dropsiding, the roof, and the chimneys. The windows were all in place and all that remained to do was the hardwood floors and ceilings for the inside. With twelve men working it didn't take long.

The Paty home with family and some friends.

Buck shook every hand and thanked them when the day was finished. He made certain that he thanked all the wives also. The men told Buck that they would be back the first rainy day to help finish the inside.

Tears rolled down Buck's face as he waved good-bye to them.

Jane and Jean fit in really well. They performed all their domestic chores and found other work to keep them busy. They worshipped Don and still acted like loving sisters.

Don, Clay, and Buck finished the northwest bedroom first. They completed the walls, floor, and ceiling in only two days. This bedroom was the largest of the three and was for Don and his two wives. It was the farthest from the fireplaces but Buck told Don, "You won't need much heat with a wife on both sides."

The next day it rained and the men from town, along with some of their wives, were there to help finish the house. "Let's go get the wagon and the team we stored," Buck said to Clay.

Don asked Buck if he cared if he made his own furniture for their bedroom. He stated that there was plenty of lumber left over from the house to do it.

"How long are you going to stay with us?" Buck asked.

"As long as you will let us," was Don's answer.

"Good, we'll have a bit of fences to build and we'll need to start on a barn soon."

Clay hitched Pet to the buggy and they headed for Thomasville to pick up the stored wagon. Mr. Lasley was home, sitting on the front porch, when they arrived. He stood up and said, "I heard you were back, so we hurried to get our crops in so you could have your team."

"We ain't quite ready for the team yet, but we do need the furniture."

"It's right where you left it. If you need any help, just yell. I'm pretty tired today. I hear you are having a dance."

"That's right," Buck answered. "You and your family will be welcome. We haven't set a date yet. I'll let you know," he said as he hurried for the barn to harness the team and get home before dark.

Once the team was harnessed and hitched to the wagon, he noticed how loose the rims were on the wooden spoke wheels.

"You better drive the wagon into the creek so the wheels will tighten up before you start home," Mr. Lasley yelled.

"Thank you, and we'll bring the team back after we make a trip to St. Louis."

"You better leave the team and wagon at Cape Girardeau and catch a boat. That's a hard trip for a team," Mr. Lasley suggested.

They followed Mr. Lasley's suggestion and soaked the wagon wheels in the creek. In practically no time, the wheels had expanded and the rims were tight again. They barely made it home before dark.

Jane and Jean brought out a kerosene lantern to help them see to unload. When they finished unloading, Buck said, "There is one bed and our best mattress missing."

"Oh, Dad, I forgot to tell you, that's the one I have in my photo studio."

After everything had been unloaded and dusted, the house still looked vacant. Buck placed his deceased wife's big pump organ in one corner of the family room. It was the most elegant piece of furniture he had. The dining room table, buffet, and chairs also looked pretty good after they were dusted.

The two beds were set up in their respective rooms, but the mattresses and covers would have to be aired. They smelled terrible.

There was an easy chair and one night table for each bedroom, and four chairs and one library table for the family room.

Buck found a pencil and some paper in the drawer of the library table. He pulled up a chair and began making a list of things he would like to buy in St. Louis. He sat for a while, arose and walked through the house, came back, and wrote some more. Finally, he could think of nothing else.

"Tomorrow, we will take the team as far as Cape Girardeau. We'll leave them at the livery stable and travel either by boat or train. Clay, I think it would be good for you to go with me," he said, "I'm sure you need photo supplies."

The next day, they were up early to start their journey. Buck told Don he would try to be back in two weeks and asked if he needed anything. He also handed Don a check and said, "Clay told me how much you earned. I suggest you open a checking or savings account at the bank. You may use the buggy and take your wives with you if you like. Good-bye and take care of things. If you have time, build a fence around the house."

"See you when we get back," Clay said with a salute to the brim of his hat.

As soon as Clay and Buck were in the wagon, Buck said, "We should go by and see Lucy. Do you realize we haven't seen her in almost a month. I would like to check on Delia also."

They first drove by the Thomases only to find out that Delia was no better. Buck expressed his sorrow and asked if there was anything he could get in St. Louis for her.

"Not unless they have something new that will cure consumption," Mr. Thomas answered.

"I'll check and see. Have you seen Lucy?" Buck asked.

"Not in a long time. I imagine she is staying busy at the hospital."

Buck climbed back into the wagon and waved as he spoke to the team and pulled the rein to turn around and head for the hospital to find Lucy.

∽ ELEVEN ∽

O n the way to the hospital, several people waved but Buck only recognized one who helped on the house. He commented to Clay, "I suspect they heard about the dance and want to be invited."

At the creek, they stopped while the team had a long drink of the cool, clear water. In fact, Clay got down and had a drink also, upstream from the mules.

"Come on," Buck said. "We'll never get to St. Louis." Clay slowly climbed back into the wagon and they went on to the hospital. The first person they saw, Buck stopped to ask about Lucy. The man lowered his head and pointed to the last tent in a row of five. "She mostly stays down there," he said.

Buck and Clay both looked at each other with a befuddled expression.

When they reached the tent, Buck tied the team to a small tree where there was grass to allow them to graze.

The flaps to the tent were both closed. Buck asked in a raised voice, "Lucy, are you in there?"

There was no reply at first but he could hear movement in the tent.

"May we come in?" he then asked.

Finally, he heard Lucy say, "Come on in. I'm not feeling well."

Buck pulled back a flap and he and Clay squeezed through. Lucy was lying on a cot with a sheet over her. She looked at both Buck and Clay and turned and faced the outside wall of the tent.

"What's wrong?" her dad asked as he went over and sat on the edge of the cot. He placed his hand on her shoulder and rolled her back toward him. It was very obvious what was wrong.

She was so young. The tears were streaming down her cheeks. Her breasts were large and her stomach was bulging. Clay saw the problem but didn't say anything.

Buck just sat there for a few minutes before he leaned over and pulled her to him. He kissed her on the forehead and said, "Lucy, Baby, this is your father and my love for you is unconditional. You can always count on me. I'm just glad you ain't sick like Delia." Buck said, "Is Pete the father, and where is he?"

"That's one of the problems, Dad. As soon as he found out I was pregnant, he left and I haven't heard a thing from him. Oh, Daddy, I was so foolish but I thought he really loved me. He only used me. I can see that now. I nursed him back to health and now this is the way he shows his appreciation. What am I going to do?"

Again Buck sat for a few moments, still holding Lucy by the hand and stroking her hair. "I'll tell you what we are going to do. You are coming with Clay and me on a buying spree in St. Louis."

"Can I get rid of the baby there?" Lucy asked.

"Don't you want the baby?" Buck asked.

"I thought you probably didn't," Lucy answered. "Yes, I want the baby."

"Enough said. Get your things together and I'll tell them you are going with your father."

For the first time since Pete left, Lucy showed some enthusiasm. She hopped from the bed and shook the pillow from its case thinking she would pack her belongings in it. She suddenly realized, "I can't get into any of my clothes!" and fell back onto the bed and began to sob.

"Don't worry, Lucy," Clay said as he removed his coat and

shirt. "Here, wear my shirt and leave your skirt unbuttoned. We'll get you something in St. Louis."

"I can't go to St. Louis looking like this," she said as she pulled on a skirt and put on Clay's shirt.

When Buck returned, he saw how awful Lucy looked and said, "We'll stop at the store and you can get a complete outfit while I go to the bank."

At the bank, Buck withdrew three thousand dollars which left him only one thousand in the bank. He hadn't dug up what he buried and wouldn't for a while.

When he returned to the store, Lucy decided on a full-bodied, floor-length dress that could be worn either with a belt or without. She also had a new pair of shoes and a new winter coat. Everyone in the store admired her and no one knew that such a young lady was expecting.

Clay paid Mr. Hass all he owed him with a check in the amount of one hundred dollars. His change amounted to thirty-five dollars and two cents. Buck said that he needed some cash for his trip to St. Louis.

Buck stuck the money in his bib pocket and called to Clay and Lucy. "Let's go see the big lights. Come on," Buck said as he helped Lucy into the wagon.

It was almost noon when they finally got underway. A few miles out of town, Lucy asked, "What are we having for lunch?"

Clay and Buck looked at each other with a blank expression. Buck slapped his forehead and said, "I guess I had too much on my mind. I completely forgot to bring food and there's no telling how far it is to the nearest house."

They hadn't traveled far when Clay spied wild hazelnuts. Usually by late September the chipmunks and squirrels had them all gathered but this was a big thicket and there were several still on the bushes. They stopped the wagon and all three got out. In a very short time, they had all they could carry in their pockets and Lucy held the tail of her dress up to form a basket in which they piled many more. Back in the wagon, Clay selected two flat rocks to crack them with. He sat in the back of the wagon and was busy cracking them and handing them to Buck and Lucy.

"Back in Louisiana we called them filberts and they were larger, but I think these taste better," Buck commented.

"I think so, too," Clay commented. "I have also found a very easy way to get them."

"How's that?" Lucy asked.

"In the fall when their covering turns brown, you go to where they grow and sit real still. The squirrels and chipmunks will gather them. You watch where they store them for the winter and then you go get them all hulled and clean."

"That's terrible," Lucy scolded.

"It's called survival of the smart ones. Let them get smart. What do you think God put them here for? Certainly not to eat."

Late that evening, they camped by a small creek so the mules could have water and graze on the green grass along the bank. They finished eating their hazelnuts and made their bed in the bottom of the wagon and stretched the tarp overhead, draping it over the seat and sideboards of the wagon. It wasn't very comfortable but they were off the ground and away from snakes and other crawly things.

The next morning they were up early and on their way by the time the sun started to peek over the hills. It was cool down by the creek making them realize that fall was here and it wouldn't be long before winter.

About the middle of the afternoon, they came to a small settlement called Piedmont. They found a place to eat and asked questions. It was another day and a half to Cape Girardeau and they could probably find what they were looking for there.

Buck thanked them for the information. He then asked where he could buy something for them to eat on the way. The lady in the eatery said, "I can fix you something if you like. I have cheese, summer sausage, and plenty of bread."

"Sounds good to me," Buck answered. "Fix enough for three people for four meals. If you have any fruit, put some in."

"I have canned peaches," she answered. It was less than ten minutes before she set the package on the table. Buck paid her and left a dime on the table when they left.

They were barely out the front door when the lady opened the door and yelled at them, "Here, you left a dime on your table!"

Turning back toward her, Buck said, "That's for you, Lady."

She threw it at him and said, "I don't take money that I don't earn!" She slammed the door and went back inside.

Lucy picked the dime up and said to her dad, "I'll take it. That's the first money I've seen since we buried ours."

When it began getting dark, they started looking for a place to spend the night. This time it was a large river that they came to. Buck wondered if they would be able to cross it with the team and wagon. It was too dark to see. They watered the mules and staked them out again where they could graze and also reach the water to drink. Clay gathered some wood and they started a fire so they could see to eat. He dragged up two old, dried logs for them to sit on. He commented that they must have been cottonwood because they were so light. They sat on them while Clay piled more wood on the fire.

Lucy opened the package of food and was pleasantly surprised at what she saw. Not only was there meat, bread, and cheese, she had included three fried peach pies and some molasses cookies. It was hard to leave anything for tomorrow; everything was so good.

"You got to learn to cook like that," Clay said to Lucy.

They ate well over half of the food and decided they would skip breakfast so they could get an early start and have the remainder for lunch tomorrow.

The sky clouded over during the night and really looked like rain when they finally woke up the next morning.

Buck pulled his watch from his pocket and excitedly exclaimed, "My God, it's almost eight o'clock! Hurry and get around. We must be on our way!"

"I got to go bad," Lucy said as she climbed out of the wagon.

She didn't even put on her dress or her shoes as she headed for a hiding place.

The team was harnessed and hitched to the wagon and Lucy still hadn't returned. Buck yelled, "Lucy, are you all right?"

"I'm in a mess," she yelled back. "I almost waited too late and I don't know if this is Virginia Creeper or poison ivy. I don't have anything to clean with."

"Go down to the river, strip and wash," Buck answered. "But hurry."

Lucy did hurry. Soon she was back at the wagon with a smile on her face. She quickly slipped on her dress and climbed in the back to pull on and lace up her shoes. As soon as she was seated in the back, she said, "I'm ready, Dad. Sorry to hold you up."

"That's O.K., Dear, but remember, if you don't go when you gotta go; you may find that you have already gone."

"I'll try to remember that," Lucy replied. "Where did you hear that?"

"Didn't hear it. Comes from past experience."

Lunch time came but they decided not to stop since they already watered the team two times. "I was sure surprised that the river wasn't deep, only dingy. Wonder what its name is," Buck said, referring to the river where they camped for the night.

Lucy said, "I don't know what its name is, but I'll remember the spot. Move over, I want to sit up front for a while. I'm tired of lying down. It don't look so much like rain now, does it? I think I'll have something to eat," she added.

"Fix us all something," Clay added. "Fix it before you get up here so we won't be too crowded."

Lucy divided the cheese, sausage, and bread into three equal portions. She counted the cookies and saw that there were four. She counted two for herself and handed her dad and Clay one each.

"How come you get two?" Clay asked.

"I'm feeding for two," Lucy replied.

After they had choked down all the solids, Lucy poured a cup of water from a fruit jar that they had kept in the wagon. They all washed the food down and felt much better. "Do you still want up here?" Buck asked.

"No, I think I'll take a nap now," Lucy answered. "If you can miss a few of the bumps in the road."

Clay glanced back in a few minutes and was sure that Lucy was asleep. "What are we going to do with the baby?" Clay whispered to his dad.

"Keep it, naturally," Buck replied.

"Don't they have names for girls who have babies without getting married and what is it they call the baby?"

"Sometimes you just have to suck it up, Son. Yeah, they have names, but we don't."

"What do they call the babies?" Clay asked.

"Some call them woods colts."

"What does that mean?" Clay asked.

"Well," still whispering, "when horses run on the open range and a mare has a colt, no one really knows who the father is."

"Isn't there another name for them, one that starts with a 'b'?"

"Yeah, there is, but we don't use that word," Buck replied. "Quiet, she might hear us."

"I already heard you," Lucy said as she sat up. "I love you, Dad. Now can I sit up front?"

Buck pulled back on the reins and yelled "Whoa!" to his team. "Come on, Baby. I don't want you to fall while climbing up here."

Clay scooted over to make room for Lucy between them. Looking a little embarrassed, he said, "Sorry, Sis."

Buck leaned over and kissed her on the cheek once she was seated. "I love you, Sis," he said.

The clouds gave way to a bright fall sun which was at their back and still holding high in the western sky when they saw what must be Cape Girardeau. It was much larger than Buck expected. He barely entered the settlement when he saw a large livery stable on his left. He pulled in and began asking questions. "How long can we leave the team and wagon here?"

"As long as you like. It's fifty cents a day for feed and care."

"Is there a floppery or a place to sleep in town?"

"There's better than that. We have a new hotel that even furnishes hot baths."

"Is there a furniture store in town?"

"Only used," the attendant replied.

"What time does the boat leave for St. Louis?"

"Every morning at eight A.M. sharp."

"How long does it take to reach St. Louis?"

"You'll be there before noon the next day, and one leaves St. Louis every day for points south. It only takes one day downstream from St. Louis to Cape."

They left the team and wagon at the livery stable and walked downtown to the hotel where they checked in and asked for a room with two beds and a bath.

"What time do you want your bath?" the clerk asked.

"Does it matter?" Buck asked.

"It does if you want your water warm. We have to fill the tub," the clerk said sarcastically.

"Oh, I didn't know that," Buck answered. "I guess we'll have it about eight o'clock. Do we have to order our meals well in advance also?"

"No. You can eat any time you please," the clerk answered in a much more pleasant tone. "The room will be two dollars a night with a bath. You must pay in advance."

Buck opened his bib pocket and handed the clerk a twenty-dollar gold piece.

"I'm sorry, sir, but I don't have change for that," the clerk said.

"Then you'll have to catch me in the morning," Buck answered.

"Perhaps after you have dinner, you will have the correct money," the clerk offered.

"Perhaps," Buck answered as he picked up a key from the

counter to room 201.

The clerk looked at the three as they walked out the front door realizing that they weren't the country bumpkins he thought them to be.

Outside, they asked the first person that they saw where the furniture store was. The lady they asked turned and pointed north and across the street. "That's it over there," she said. "It ain't much of a store."

"Do you have a ladies' clothing store?" Buck asked.

"Sure do, and it's a good one. Miss Betty's. She makes most of her own clothes. If you have time, she can work wonders with a piece of cloth, a needle, and a thread. She could even make your little girl not look pregnant. It's behind you and in the next block," she said as she stuck her nose back in the air and twisted on down the street.

Buck looked at Lucy and saw a tear start to emerge from her left eye. He reached over to her, and with his finger, removed it. "Come on," he said, as he turned around and headed for Miss Betty's.

"Now, Lucy, when we get there, I don't want to see any more tears. Order you three outfits. Two for growing pregnancies and a beautiful one for after the baby is born to wear to dances and to church."

At Miss Betty's, it was a different story. She greeted them at the door and offered them a seat by the window where she had a coffee table and four easy chairs sitting on a beautiful Oriental carpet.

"How may I help you?" she asked.

Buck spoke up to let her know they were on their way to St. Louis and would be back in three days. "My daughter here, her name is Lucy. The baby's father is in the Confederate army. She wants two pregnancy dresses and one for after the baby. Something that she will look good in at dances or at church."

Betty looked a little shocked. "That might be a problem. You usually don't wear the same dress to both places."

"I should have realized that," Buck answered. "Get her one for each. Can you have them finished by the time we return from St. Louis?" Buck asked.

"They will be ready even if I need to hire some help."

Buck turned to Lucy and said, "Clay and I will go to the furniture store while you and Miss Betty make your selections."

As soon as they were out the door, Miss Betty motioned for Lucy to follow her. She placed her hand on Lucy's shoulder and asked, "How much do you have to spend on these garments?"

"I only have a dime," Lucy said.

Miss Betty removed her arm and stopped in her tracks.

Lucy smiled and said, "Money is no problem, My dad has plenty and it is in gold."

"Well, come on, then," Miss Betty said, smiling again. She showed Lucy what was on the racks that she made herself, then picked up a catalogue to show Lucy what she could make for her.

Lucy finally stopped looking and turned to Miss Betty and said, "You are better at this than I am. Why don't you measure me and make the selections for me."

"I'd be happy to do that," Miss Betty answered.

Betty and Lucy barely finished with their measuring when the front door opened. Buck and Clay came in with disgusted looks on their faces. "How are you doing?" Buck asked Lucy.

"We're all finished," Lucy replied.

"How much do I owe you?" Buck asked turning to Miss Betty, as he dug for his twenty dollar gold piece. Having retrieved it, he handed it to Miss Betty.

She looked at it and said, "Oh, that is more than enough."

"Well, can you give me back five and we will settle up when we return."

Miss Betty was lucky to have five dollars, but was happy with the deal.

"Come on," Buck motioned. "We can't buy furniture here. We need to eat and check out the boat before we have our baths."

They walked down to the riverfront where Lucy saw the mighty Mississippi for the first time. She couldn't believe the enormousness of it.

The boat wasn't there yet but they were assured that it would be there in the morning and that there would be no trouble getting a ticket.

Back at the hotel, they were just in time for their baths. Lucy was in first and thoroughly enjoyed it. She stayed until the water began to get cool. When she came out, she told Buck and Clay how wonderful it made her feel.

Clay stripped off and stepped into the tub to find the water to be almost cold. "Where do you get more hot water!" he yelled.

"I'll go down to the desk and see," Buck answered, as he went out the door. At the desk, he asked the clerk about more hot water.

"That will be extra," the clerk replied. "Besides, you haven't paid for the first one yet."

Buck opened his bib pocket and took out a brown leather coin purse which he held above the counter so the clerk could see and hear as he rattled the coins. "There must be something smaller than a twenty in here some place," he commented. "Oh, yes, here is a five. Can you handle that?" he asked as he handed it to the clerk.

"With an extra bath, it will come to two dollars and ten cents," the clerk answered as he counted out his change. "I'll send someone right up with more hot water. Thank you, sir. I hope you enjoy your stay with us. Leave your key in your room when you leave tomorrow, please."

After their baths and a good night's sleep, they felt much better. They ate in the hotel dining room the next morning and was delighted at the variety that was offered. The dining room was almost full. They overheard many people discussing the boat trip to St. Louis. They wondered if most of them would be on board.

Shortly before eight, everyone paid up and headed for the boat which they could see docked less than two blocks away.

Buck inquired earlier about the fare and had the correct change in a front pocket. At the boat he handed it to the man at the end of the gangplank. "For three," Buck told him.

"Thank you for having the correct change, it helps," the man said as he motioned them forward.

The boat was a big two-decker with an enormous paddle wheel powered by a steam motor. This was a new experience for all of them. They went up the stairs and to the front of the boat where they found three chairs. Buck pulled out his watch, and sure enough, at exactly eight o'clock, the gangplank was raised, the steam whistle sounded, and they could hear the big wheel begin to churn.

They spent most of the day just talking and watching along the big river. They saw a few Indians, lots of wild game, but no soldiers.

Only two left to go eat. They didn't want to lose their choice spot on the boat. Clay held the seats while Buck and Lucy had something to eat. They then held Clay's seat while he ate. They did the same for visits to the toilet.

The night was really long since they dozed off and on all day. It seemed like morning would never get there.

When daylight did arrive, they could see what looked to be a black cloud up the river ahead of them. When they came closer, it turned out to be smoke from brush a farmer was burning while cleaning his land.

When they finally arrived and the boat was tied securely to the dock, Buck, Clay, and Lucy were the first to disembark. They only walked a few feet when Buck saw newspapers being sold by an old man. "Hold it a minute," he said as he walked over and purchased one.

When he returned to Clay and Lucy, he said that the old man said it was only about two blocks to a big store where you could buy most anything.

Buck opened the paper to see the front headlines which read, "Black Regiment from Kansas Mops up on Confederates." He went on to read where they killed hundreds in a hard fought battle near Camden and Poinson Springs in Arkansas. Under the command of a white man, Captain Williams, they fought with vengeance, having no mercy. They captured some Confederate soldiers and sent them back to their units with a message that read, "Unless the Confederates began treating their prisoners better, we will take no prisoners."

This message must have been effective, for the Confederates hightailed it out of the area, heading for Hot Springs, where they hoped to hitch up with help. Captain Williams and his crew were in hot pursuit.

"It sounds like the worm has started to turn," Buck announced. "I'm sure glad I'm out of it. I guess they won't come looking for me. They are still a long way from Missouri."

They walked down to the big store, and it seemed like many stores in one. The offices were in the center and there were aisles running in every direction from the hub. Between the wide aisles was everything imaginable.

They walked down the furniture aisle first, where each picked the easy chair of their choice. They all picked large, leather-covered chairs. They then agreed on two tuft couches with curved, wood-accented arms and back. They chose one large Oriental rug for the family room and library. Foot stools, a coffee table, and other small pieces like an umbrella holder, a coat and hat rack, and some beautiful fern stands were also chosen.

Lucy kept going back to look at a large, wood cookstove. It had a large oven door with a thermometer mounted in the center. There was also a large, two-compartment warming closet above the cooking part. There was a big water reservoir with a turn-down spout all behind a large, yellow enamel door with a nickel-chrome trim on the extreme right side. The entire front of the stove was covered with yellow enamel and chrome. It was the most beautiful thing any of them had ever seen.

Buck called a salesperson back to ask the particulars. He was shown the damper on the back of the heating surface as well as the damper on the side of the firebox. He also lifted the three large caps above the firebox to show how large it was and pulled out a tray under the box to show how easy it was to remove ashes. The salesperson finished by saying, "It is made right here in St. Louis, and I'll put it up against any cook stove you can find anywhere."

"How much is it?" Buck asked.

"You're not going to believe this," the salesperson answered. "Thirty-five dollars only because we want to let people find out about them. We just began handling this brand and need some sales as well as advertising."

Buck replied, "We'll take it. Let me show you what else we want, we have just completed a new house and are furnishing it."

After they made their rounds with the salesperson and pointed to their selections, Buck asked, "Can you get all this on the boat going to Cape Girardeau tomorrow?"

The salesperson reached over and excitedly shook all their hands as he said, "For an order like that, we'll work all night if we have to."

"What will be the total bill?" Buck asked.

"Just a moment; I'll have to figure it up."

In a very short time, he said, "The entire bill comes to four hundred seventy-five dollars and sixty-five cents."

Buck said, "That's a lot. I didn't bring quite that much with me. Can you take a check on the Thomasville Bank?"

"Just a moment, I'll have to see," he said as he walked over to an old, gray-headed man sitting behind a desk in the hub smoking a cigar. He leaned over to have a look at Buck and yelled, "Who is the banker there?"

"Mr. Weaver," Buck replied.

"How much do you want to write the check for?" the old man asked.

Buck took his coin purse out and started counting his gold.

The gold really got the man's attention. He slowly got up from his desk and walked over to Buck to shake his hand.

"I would need to write the check for twenty-five dollars," Buck said after he calculated how much he would need for the return trip.

"No problem," the old man said. He then turned to his salesman and said, "Get some help and get it on the boat." He turned back to Buck and said, "Tell the clerk down at the

Missouri Hotel that your lodging tonight is on Dick Buch.
Thanks for your business and tell Mr. Weaver hello for me."

"Thank you," Buck said as he wrote the check and counted
out his money.

Clay spoke up and asked where he could buy supplies for
his photo shop.

"What are you looking for?" the salesman asked. "We just
began carrying photography supplies. Try aisle number
eleven. We have a lot of post cards for printing pictures. We
have about anything you might need; developing fluid, phos-
phate for artificial light, and stuff like that."

Clay was soon back with an armload of supplies, looking
pleasantly surprised. "Can we afford this?" he asked his dad.

"If they can take a check we can," Buck replied.

"No problem," the old man said again as the salesman figured up Clay's purchases. It came to thirty-eight dollars.

Clay saw the ticket and told his dad that it would last a
long time. "Leave it with our furniture," Clay said as he
pushed all the supplies into one large pile.

Buck wrote another check, thinking, "We are going to have
to make another deposit soon."

At the hotel, they were again pleasantly surprised. The
bath tub didn't have to be filled by hand. With the turn of one
handle cold water came out. With the turn of another handle
hot water came out.

When Lucy emerged from the bathroom, she asked her dad
if he thought they could have a bath like that one in their new
home.

"We'll see about it," Buck answered.

They were up early the next morning, anxious to see if all
their purchases were on board the boat. When they boarded,
they identified themselves and were told where their cargo
was stored. It was on the lower deck, covered with a tarp. A
note was on it with directions that it should be unloaded at
Cape Girardeau.

The return trip to Cape Girardeau was uneventful. They
arrived two hours before dark, which gave Buck and Clay

enough time to get their wagon and load their freight. The wagon was stacked full. Buck began to wonder if he'd be able to fit it all, but after a few re-arrangements they could see they were going to be able to get all their belongings on the wagon. Now all they had to worry about was getting it all home undamaged. They all were proud of their selections, especially the cook stove.

Lucy went over to the hotel and rented a room while Buck and Clay cared for the wagons. While she sat in the lobby waiting for Buck and Clay, she was the focus of lots of stares and snide remarks. Finally, she stood up and removed all doubt she was pregnant. She placed both hands on her waist near her back and paraded back and forth. When she could stand the stares and giggling no longer, she stopped and announced, "The baby's father is in the army." She directed her remark to anyone who was listening and particularly to two middle-aged, well-dressed ladies seated by the front window.

"Well, I'll declare," one said to the other as she opened her collapsible fan and gave herself a slight breeze as she whispered, "She can't be over fourteen."

Lucy's face turned red as she walked over to them and said, "Why don't you ladies go kiss a mad dog." She then twisted up the stairs to her room.

Buck and Clay soon came to the hotel and checked with the clerk to see where their room was. Buck paid for the night and said that they would be leaving early the next morning. He also asked if they could have their dinner sent up to their room and what time they were open for breakfast.

The clerk said they could order food to their room any time and offered Buck a menu.

"Great," Buck answered. "We'll have three of the blue plate specials tonight with one coffee and two iced teas. Tomorrow at six A.M., we'll have the breakfast special and for lunch we'll have a picnic lunch to go. Oh, we want the picnic lunch at six A.M. also."

The clerk quickly did some figuring while looking at the menu and said, "That will be five dollars and twenty cents, and if you wish, you may tip the one who delivers your meals or I can add it on to your bill."

"We'll take care of our own tipping," Buck answered as he handed the clerk the correct amount.

As they turned to go up the stairs, Clay asked, "What's tipping?"

"If the one who brings you the food does a good job, you can pay him a little extra if you like."

When Buck and Clay knocked on their door, Lucy opened it immediately, obviously still mad. "I wish I had my new clothes," she said. "There are two old bitties down in the lobby I'd like to show off for," Lucy scoffed.

"Betty might still be open. I'll run and see," Buck said. As he started to leave, he said, "I forgot about them. If we can't get them tonight, we'll probably have to wait for them tomorrow."

Buck hurried down the stairs and through the lobby where he saw two floozy looking ladies sitting by the front window whispering to each other every time a man passed. It went through Buck's mind that their husbands were probably in the army and they were lonesome. It never entered his mind that they might own the hotel or be waiting for their husbands to get off work. He did, however, wonder what they were saying about him.

At Betty's shop, the door was closed and locked but he could see a light through the curtains in the back. He knocked at the front door first gently, then hard. The curtains parted and Betty came to the door with a candle in her hand. "Who is it?" she asked.

"Buck Paty. We got back from St. Louis quicker than we thought. I was wondering if you had Lucy's dresses finished."

Betty unbolted the door and invited Buck to come in. "I was just finishing the last one," Betty answered. "If you could stay thirty minutes, I'll be finished. Would you like a cup of coffee?"

Buck followed Betty through the curtains into the back-room where she worked. She motioned to an easy chair by the curtains and asked Buck to be seated while she prepared him a cup of coffee. Betty returned in practically no time with the coffee and immediately began sewing on Lucy's dress.

As soon as it was completed, she gently folded it and placed it in a box on top of the other three.

Buck paid her and excused himself saying that they hadn't had dinner yet and they would be waiting on him. Buck went out the door wishing that he could spend more time with Betty. He really liked her looks as well as her personality.

Back at the hotel, their dinner had just arrived, but Lucy couldn't wait to try on her dresses. She had never seen such beautiful material and the patterns were gorgeous. She slipped on her pick of the two maternity dresses, combed her hair, and went out the door.

Sure enough, the two bitties were still sitting at the windows. She pranced over to them and asked, "Do you gals know where a lady can find some action tonight?"

They both looked at her, then stood up and huffed away. Lucy yelled after them, "By the way you two look, I thought you would know." They both went out the front door, and Lucy, laughing, headed back up the stairs.

"Where did you go?" Buck asked.

"To have a little fun," Lucy replied.

They finished their dinner and went to bed early.

The next day, Lucy, Clay, and Buck had breakfast at six and were soon on their way home. The sky was clear and the sun was rising over the mighty Mississippi.

They traveled from sun-up to dark each day and made the trip in a little less than three days. They were anxious to get the furniture and rugs in the house without getting them wet.

Don built a fence around the house and built a sidewalk from the yard gate to the front porch out of leftover flat rocks and pieces of unused boards. He had even built a front gate.

Jane, Jean, and Don moved from the studio into the northwest bedroom. Don built the bed extra large. Jane and Jean constructed a mattress to fit it from a spongy moss that grows wild and in abundance on the north rocky hillsides. It looked pretty good and they said it was comfortable.

Lucy liked the looks of their bedroom. She asked Don if he

would fix a baby bed next to hers in her bedroom. Don was glad that she asked him, hoping that he would soon need to build one for his bedroom.

The house was completely squared away in two days.

Jane and Jean were amazed at the new cookstove, even though they didn't know how to use it. They never cooked a meal or baked a pie in their life. All the cooking they did had been over an open fire in a pot.

Buck soon decided that he needed someone to teach them how to cook and also teach them a few social graces if they were all going to live in the same house.

The next day, Buck decided that it was time to have the housewarming dance. He hitched Pet to the buggy and headed for Thomasville. Before he went, he sent Don and his wives to check the corner stakes of their claim. He told them that it was a nice warm fall day and they should get away for a while.

As soon as they were out of sight, Buck dug up the money and counted out another ten thousand dollars and buried the remainder back in the same place.

The first stop in town was at the bank where he deposited the entire amount. Mr. Weaver was happy to get his money but really looked at him suspiciously.

Buck told Mr. Weaver that he was ready to have the party and that he needed to hire some musicians. He also wanted to hire a good cook to teach Lucy and Don's wives how to cook.

"I'd gladly pay someone to plan the dance if you could recommend someone."

"Well, let's see, how much are you prepared to pay?"

"I'd give someone a hundred dollars to take care of everything; food, drinks, and someone to cook." Lucy, Jane, and Jean will help.

"I only work five days a week," Mr. Weaver commented. "I suppose I could manage your dance if you have it on Saturday."

"Well, let's see," Buck said. "Today is October the second. Could you have it ready in two weeks?"

"Sure could," Mr. Weaver answered.

"You take care of everything," Buck said as he wrote him a one hundred dollar check.

The two weeks passed in a hurry. Mr. Weaver sent out a woman named Mrs. Murphy with all the groceries imaginable. She was to teach cooking to Lucy, Jane, and Jean. Mr. Weaver made an excellent selection. Not only was she kind and patient with the girls, she was an excellent cook and they were eager to learn. Jane specialized in making bread. Jean liked to make sweets and Lucy made lots of pasta dishes along with meats cooked in a variety of ways.

Mrs. Murphy was crazy about the stove and said she must have one like it.

In practically no time, there was food stacked everywhere. It looked like they had cooked for at least a hundred people.

Jane was wearing her Mona Lisa smile all the time and even Jean managed to smile a little. It was both a happy and busy two days for all of them.

Jane and Jean went to the woods and gathered some fall flowers. They found gold seal and blue and lavender wild carnations from which they made some beautiful arrangements. They placed them in jars around the room.

∽ TWELVE ∽

Time passed quickly and the day of the party was already at hand.

Mrs. Murphy prepared for fifty people. Many nibbles were prepared for before the main meal. Buck bought lots of apple cider. Some had spirits and some didn't. This was for the meek. He had plenty of hard stuff for the more serious drinkers.

The big Oriental carpet was rolled and stashed against the side of the room. One corner was cleared and ready for the musicians. The bar was set up in the corner the farthest from the fireplace. Everything was ready.

People began to arrive a little after four P.M. The musicians didn't arrive until much later, then they screeched and plucked for at least thirty minutes before everything was tuned to suit them.

Buck, Clay, and Lucy stood near the front door and greeted people as they came. Many of the guests they didn't know, but they introduced themselves and welcomed them to the dance.

The word got around that some rich folk from Louisiana settled on Spring Creek. Everyone had to see for themselves. After seeing the furniture, the cookstove, and after peeking at the Oriental carpet, they all wanted to get to know them. The house was beautiful and tastefully decorated.

The musicians finally broke into a fast hoe-down with all the women lining up on one side and the men on the other. The

Virginia Reel was always popular as an ice breaker. They then did another ice breaker to the sound of "Oh Johnny." In this dance you change partners with each jingle.

The music then changed to a waltz. Not very many people were shy and after a few spirited drinks, they lost all inhibitions. Even Lucy danced every dance.

Buck announced that the food was in the dining room where everyone could help themselves and would be served by Jane and Jean. Everyone had a great time and no one got drunk.

It was almost midnight when they started to leave for home. The night was dark but the horses seemed to be able to see much better than the men. Some of the buggies carried kerosene lanterns which helped them see better. The dance was the talk of the town and everyone agreed that a good time was had by all.

Clay came to town one day soon after the dance and brought his camera. He put up signs all over town displaying samples of his work. He offered the postcard pictures for fifteen cents each. The first day, he took thirty-two pictures and promised he would be back the next day with the prints. He could then take more pictures if anyone wanted them.

When he brought the pictures, the word soon got around. They were the best anyone had ever seen in Thomasville. Clay took more pictures and more orders for the ones he already developed.

The postcards were far ahead of the tin types. Everyone wanted them to mail for Christmas. There were many orders. He told the people it would be three days before he could develop the film and deliver the pictures.

By evening, Clay was tired but excited over the enthusiasm shown. He told the people that he had a studio in his home and he could take pictures any time they wanted. He also asked them to tell their friends. In almost no time, Clay was very busy and needed help. He taught Lucy and Don to help him.

Buck decided to build a pole barn with several stalls downstairs along with a grainery and a place to hang tobacco. The loft of the barn was large enough to handle lots of hay and corn fodder.

When the weather permitted, they cut large red and water oak blocks with a cross cut saw. They hauled them to the front porch of the house where they could sit in the dry to split shingles for the barn. They used a frow and a wooden mallet to slice wooden blocks into sections to use for the roof. By spring, the barn was finished along with some rails to start the fence for a corral.

Everything was really looking good. Buck was ready to buy some cattle, hogs, and some chickens. He hadn't been this happy in a long time. He would really like to find someone suitable to marry. He often asked about Miss Thomas but the news was never good. She was still very sick and became even thinner. Her cough and chills were worse. Buck wanted to see her to tell her how he felt about her but he was afraid he would catch what she had. He checked in St. Louis but the doctors said "there was no new medicine."

~ THIRTEEN ~

*I*t was late one evening during the end of November when Lucy came to her dad's bedroom holding her stomach and crying. "I'm sick," she said as she sat on the edge of her dad's bed. She had only sat there for a short while when she had a definite contraction.

Buck jumped out of bed and pulled on his clothes. He knocked on Jane and Jean's door and told them to hurry and get up. Lucy was in labor.

Jane built a fire in the cookstove while Jean wet a cloth and tried to soothe Lucy's brow. Buck grabbed a kerosene lantern, struck a match, and lifted the globe to light it. Once lit, he headed for the buggy and Pet. He harnessed her in a hurry and asked her to hurry as he slapped her with the reins as soon as she was hitched.

They covered the few miles in what was probably record time. Dr. Pace was the only doctor that he knew. He pulled up to the dark house and knocked hard on the front door and rattled the screen loudly.

A light came on and moved toward the front door. Mrs. Pace asked, "Who is it?"

"It's Buck Paty. Lucy is fixing to have a baby."

"All three of the doctors are at the hospital. They have a new bunch of wounded soldiers. I'll go with you if you like. I have helped deliver a lot of babies."

"Please hurry," Buck answered.

"I'll leave a note and be there as soon as I can dress. How cold is it?"

"Wear a heavy coat and bring a blanket. It's pretty cold."

The lantern burned bright now and Buck could see tiny flakes of snow beginning to fall. He knew the temperature had dropped but the sky was clear when the sun set. It must have been one of those fast moving fronts. There were some mare's-tail clouds reaching from the west when he went in about six o'clock, but it certainly didn't look like snow.

When Mrs. Pace came out of the door, Buck hopped down to assist her climb to the seat. "Is that snow I'm seeing?" she asked.

"I'm afraid so," Buck answered as he climbed in, picked up the reins, and yelled, "Gitty up, Pet, we're in a hurry."

"I brought along the doctor's black bag. I hope I got the right one. He has a special one for delivering babies."

She set the bag between them and opened it. "Could you hold the lantern over here so I can make sure?"

Buck removed the lantern from its hanger on the side of the buggy and held it closer to Mrs. Pace.

Buck looked inside and felt sure she had brought the wrong one when he saw all the metal forceps.

"Yep, it's the right one," she said, but Buck already started pulling back on Pet's reins feeling sure they would have to go back for another bag.

"What are those metal things for?" he asked as he encouraged Pet to go ahead with a few clicking sounds from his mouth.

"Oh, those are for emergencies, when they have to take the baby and there isn't enough room for the hands."

Buck frowned and mulled over in his mind what he saw and how they could be used.

When they pulled up in front of the house, there were many lights on. The snow was coming down a little harder but there was not much accumulation.

Mrs. Pace went into the house while Buck tied Pet to the yard fence. When he opened the front door, he saw no one, but he heard a funny sound coming from Lucy's bedroom. The room was full of people sitting on the edge of the bed.

Buck walked over and looked at Mrs. Pace, Jane, and Jean who were sitting on the front side of the bed. Don and Clay were sitting on the foot.

Buck was astonished but pleasantly surprised at what he saw. A baby was nursing Lucy. The noise it was making was what Buck heard when he came in the front door.

Lucy looked up and saw her dad. She lifted the baby from her breast and extended it straight up to her dad. "Here, Dad, hold your granddaughter."

Buck took the baby and walked over close to the kerosene lamp so he could have a better look. "She's going to be a heart breaker," Buck said, loud enough for all of them to hear. "Have you named her yet?" Buck asked as the baby started to nuzzle his shoulder looking for more to eat.

"Her name is Ivy Amonette," Lucy answered. "Give her back to me. I don't think she finished dinner."

Buck handed her back and moved to the foot of the bed where he could see better.

"All of you go back to bed," Mrs. Pace said. "Lucy is tired and needs some rest. I'll sleep with her tonight so I'll be close if she needs me."

Buck started to bed but remembered Pet and went outside with a lantern to care for her. The snow began to stick on the ground. He carried in some wood and piled it on the fire and stacked more on the front porch so it would stay dry.

The next morning, everyone was up early, so they could see and hold Ivy. She was a beautiful baby with big blue eyes and very fine short hair, about the color of new corn silk. Both Jane and Jean made little gowns for the baby with a drawstring in the bottom.

Mrs. Pace reached into one side of the doctor's black bag and pulled out a beautiful little dress with a bonnet. She said the doctor always carries a girl's outfit in one side and a boy's in the other.

Lucy looked and looked at it when Mrs. Pace handed it to

her. Lucy reached to Mrs. Pace and pulled her down to whisper in her ear, "I'm glad the doctor wasn't home."

The next day, Buck took Mrs. Pace home a little before noon. The snow accumulated to about four inches. He couldn't help but wish Mrs. Pace wasn't married. He would love to put his arm around her and pull her close. He wasn't thinking about sex but would just like to feel a warm body next to him. His mind was still wandering when they arrived at her home. Buck jumped down, tied Pet, and went to the other side of the buggy to help Mrs. Pace down. "How much do I owe you?" he asked.

"I don't charge. Only the doctors charge," she replied.

"Is the doctor home?" Buck asked as she opened the door. The house was very cold and it was obvious that the doctor wasn't there. "I'll build you a fire," Buck said as he walked in and began to put some kindling wood in the fireplace. Buck turned to her and asked, "Do you know what is wrong with Miss Thomas?"

"She probably has tuberculosis," Mrs. Pace answered. "Some doctors call it consumption. It is such a wasting disease. Very few ever survive it but sometimes it takes years before it kills the person."

"Do you think John and Matilda would let me see her?" Buck asked.

"I suppose they would, but don't get too close and don't eat or drink anything while you are there," Mrs. Pace added.

Buck thanked her, turned and walked to the Thomases. The walk had the snow removed across the porch to the door. He knocked and Matilda answered.

"So good to see you. I've been wondering about Lucy. I'd like to ask you in, but I'm afraid you might get sick too."

"I'd like to take that chance," Buck said. "I'll not touch anything if you'll allow me in."

Mrs. Thomas opened the door wider to allow Buck to come in. "Thank you," he said as he walked past her toward the library and Mr. Thomas. Mr. Thomas turned to see who was approaching and was obviously happy to see Buck. He feebly got to his feet and stuck out his hand which Buck took and shook vigorously.

Buck sat and brought him up to date on everything. "Sure wish you could have made it to the dance," Buck said.

When the conversation began to slow, Matilda came in with a tray of tea and cookies. Buck thanked her as he hesitated before taking any.

He had almost finished when he heard a faint voice from his right say, "Who is it, Mother?"

"It's Buck Paty," she answered.

"Ask him to come in, Mother. He can sit by the door."

Matilda realized that Buck heard her request. She shrugged her shoulders and looked toward Buck, motioning reluctantly toward the bedroom door.

When Buck saw her, he thought she was still beautiful and had to fight the urge to go over to the bed and give her a big hug and kiss. Instead, he sat in the chair by the door approximately eight feet from her bed.

"Tell me about Lucy," she said.

Buck told her about the new baby, the house, and everything else that he could think of that might be of interest to her.

Delia opened her eyes wider and said, "Thank you so much for coming."

Buck stood up so he could see her better and said, "All people don't die with consumption. You have to get well. There are many things I would like to show you and share with you. When spring gets here and you can get outside, it will make a difference."

"Is that a proposal?" Delia asked.

"It sure is," Buck said as he lowered his head not sure what else to do or say.

"Would you believe, that is my first. I guess everyone thought I wasn't interested. You can't imagine how many sleepless nights I've spent. Yes, some of them thinking about you."

Buck was elated and wished that she could get well.

The next spring, Delia did become a little better. She was

able to get out of bed and spent much of her time sitting on the front porch. She dreamed about getting well and going back to work at the hospital. They needed her so badly. She also dreamed about Buck.

The doctors all agreed that the fresh air and sunshine was doing her good. Buck often stopped and had long talks with her. She finally decided to go with Buck to see his place, but first she wanted him to drive her over to the hospital to have a look.

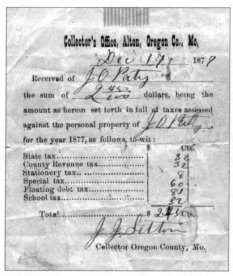

tax receipt

John and Matilda both opposed her expedition but didn't say no. Buck picked her up early one morning in June and drove her over to the hospital where she saw only a few people that she recognized. They were happy to see her and asked, "When are you coming back to work?" Everyone encouraged her by telling her how good she looked and that she must have her illness whipped.

Delia knew how she felt but smiled and thanked them for the kind words. Buck excused her by saying, "We got to be going. We are going to my farm to see Lucy and her new baby."

Some looked shocked to hear that Lucy had a baby, but everyone wanted to know about them.

They crossed the creeks on the way back through

Thomasville. Delia sat very erect and enjoyed being out to see things beyond her front porch again. She turned to Buck and said, "I didn't think this would ever happen. I have been so sick and weak. How can I ever thank you?"

"Just continue to get well," Buck answered as he pulled back on the reins and to the left where he saw Alpha Roberts standing in front of the company store.

Mr. Roberts recognized him and tipped his cap to Delia and said, "It's good to see you out. I hope you are well. I'll tell my wife and girls I saw you. They have been helping over at the hospital lately. Lots of new patients," he stated.

"How are my boys, John and Bill?" Buck asked.

"They are fine. I'll tell them you asked."

"Tell them I'll be over to see them soon," Buck answered as he said good-bye and drove away.

They were barely out of town when Delia scooted over close to Buck and laid her head on his shoulder. He liked the feeling but was concerned about contracting what she had. He didn't say anything as he grasped the reins in his right hand and stroked her head and hair on his shoulder.

When they pulled the buggy up in front of Buck's house, Delia opened her eyes and looked around. She made a feeble effort to get out of the buggy but needed help. Buck was more than willing to help her. She collapsed into his arms as she leaned over the side. Buck carried her up the walk, across the porch, and into the library where he placed her on one of the new couches.

Jane quickly came to Delia's aid and propped her head up with some pillows. Lucy came running from the back of the house when she was told that Miss Delia was here. Lucy hovered over her, kissing her on the cheek while scooting a seat beside her.

"You have no idea how much I have been wanting to see you?" Lucy said as she leaned over and kissed her again.

"Me, too," Miss Thomas said very weakly. "I hear you have a new baby. May I see her?"

Lucy jumped up and ran to her room where she woke Ivy

from a nap. Lucy quickly brushed Ivy's pretty blonde hair and carried her into the library where Delia could see her.

Delia opened her eyes wide and said, "She is beautiful and I know who the father is. He was a handsome young man." Miss Delia then closed her eyes and leaned back on the pillows. "We'll let her rest for a while," Lucy whispered as she shooed everyone away. "She must be very tired."

Everyone went on about their chores. Jean brought Delia a drink. She opened her eyes and took a long, slow drink before she went back to sleep.

It was getting dark and Delia still had her eyes closed. "Save her some food for when she wakes," Buck said as he left the dinner table and took an easy chair close to Delia. He lit his pipe and sat there staring at her.

Buck finished one pipeful and was loading another when Delia opened her eyes and looked at him.

"May I have another drink of water?" she asked.

"You sure may, and how about some dinner?" Buck asked.

"I really need to go to the toilet first," she said as her face flushed.

Buck yelled, "Jane and Jean come here."

They immediately came from the kitchen where they were cleaning up after dinner. "Miss Delia needs to go to the toilet," Buck announced.

"Would you like to go outside or in the chamber?" Jane asked. "Sometimes there are snakes out after dark."

"I guess I'll use the chamber or slop jar, whichever is the handiest."

Jane and Jean helped Delia to her feet. With one on each side of her, they walked, or rather almost carried her to their bedroom, closed the door and removed the chamber from beneath the bed. They helped Miss Thomas raise her dress and lower her bloomers. They then had to hold on to her as she squatted on the pot. They still held on to Miss Thomas as she apologized for being so much trouble.

Jean held her nose and Jane turned her head as far away as possible but still held on to her.

"Hold on while I get something to clean her with," Jane said.

She soon returned with some tissue and a warm basin of water with a washcloth and a towel. When Miss Delia was finished and cleaned up, she felt much better. Jane and Jean led her to the dining room where her place was still set. Her filled plate was in the warming closet of the stove and they poured her a big glass of cool mint tea fresh from the spring.

Miss Delia sat at the foot of the table and reached for each of the girls. They gave her their hands which she squeezed and offered, "Thank You, God, and thank you, girls, I love you."

This was the first thank you Jane and Jean ever received.

Delia ate some of everything on her plate. She really enjoyed the wild greens and the bread and butter. This was the most she had eaten in a long time.

After she ate, she said, "I guess I better go home, but I wish I could stay."

Buck was standing at the door and overheard her.

"Why can't you stay?" he asked.

"It wouldn't look right and my mother and dad would worry."

Buck walked over to her and said, "I'll go there right now and tell them that you are staying." Without waiting for an answer, he walked back to the library where he picked up his cap and went out the door. He found the lantern on the front porch, lit it, and went to get Pet harnessed and hitched to the buggy.

Again he asked Pet to hurry, slapping her on the back with the leather reins. All the way to Thomasville, he dreamed of Delia. He dreamed of how she became well in short time, how he loved her, and what a wonderful wife she would be.

He was at the Thomases before he realized it. There was still a light in the house. No doubt they were worried and were waiting up for Delia's return.

They heard the buggy and met Buck at the front door looking past him for Delia. Matilda asked, "Where is she?" with a terribly concerned look on her face.

"She's fine," Buck assured her with an arm on her shoulder. "May I come in?"

Inside, Buck told the entire story. He told her how Delia went to sleep on the couch, but after a meal she said she wished she could stay longer. "I told her she could stay as long as she liked," Buck stated. "Both of you are welcome to come out any time."

"See, Mom, I told you she was fine," John said. "We'll be out in a day or two," he said as he went back to his easy chair.

"I'd better be getting back," Buck said as he put his cap on and went out the door.

When he arrived home, Jane and Jean put Delia to bed in Buck's room. Buck took her place on the couch.

Delia's stay was extended from days to several months. Some days she felt pretty good and sat on the front porch, looking at the morning sun rising over Spring Creek. She received excellent care which her mother and father were unable to provide her at home. At least once a week her mother and father came out to see her.

Summer gave way to fall and fall to winter. Delia's health improved all summer and fall but as winter came she became worse. She went down fast and really hit a new low.

Lucy made sure that Ivy never went to Delia. Even though Ivy was walking and even running, she always steered clear of Delia and her room.

It was the day before Thanksgiving when Delia finally stopped breathing. This was the saddest day in all their lives. Everyone cried until there were no more tears.

Buck really dreaded telling John and Matilda, but he wrapped Delia in their best quilt and laid her gently on the floor of the buggy with her head up front.

Everyone dressed and informed Buck that they wanted to go to town with Buck. Don, Jean, and Clay sat in the back. Two were on each side while Lucy and Ivy rode in the front with Buck.

As soon as they arrived at John and Matilda's, everyone in town knew what happened. Buck, Don, and Clay carried her into the house and laid her on a couch.

Matilda only cried a short while until she asked, "Will someone help me lay her out? Buck, will you and Don put another leaf in the dining room table and bring it to the front room of the house where it is the coldest?"

She asked Jane and Jean to go to Delia's closet and select the prettiest dress. Matilda selected her best table cloth and all her pretty needlepoint pillows. Jane and Jean dressed Delia after they washed her and fixed her long hair into a bun on top of her head with short ringlets on each side. Once she was dressed, they placed her on the table with a soft down pillow under her head and the pretty pillows along each side.

Matilda went to Delia's room where she found some lip rouge and some slightly colored powder. She returned and applied a small portion of the powder and the lip rouge very carefully. When Matilda finished, Delia looked good.

Word was sent to Mr. Shirrell, the casket maker, that they wanted a mummy-shaped pine casket, lined and well padded with white silk.

It was decided that the funeral would be in two days in the community building. She would be buried in the newly dedicated Bellow Cemetery. John selected a spot under a large walnut tree. As soon as the spot was selected, the men, who were usually known as the "spit and whittle club," were there with their picks and shovels to take turns digging the grave.

When the day arrived, and preacher had many adulations for Delia. She was truly a remarkable and extremely kind person. Everyone in Thomasville was there, and when the preacher finished, there wasn't a dry eye in the house. Delia was truly a person that no one could say a harmful thing about.

Everyone followed the procession as the men took turns carrying her the last mile on their shoulders. Some of the women gathered wild ferns, that would stay green all winter, to place on her grave.

After the coffin was lowered into the grave and everyone tossed in a handful of dirt, the club used their shovels to finish filling the grave while the sun made sporadic appearances from behind clouds. This was the first time in many days that the sun made an appearance. It looked like God was saying, "A job well done, come on home."

After the funeral, everyone walked by John and Matilda to offer their sympathy. In return, they asked everyone to come by their home for coffee and something to eat.

They all made their way to John and Matilda's house, some on foot, some on horseback, and some in their buggies.

Mrs. Thomas was a gracious host. She welcomed everyone and thanked them for coming and offering their kind words.

It was almost dark before everyone finally said, good-bye and went home.

~ FOURTEEN ~

uck went into another period of depression but Ivy
didn't allow him to ignore her. She was always in his
lap, hugging, kissing, or doing whatever necessary to
make him pay attention to her.

Before long, green sprigs of grass bursted through the
leaves and dead grass of winter. Buck decided it was time to
buy some hogs and cattle. He dug up his buried money again
and made a withdrawal of five hundred dollars in gold.

The next day, Buck made the trip to Thomasville. Clay and
Don came along and rode the mules. He planned to buy what
he could and drive them home where he would hold them
inside the barnyard fence for a few days to gentle and feed
them before they were turned out on the open range.

In Thomasville, they purchased thirty-two cows and one large
white-faced bull. They also purchased four sows and one big boar.
It didn't take them long to decide that they needed help driving
them home.

Buck hurried to the store and announced what he needed
and that he would pay a dollar to anyone who would help
drive them to his barnyard. They all jumped up to go with
Buck. Three had horses and the other six came on foot.

It was unbelievable how much a few extra hands helped. In
less than two hours, the stock were all inside the barn lot and
the gate closed behind them. The hogs were herded into the
barn because Buck thought they might get through the rail

fence. He threw them a few ears of corn and poured a bucket of water in a trough for them.

Buck gave one man a ten dollar gold piece and told him he could break it at the bank and pay the rest of them. "With the extra dollar, buy them a drink at the store," Buck said.

The cattle and hogs soon settled down and Buck felt sure they would stay close when he turned them out on the open range. After he turned them out into the forest he would see some of them every once in a while. The summer soon passed and it was time to bring them in and hold them in a field that he and Don had fenced. They fenced another field where they planted corn and other grains.

Buck, Don, and Clay began looking for their stock. They found twenty-three cows with twenty calves and they also found their bull. After three more days they found no more cows, so they gave up and took them home hoping the rest would come on their own.

The oak acorns, which hogs love, began to fall so they decided to leave them on the open range for a few more weeks. When they decided to look for the hogs, they could see many places under the oak trees where the hogs rooted for hidden acorns. When they finally found them, all four of the sows and the boar were there, but there were only twelve pigs, and they were as wild as could be. They looked like they might weigh as much as forty pounds. Some had long tusks sticking down below their lower jaw, making it hard for them to eat.

After they finally got them home, Buck decided that he would keep the hogs in pens until after the sows had pigs and until the next fall when the acorns began to fall.

Each year was pretty much the same for a long time. Clay had a pretty good business with his photo shop. Don was still happy even though neither Jean nor Jane were pregnant. The war was over and nobody came to look for either Don or Buck. That fall he found twenty-seven cows and calves. There were three he never found.

Buck's herd of cattle was growing. He sold steers each fall and kept the select heifers. He soon had almost one hundred cows and five herd bulls. All of these animals came in five years from the original thirty-two cows.

He noticed many head of cattle on the open range and found it hard to figure out which ones were his. That fall, after he gathered what he thought were his into the fenced area near the barn, he went to Thomasville to the blacksmith and asked him to make him some branding irons. He had four made with the initials "BP" so he would brand his cattle and identify them.

As soon as Buck had all his fall jobs finished; branding, castrating, and selling the steers and undesirables, he told the family that he would be gone for a few days. He had an idea that he wanted to discuss with all the farmers who ran cattle on the open range.

The first farm he stopped at, he explained his idea. He wanted to build a big pond, a corral, and bunkhouse at a spot near Spring Creek. He wanted all the farmers to help, each fall on a designated day, to fan out on horseback and drive all the livestock toward the big corral. They would castrate and brand all their stock, then separate and drive their cattle home for the winter.

The farmers were so enthused about the idea that Buck pulled a calendar from his pocket and named the dates to meet and build the pond, corral, and bunkhouse.

Buck must have visited thirty families while he made a complete circle and gave them the dates to meet and work. He also reminded them to bring their branding irons to make sure none were alike.

Buck hadn't been feeling well for quite some time. He soon began to cough a lot and was often short of breath, but he thought it only was part of growing old.

After he returned home, he noticed that Lucy had a bad cough also. She always carried a white handkerchief to cover her mouth with and to deposit the sticky phlegm that she often coughed up.

When the time came for the farmers to gather to build the pond, corral, and bunkhouse, there were over thirty men there.

Construction of the Paty Pond. Note the teams of mules with their scrapers. When the long handle was held down, the scrapers gathered dirt. When it was released, it dumped its load.

Many brought their scrapers which looked like giant long-handled shovels on wheels hitched to a team. When the operator held the handle down, it scraped, and when he released, it dumped the load of dirt. This was the way the pond was dug.

Sometimes the scraper would hit and unexpected rock or tree root and the one holding the handle would get a jolt, often breaking the handle if the operator didn't release his hold. If it did break, another could be cut from a young hickory sapling in practically no time.

Many men brought cross-cut saws, axes, splitting mauls, and wedges. Any tool they might have needed, someone had thought of and brought.

Buck acted as coordinator or superintendent. The men who brought scrapers were naturally given the job of building the pond as soon as the trees were out and skidded to the area where they planned to build the bunkhouse and corral. In all, it took twelve days to complete the project.

Jane, Jean, Lucy, Don, and Ivy, who had just turned thirteen, did the cooking and serving. It kept Don busy making trips to Thomasville and carrying drinking water from the spring. Lucy didn't feel like doing much. She mainly sat in the shade and made suggestions. She wanted the bunkhouse built not only for men to sleep in, but she also wanted a kitchen and dining area in one end with two private bedrooms for the cooks if the women had to do that job.

Buck also suggested building a narrow chute leading from the corral to a small area with gates to use as a holding area for the branding.

While sitting around the camp at night, the men played cards and told wild tales. Ivy always found a hiding spot close enough to listen. I guess you could say that this is the place where she received her first sex education.

The men also decided on the brands they would use. Some changed their minds after Buck pointed out how it would be too easy to change them with a running iron. They never heard or thought of using a running iron.

Everyone really appreciated Ivy bringing them water. It was hard to say which they enjoyed most, the water or just getting to see Ivy. She had blonde hair and beautiful blue eyes. She was tall for her age and began to fill out in spots that were noticeable. Every man in camp talked about her, but Clay, her uncle, was the only single man there.

No one paid any attention to Lucy, Jane, or Jean. They were all becoming old and very wrinkled. Lucy's cough was becoming worse. Some days she was hardly able to get out of bed.

Buck's cough was worse also, but the excitement of building the pond, corral, combination bunk, kitchen, and dining hall gave him a burst of energy that he hadn't felt for a few days.

It was now the end of June and the rainy season was almost over. They hoped the pond would fill before the fall roundup. There had been some spotty showers, but nothing heavy enough for a runoff to put water in what was now called Paty Pond.

Every time Buck heard the name, his chest puffed out and made his breathing a little easier.

The last night in camp they finished the combination house and had a feast inside with both front and back doors open. Everyone moved their bedrolls inside and selected their bunk.

Most of them carved their names on the wooden pole frames and decided what they would need to make it more comfortable.

Jane, Jean, and the rest of the kitchen help cooked all of the leftovers.

That night they had a feast. They ate everything that was prepared and left nothing but coffee for breakfast.

At about two A.M., they were awakened by loud claps of thunder and bright flashes of lightning. Soon, the rain poured down, revealing several leaks in the roof, some above bunks. They quickly learned that the roof needed some repair.

By daylight, the rain stopped and the sun tried to break through the clouds. Some of the men climbed on top of the building and repaired the leaks.

The Paty Pond caught a good supply of water. Buck thought it would be interesting to see how well it held water and how much would be there when they brought the cattle in next fall. One corner of the corral was built almost to the center of the pond to allow the cattle to help themselves to the water.

The men agreed on the fifteenth of October as the day to begin their roundup. Everyone also agreed to pay Don and whatever help he needed to take care of food and its preparation.

Many of the men pretended to thank the cooks, but they really came to talk about and perhaps dream of next fall. Ivy really enjoyed all the attention she got but had no idea that some of the men had other things on their mind other than just being friendly. She really hated to see everyone go home. She hugged and kissed many good-bye.

After everyone was gone, Ivy helped Jane and Jean gather up what food was left and took Buck back home.

Buck and Lucy were both exhausted and badly in need of some rest.

Buck stood outside for a while and looked at a dream come true. He was very proud.

Buck and Lucy sat together in the front seat of the buggy

while Clay drove. Don and his wives brought the wagon with the tools and supplies.

Buck and Lucy looked like two very old people instead of father and daughter. They leaned against each other as they rode home.

Ivy didn't want to ride so she took the short cut home across the hills and beat the wagon and buggy home by twenty minutes. She really had a good time at camp but was happy to be home. Soon after she arrived she built a fire in the big fireplace. She knew Buck and Lucy would be chilly from their ride home and would enjoy sitting in front of the fire to warm their aching bones. Ivy was becoming very concerned about their health.

∼ FIFTEEN ∼

*W*hen the Patys and the Walkers returned to their home, Buck became very weak. His cough worsened and he had chills and a fever.

The holding tank they built at the spring was about the only thing that would run his fever back down. Don was really worried about him. No one seemed to have any ambition since Buck became ill. Clay spent most of his time in the studio and never noticed the repairs that needed to be done around him. The yard gate was off its hinges. The roof developed leaks, and the yard was grown up in weeds.

When Ivy suggested something to Don, he said, "It doesn't belong to me. Let Clay do it."

Clay became fat and extremely lazy. He was not interested in doing anything that required physical labor. He loved his father and was very concerned about him. There were no money problems. Their bank account was growing yearly because of the many livestock that they were selling each fall, and there was still buried money.

Clay and Don didn't get along very well. Don's wives seldom called him any more for meals and when they did, he was treated coolly. Ivy was still growing quickly and Lucy seldom came out of her room. Even the leak above her bed went unattended. Everyone seemed to think, "Why bother? Everything will be O.K. tomorrow." Buck had truly been the magnet that held them all together. When he asked them to do something, they did it without a question or complaint.

It was late September when Buck awoke everyone late one night coughing really hard. He coughed for sometime when Clay finally decided to go see if he could help and brought him a cup of cool water to wash his face. When Clay got dressed, Buck stopped coughing, so he went back to bed. Hearing nothing, he was soon asleep again. He didn't get dressed the next morning even though he was awake. He listened for a sound from his dad's room and he was startled by a knock on his door.

"Come quick," Ivy said. "Buck is dead."

Clay wasn't prepared for what he saw when he entered his dad's room. The bed was covered with blood. He must have burst a major blood vessel and blew it all over the bed while he coughed. Blood had run out of his nose, ears, and mouth. Even his eyes looked like they had been bleeding. "Everyone, get out!" Clay shouted. Looking at Ivy, he said, "Bring me water, a washcloth, and towels."

As soon as they were gone, Clay closed the door. He stripped his dad and lay him on a quilt on the floor. He then stripped the bed and replaced the bloody sheets and pillow cases with fresh ones from the closet.

Ivy knocked on the door and brought Clay the water, washcloth, and towels. Clay took them and set them on the floor next to Buck. He then handed Ivy all the bloody clothes and bedding tied together in one sheet. "Take them down to Spring Creek and throw them in to soak. Anchor them down with rocks in the cold, running water." Clay then closed the door and picked up the washcloth. He began to clean his father. He washed and scrubbed every speck of blood from him. He even washed and dried his father's hair.

When he had him cleaned, he selected his father's best dress clothes and dressed him.

The bed was made to look comfortable with a fluffed goose down pillow and folded quilts.

When he completed his work, he cracked the door again and yelled for Ivy to come in. Ivy looked and looked while tears flowed from her red eyes. She then turned to Clay and said, "They are both gone now, Clay. Mama won't last long. What are we going to do? I couldn't have done what you just did. I just couldn't do it," she repeated as she threw her arms around Clay's neck and said, "I love you."

Clay, a little embarrassed, said, "There are a few more things to put in the creek." He pointed to a pile in the corner. "Have you told Lucy?" he asked.

"No," Ivy answered. "I didn't know what to say. Don and his women are just sitting in the kitchen staring at the floor."

"Tell them to cook something good and make plenty of coffee. I'll go to town and make the arrangements. You should tell your mother," Clay said.

He went back to his studio where he cleaned up and dressed for his trip to town. He allowed Pet to take her time. She, too, was getting old, and he needed the time to think. He decided to have the funeral at the house and to bury Buck at one of his favorite spots, overlooking Spring Creek and the valley. He thought about burying him at Paty Pond which he would never get to see full. Neither would he get to participate in the first roundup, which was his dream.

In town, Clay went to the company store, where he told the bad news first to Mr. Hass, then to the men in the back playing checkers. When Clay told them, all heads bowed and he could see some drops hitting the floor. "He is ready for viewing and the funeral will be at the house the day after tomorrow at ten A.M., and the burial will be at the farm," Clay continued. He then went back up front where he paid the bill and picked up a few groceries on the way out of the store.

When Clay arrived back at the house, everyone was busy preparing for the funeral. Clay unhitched Pet, hung her harness in the barn, and turned her out to pasture. Then he walked to the spot where he thought his dad would like to be buried. He laid down on the ground and pointed his feet to the east with his head to the west where he could look to his left at the house and over his feet to Spring Creek and the rising sun. He marked the spot with a rock at each corner and thought that

The last picture of Buck Paty, taken by Clay about two years before Buck's death.

the spot would please his dad.

When he arrived back at the studio, he saw horses and buggies coming from Thomasville. Clay waited outside his studio until they pulled to a stop. He saw that it was the spit and whittle club from the store with their picks and shovels, ready to open the grave. Clay thanked them for coming and asked them if they wanted to see Buck before they started working.

"Guess we better," one spoke up. "I wouldn't want to track mud on such pretty carpet. How is Lucy and the rest of the family?"

They walked around to the east side of the house where Ivy met them at the door. She asked them to come in. With her head down, she led them to Buck's bedroom. When they began to leave, Ivy asked them to please come to the dining room and have a cup of coffee and a crumpet before they began to work. Everyone thanked her and expressed their sorrow.

As soon as they finished the coffee, they were led to the spot selected for the grave by Clay, who showed them the four rocks.

They took turns, using first the pick, then the shovel. Long before dark, they were finished. Some left their shovels for filling the grave. They then headed back by the house to their buggies.

Ivy sat on the front porch watching. When she saw the men start to leave, she yelled to Jane and Jean, "Bring it now."

Ivy ran out to meet the men and asked them to please come sit on the front porch and have some lemonade or some coffee and more crumpets.

Everyone was charmed by Ivy's beauty and her kind and thoughtful behavior.

While they sat on the porch, Ivy took the trays from Jane and Jean and passed them among the workers while very softly telling how much she appreciated them and invited them back.

As soon as everyone was gone, Clay and Ivy went back into Buck's bedroom and sat on the foot of his bed for a long time.

"What did your mother say?" Clay asked.

"I haven't told her. I just couldn't," Ivy replied.

Clay jumped up, obviously disgusted, and went immediately to Lucy's room. Her door was closed but she knew something was going on.

When Clay came in, Lucy opened her eyes and looked at him before she asked, "What is going on, Clay?"

Clay went over to Lucy's bed and sat on the edge. When he

sat down, he leaned over his sister and placed his hand on the bed across her. He felt a wet bed and could smell urine.

"Lucy," he gently said, "Dad died last night. He is laid out on his bed. Are you able to go see him?"

"If you'll help me, I think I can make it," Lucy weakly uttered.

"Wait just a moment," Clay said as he went out of her room and closed the door. He picked up a chair and set it by Buck's bed. He then called for Ivy to bring water and towels again.

Clay, as he appeared at the time of his father's death.

It scared Ivy when she heard Clay yell for her. She

had never heard Clay speak in such a stern manner before. "Also tell Don and his two witches I want to see them NOW!" This really scared Ivy. They all rushed to see what the problem was.

When they were all there, Clay said, "Sit down. Things are going to change around here. Lucy's bed is wet. She smells like piss. I don't know if the moisture is from her or the leak in the roof. Ivy and I are going to clean her up and move her into Dad's room for a while. Don, you take some singles, a hammer and nails, get on the roof, and, by damn, fix it."

Don wanted to talk back to Clay, to let him know that he hadn't been paid in months and he was afraid to climb on the roof, but decided this wasn't the time.

"Jane and Jean, you strip her bed. If the mattress is wet, get Don to help you carry it out in the sun. I'm not interested in your aches and pains. Now get with it unless you want to look for a new place to eat and sleep."

They both picked up the hems of their dresses and stomped out of the room—the Mona Lisa smile turned to a frown.

"I want it done as soon as Ivy and I get her out of the room," he yelled after them, "and I better not find her in this mess again."

Ivy and Clay stripped Lucy. Ivy washed her all over and soon discovered where some of the foul odor was coming from. As soon as she was washed, Clay set her in a chair while they dressed her. Clay brought a toothbrush with some baking soda and a glass of water. He even scrubbed her mouth and teeth before carrying her into Buck's room.

He set her in a chair with the back toward the foot of the bed so Lucy could look at Buck in the face.

"He doesn't even look sick now," she said. "I wish I could go with him."

Don was hammering away on the roof. There must have been several rotten shingles, Clay thought. He couldn't believe that his sister was in such a mess. He thought Ivy was seeing after her and Ivy thought Jane and Jean were. Anyway, things

Lucy Paty, a short time before her death. She was the youngest Gray Lady ever to work at the Civil War hospital in Thomasville. In her later years, she was often called "Lady Gray" with utmost respect from those who knew her during the Civil War.

would be different now.

Clay went back to Lucy's room and saw a big wet spot where she had been lying. He again yelled for Jane and Jean. There was a feather bed on top of a corn shuck mattress. He pulled the feather bed off and onto the floor and couldn't find a wet spot underneath.

Clay looked up to see Jane and Jean standing in the door. "Get hold of the mattress," he yelled. Jane started to say something about her sore hands but Clay soon changed her mind with, "Get hold of it, dammit, I'll handle one end."

They reluctantly took hold of two corners while Clay got the other end. Out the door they went, dragging it on the floor. Clay told them in no uncertain terms that they were going to mop up the streaks they were leaving. They both picked up their corners much higher so they wouldn't make any marks on the floor.

Outside, they hung the feather bed high on a wire clothes line. As soon as it was on the line, Clay brought buckets of water and dashed it onto the mattress.

Back in the house, Jane was mopping the floor, grumbling all the time. Lucy was still sitting by Buck's side, crying. Clay asked her if she would like to sit in the library or on the front porch for a while.

"I would like to sit on the porch," Lucy replied.

Clay and Ivy helped her to a chair on the front porch from where she could see the pile of dirt where Buck was to be buried. Lucy looked at the spot for a long time. She finally said

Ivy, at the height of her career. Many men came to visit her. One, a medical doctor from Birch Tree, was her favorite.

very softly, "I'll be joining you soon." Then she turned to Clay and said, "I want to be buried beside him. I wish Mother could be moved here to be with us."

"I'll tell you what I'll do," Clay replied. "I'll move her remains here. I want to be buried there too." He said making sure Ivy heard him.

Lucy began to get cool as the sun loweredbehind them. She asked for a cover or to be moved back into the house. "I could use the chamber too if I had some help," Lucy whispered. Clay yelled for Jane and Jean to bring the chamber and help Lucy.

When they came back inside, Clay went to the porch and carried Lucy to the larger couch in the library. He set her there and went out the back door to check the mattress which he still found very wet.

Don finished repairing the roof and sat at the kitchen table with a cup of coffee and a sorrowful look on his face. "Just what is wrong with you?" Clay asked, picking up a cup of coffee and sitting at the table.

"Lots of things," Don answered. "I don't have any kids to care for me. These two old biddies probably gave me venereal diseases. I don't care anything about them any more. I have no money and haven't been paid since last fall."

"Sorry I asked," Clay said. "How much does my dad owe you?"

"Well over a hundred dollars, and Jane and Jean never got any pay. They deserve something, surely."

"We'll discuss it after the funeral," Clay said. "I'll make it right then."

After dinner that night, Lucy was moved back to the couch after Ivy brushed and set her hair. She let them know what dress she wanted to wear for the funeral the next day.

Early the next morning, the living room and library were quickly converted into a church with Buck placed on a couch up front beside a fern stand where the preacher would be. Everything they owned that could be sat on was placed in the big room facing Buck.

The funeral was supposed to be at ten A.M. but it was only 8:30 when people began to arrive. A long time before ten, the room was full and people began sitting all over the front porch. Somehow, all the farmers who ran cattle on the range and the entire population of Thomasville made it there, Clay thought. It was a great tribute to his father.

The preacher hardly knew Buck, and he invited a farmer to say a few words about him. Old and feeble John and Matilda Thomas stood and gave a brief summary of what they knew about him. Mr. Weaver from the bank and Mr. Hass from the company store also testified to his truthfulness and how he always paid his bill.

Clay asked the Spit and Whittlers to come in from the porch and carry Buck to his final resting place, telling them that this would make Buck happy.

Ropes were used to lower Buck into his grave as everyone looked on. Many brought flowers, some in glass jars and some with the stems wrapped with a wet cloth.

Everyone stood around until the grave was completely filled and rounded up with dirt. Then, they each found a special place for their flowers.

Clay didn't ask them to stay and eat because he knew there wasn't nearly enough for all of them.

After they were gone, Lucy could see the huge mound of flowers and the tears began again and continued until she began coughing hard.

Clay brought her a spoonful of fresh honey and a glass of water which helped. The next day, the feather bed had dried and Lucy moved back into her room for the night.

With better care, Lucy was improving. Each day they got her up, helped her to the pot when she needed to go, and made sure all her needs were fulfilled. There was no more leak above her bed.

Clay and Don settled their differences, and Jane and Jean knew what their chores were to be if they expected any pay. Clay agreed to give Don six month's pay which would amount to one hundred twenty dollars cash and the two wives were to receive five dollars a week beginning now if they did their assigned jobs. Ivy was to see after her mother and was allowed to write checks for what groceries and other necessities they needed.

Soon, Ivy was having callers, some from Thomasville and some from as far as Birch Tree. The farmers spread the word about the young and lonesome lady who lived on Spring Creek. Ivy would often leave and be gone for two or three days.

Clay and Lucy worried about her, but nothing seemed to make any difference. She was young, beautiful, and she liked male company.

Clay more or less lost interest in everything. He no longer participated in the fall roundups and brandings. Don, his wives, and Ivy went a few times, then Don decided his pay was the same no matter if he helped or not.

Ivy wasn't the only one who enjoyed the fall roundups. She got to mix and see if there were any new men. She culled none, but was never able to put her brand on any.

Old Doctor Davies from Birch Tree was her best male friend. He came to see her all year long. She asked him one night if he would marry her and his answer was, "I'll think about it."

Ivy didn't tell him she was pregnant. At least she thought she was because she was at least three weeks late.

One morning, Jane and Jean came to the kitchen and just sat at the table with their heads down and didn't look at each other. Ivy came in, ready for breakfast for her and her mother. She immediately noticed them and asked, "What's wrong?"

"You tell her," Jane said.

"Don's gone," Jean said, not raising her head.

"Good riddance," Ivy answered. "He didn't do anything, anyway."

Both Jane and Jean started to cry and went back to their room.

Ivy went out the front door and around to Clay's studio. The weather was below freezing, but the day would warm up as soon as the sun got a little higher in the sky.

Ivy banged on Clay's door, but no one answered. She thought, "Oh, no, he hasn't taken off too!"

She opened the door and found her lazy uncle in his dirty bed with the covers pulled over his head. She walked over and jerked the covers back and saw he hadn't even bothered to remove his clothes.

"Get up, you lazy butthole," she yelled. "Don is gone and the house is cold. You'll have to build some fires. Jane and Jean went back to their room crying. Mom is feeling worse. Now get up. I mean now!" she yelled, yanking the cover completely from the bed and onto the floor. The odor struck her when she pulled the covers off. "My God," she shouted. You must like to smell your farts. It's about time you snapped out of it, Clay," she said as she went out the door.

On her way back up to the porch, she detoured by the woodpile where she picked up some kindling and a few sticks of wood.

She placed an old piece of wrapping paper in first, and laid the kindling and wood on top. She struck a match to the paper and soon had a fire going in the cookstove.

By the time Clay made it up to the kitchen, she fried some bacon and eggs. There were left-over biscuits in the warming closet and butter and jelly in the pantry. She forgot the coffee, which was the first thing Clay looked for. He picked up a cup and walked over to the stove looking for it.

"Where's the coffee?" he asked.

"The same place as the fire in the library."

Clay knew exactly what she was referring to. No fire, no coffee. Clay slowly went to the fireplace and began building a fire.

By the time the fire began to warm the house, he could smell coffee boiling on the cookstove. "Go bring Mother in and see if Don's pokes are going to eat," Lucy said.

Clay soon returned, assisting Lucy to the seat nearest the cookstove. Jane and Jean soon followed and seated themselves at the table. Ivy stopped what she was doing and placed both hands on her hips and said, "I'm the one around here that does not get paid, and I'm doing all the work." She finished filling her mother a plate and set it before her. She poured two cups of coffee and set one in front of her mother. She then filled another plate as everyone watched and wondered who it would be for.

Ivy picked up the cup of coffee and went to the empty chair at the foot of the table where she sat with her food and began to eat.

Everyone looked at Ivy with a sorrowful expression as if to say, "Aren't you going to wait on us?"

Ivy finished a mouthful and took a sip of coffee, then said, "There's some more on the stove if you are hungry."

"Bullshit," Clay remarked, dragging himself away from the table with his cup to the cookstove where he filled it and filled a plate, taking most of what was left.

"Would you get me some?" Jane asked Jean. "My hands are swollen and so sore."

Jean dragged herself to the stove where she really had to stretch the pots for both of them to have anything to eat. They had to split the one remaining biscuit. However, there was plenty of coffee.

While seated at the table, Ivy began to complain about never having any money. She asked how much they made from the last roundup.

"I don't know," Clay said, "I didn't go. I took care of Lucy. How much did you make?" he asked Ivy sarcastically, "and how much did you two make?" he asked, indicating Jane and Jean. "Don never brought any cattle home, nor did he give me any money."

"Bullshit," Ivy said, "I don't believe you. He was selling stock to anyone who would buy. He said you told him to sell out."

Clay looked shocked. "So that's the reason he's gone. I'll go see about that, if Pet and the old buggy will make it to the sheriff's office." He finished his cup of coffee, pushed back his chair and said, "I'm going to town!"

By the time he harnessed Pet and hitched her to the buggy, the sun was warming things up pretty good. Pet's old harness dried out from lack of oil and was simply coming apart.

Clay and Pet barely made it to town and to the sheriff's office by going slow and careful. At the sheriff's office, Clay explained what happened and asked if he had seen Don Walker around.

The sheriff answered, "Yes, I have seen him around, but not today. You should go to the bank and see if Mr. Weaver knows anything.

Clay asked the sheriff if that wasn't his job, but the sheriff never answered. He just stared at him.

At the bank, Clay asked Mr. Weaver if he had seen Don Walker lately. "Sure have," Mr. Weaver answered. "He opened an account here with quite a large deposit. I remember he had a large check from you and several from local farmers. I think he deposited well over one thousand dollars."

Clay's mouth fell open as he said, "That crooked bastard. I did pay him some back pay. He sold my cattle at the roundup. By the way, how much do I have in my account?"

Mr. Weaver looked it up and told him that he still had over eight thousand.

Clay started to leave, but he turned back to Mr. Weaver and asked, "How much did you say Don had in his account?"

"A little over one thousand," Mr. Weaver answered.

"I only wrote him a hundred and twenty dollar check for back pay." Clay walked next door to the company store where he found Mr. Hass unloading a big load of supplies from his new truck. He walked to the truck, really looking it over. He opened the door and checked everything inside. He jumped back when he turned a knob and heard a voice say, "Top of the third with two outs. Russell is really burning them in there today." He quickly turned the knob the other way and the voice stopped.

Mr. Hass saw what happened and told him that it was a radio. He could hear people as far away as St. Louis.

Clay never heard a radio before. Mr. Hass further explained that one of the Lewis boys from up the river even played for that team.

He really had Clay's attention. He knew the game of baseball and could imagine spending a lot of lonely time listening to the radio.

"How much did this truck cost?" Clay asked.

"This is one of the best ones," Mr. Hass answered. "It has everything; an electric starter, radio, balloon tires, and blue paint. I gave almost nine hundred dollars for it."

"How hard is it to drive?" Clay asked.

"I bought it at Alton and drove it home. It's easy. Brakes, clutch, gas pedal to control speed. Three gears forward and one back. I could teach you in thirty minutes."

"What'll you take for it?" Clay asked.

"I need it and don't care about selling it," Mr. Hass answered.

"Would you take a thousand dollars for it?" Clay asked.

"I have a lot more supplies to haul. In fact, I'm thinking of starting a delivery service."

"I'd throw in Pet and the buggy," Clay almost pleaded. He really wanted the truck.

"How could I turn that down?" Mr. Hass asked. "As soon as I finish unloading, we'll go to the bank and she is yours."

Clay smiled a big happy grin and he even helped to unload. Mr. Hass was right. It only took Clay a very short time to learn how to drive. He could even shift while going up a hill with very little jerking.

Ivy was outside at the woodpile when she heard and saw him come out of the forest. She dropped her armload of wood and ran into the house. She looked out the window and saw Clay get out. She jerked open the door to run out to see what it was that turned him loose. Jane and Jean stood on the front porch, not daring to get any closer.

Clay slowly and methodically explained everything to Ivy and asked her to get in so he could take her for a ride.

As soon as they were in, Clay turned the radio on. The sound of music made Ivy look around until Clay explained and told her where it was coming from. Ivy really liked the radio idea. She recognized the song and began singing along.

Clay started the truck and turned it around and headed back to Thomasville. Ivy couldn't believe how fast it would go. She never traveled that fast before.

Clay didn't think of what made the car go, so he stopped at the store and asked Mr. Hass, who explained what fuel was and how far it would go on a tankfull. He showed Clay how to read the gauge and how to check the oil. Clay was really glad he came back to town.

"How much do they cost?" Ivy asked on the way home.

Clay told her and he also told her what he found out about Don, saying that he had been to the sheriff and was thinking of having him arrested. He hoped they would hang him if he did have him arrested.

Back at the house, Clay told Jane and Jean what he had found out about Don and the he was probably going to have him arrested.

The next morning when Ivy got up, the house was cold again. She again went around the house to where Clay parked his truck in front of his studio. Clay was sitting in the truck, slapping the steering wheel in time with the music.

Ivy opened the passenger door, climbed in and began slapping her leg. "Let's go to Thomasville for breakfast," she suggested. "I saw a new cafe across the street from the store."

"What'll we do about sis?" Clay asked.

"We'll bring her something." Ivy answered.

Clay turned the key on and stepped on the starter. The truck started on the first revolution.

"We'll have to hurry," Clay said as he shoved down harder on the fuel pedal. "The house will be getting cold and those two bitches won't build a fire. They'll just lay in bed."

Ivy and Clay pulled up to the new cafe and found it to be to their liking. They both had hotcakes and sausage, which they were definitely not used to. Clay asked for a second stack and for one to go. He must have drank six cups of coffee, saturated with sugar and milk.

When they started to leave, the lady who served them introduced herself as Cecilia Williams and said, "I hope everything was all right."

"Well," Clay said, "the second stack wasn't nearly as good as the first."

Cecilia looked startled until she saw Clay smile and she caught the joke.

"The sugar must have been O.K.," she replied. "I see the bowl is empty. Come back again," Cecilia commented as they left.

Back at Spring Creek, Ivy carried her mother's breakfast in and set it on the table. The house was cold with no fires anywhere.

Clay came in with wood for the cookstove as Ivy went to get her mother and check on Jane and Jean. She first knocked on Jane and Jean's door, but heard no response.

"Time to get up before you freeze your knobbies off," Ivy yelled. Still, she didn't hear any response. Gently, she eased the door open to have a look. The bed didn't look like it had been slept in. On closer examination, she found that two pillow cases were missing. Looking around the room, she discovered that their clothes and personal items were also gone. Ivy figured that they loaded all they could carry into the pillow cases and lit out the night before.

Ivy went across the way to her mother's room and found her

with all the available covers pulled up around her and fast asleep. She gently shook her awake and helped her get dressed.

Lucy was pleasantly surprised when she sat down beside a warm stove. Clay set the stack of hotcakes with sausage, butter, and maple syrup beside her.

"Clay and I ran into town in his new truck," Ivy said.

"What's that?" Lucy asked. "I didn't know Clay could still run. All I ever see is movement like a turtle."

Clay tried to explain but finally told her that she would have to see it and that he would take her to town when spring came.

After Lucy finished her breakfast and took a few sips of coffee, Clay told her about Don and his wives. Lucy didn't say anything for a while, looking as if she were going into shock.

Finally, she asked, "What are we going to do?"

"We'll make it, Sis," Clay said kindly. "I'm having him arrested and I hope they give him the works."

Clay suddenly sat up straighter and said, "I'll bet those two bitches have gone to warn him. I think I better go back to town."

"Wait a minute," Ivy said with her head down. "I have some more bad news." Both Clay and Lucy looked at Ivy, giving her their undivided attention.

"I'm pregnant," Ivy said, as she raised her head to catch their reaction.

Neither said anything until Clay broke the silence with, "Maybe you will stay home more."

"I don't want a baby and he won't marry me," Ivy said emphatically.

"Do you know who the daddy is?" Clay asked.

"I think it must be Dr. Davies, the best I can figure. I asked him to marry me, but I can tell he won't. He said he would have to think about it and that was three weeks ago."

"He's not going to marry you. He's rich I hear. He has a hotel on the Current River, a drugstore in Birch Tree, and no telling how many farms. He probably has a girl in every town," Clay chided.

Ivy began to cry when her mother asked, "How far along are you?"

"I haven't had a period in three months," she answered as she pulled back from the table and walked over to pick up her mother's plate.

Lucy gently took Ivy's hand and pulled her down so she could give her a hug and kiss on the cheek. I know exactly how you feel, Dear," Lucy said. "We love you and it will work out fine. Don't worry. My love for you is unconditional."

⌒ SIXTEEN ⌒

"I'm going to town to find Don and I may be gone a few days if I can work it out," Clay said.

"What are you going to do?" Lucy asked. "I hope it ain't anything drastic. Don has been awful good to you."

"If I can find Don I may take him with me to get mother and bring her body here to bury alongside dad."

Big tears formed in Lucy's eyes as she turned to Clay, "Oh God help you," she said as she feebly reached upward with both hands. "Please hurry Clay," she said as she reached for him to give him a kiss, tears rolling down her cheeks and dripping on the table.

Clay couldn't hold back tears as he said, "I'll go get her even if I have to go by myself. It shouldn't take more than a week. I'll hurry," Clay said as he went out the door to look for picks and shovels to throw in the back of the pickup truck.

When he reached Thomasville he went straight to the sheriff's office to see if he had picked up Don yet. The sheriff told Clay that he couldn't pick him up unless he made a formal complaint and swore out a warrant.

"Forget it," Clay said as he turned to leave. "I'll take care of it myself. Do you know where he is?"

"I hear he is camped out somewhere up Birch Tree hollow."

"I'll find the bastard," Clay said as he slammed the door.

It didn't take him long to find Don's camp but no one was there. Clay yelled as loud as he could, "Come on out Don, I know you are near. If you don't come out I'll go to the sheriff and have you arrested and you know what they do with cattle thieves. You have five minutes, come on out and let's talk."

He heard a noise to his left and saw Don crawl from behind a pile of brush.

"Come on, I'm not going to shoot you," Clay said.

Don stood and walked very slowly toward Clay with his head down, never looking at him. When he was close he stopped and just stood shaking his head.

Finally he said, "I know I shouldn't have done it but I needed to get away. I can't stand them two bitches I married. They can't have kids. The only thing they gave me was V.D. I'm getting old and will soon need someone to take care of me. I know that's no excuse for what I did but that was what I was thinking. Can you forgive me?" When Don raised his head to look at Clay, tears streamed down and he put on his most pitiful face.

"I'll think about it," Clay said. "Come with me. I have a trip to make to Louisiana and need some help. We'll figure out something."

Don slowly followed behind Clay to the truck where he got in, still wearing his chin on his chest.

"Have you had anything to eat?" Clay asked.

"Not in three days. I haven't been hungry, been trying to decide what to do. I was afraid to go to town."

Clay pulled to a stop in front of Cecilia Williams' cafe and told Don to go in and eat a good meal and he would be back to pick him up soon. "Do you have any money?" Clay asked.

"I got plenty of money," Don said as he got out of the truck.

Clay went to Alpha Roberts to ask about Bill and John. He wanted to take them with him to do the work.

Alpha was happy to see Clay and thought it was a good idea to take Bill and John because they had been very sad lately. They didn't get to see Buck before he died and often asked about Clay and Lucy and why their parents hadn't come for them yet. They were really feeling pretty low. "This should be a boost for them," Alpha said. "I'll go get them and bring them over to the cafe. I'm sure Cecilia would love to feed them. Did you know that she is my youngest daughter?"

"No, I didn't," Clay answered. "We'll wait for you at the cafe. I could use something to eat myself."

"I'll have them there in a few minutes. Oh, how long you going to be gone? Do they need extra clothes?"

"We'll probably be gone a week. I'm going to get Mother and bring her home to be with Dad."

Alpha looked shocked but walked away.

Clay took his time eating because he knew that Bill and John would have to eat.

Bill and John were both happy to see Clay and were more interested in the trip back home than eating. They said they were ready to leave.

Cecilia already had food prepared for them which they insisted on taking with them and they graciously thanked her.

It was almost one o'clock when they finally got underway. Bill and John sat in the back with their backs against the cab. This was their first ride in an automobile and they couldn't believe how fast they were going.

When the sun went down, the temperature dropped drastically. Clay pulled over to the side of the road and stopped. He told everyone to get out and relieve themselves and for Bill and John to come squeeze up front in the cab.

Bill and John were very interested in the truck. They wanted to know how everything worked. They couldn't believe that a pull of a button would light up the road. They almost jumped out of their hides when Clay turned the radio on.

They traveled until late that night and slept in the pickup. Early next morning they were in Little Rock, Arkansas, where Clay pulled in at a big restaurant. He was really embarrassed when they wouldn't serve Bill and John inside so he ordered all four meals to go.

They stopped again for lunch and again ordered to go. It was almost dark the second day when they arrived at the old plantation. The house looked pretty much the same as he pulled up in front.

A middle-aged man came to the door with a shotgun broken down and draped over his left arm.

Clay quickly got out of the truck and identified himself and told the man what he came for.

The man stood his gun against the wall and went down the steps with an outstretched hand. "I'm Gene Pierce," he said introducing himself and shaking hands. "That's a good looking truck you have," he said walking over closer for a better look only to discover three more men in the truck.

Clay reached over and opened the door. He introduced Don, Bill and John.

Gene looked a little concerned, but did offer his hand. "I'm sure you would like to stretch your legs," Gene said, not really knowing what to say.

Bill, John, and Don took the cue and started walking toward the barn and outbuildings. Clay explained to Gene that Bill and John were raised here and were real anxious to come back. "We'll dig mother up tomorrow and not bother you any longer than necessary."

"Come on in the house. I'll tell Flo to set another place," Gene said. He saw the expression on Clay's face and knew that he was concerned about the other three.

"Don't worry about them," Gene said, "I'll send our help to take care of them."

"Do you still have slaves?" Clay asked.

"Well, you might say that. They can't find anywhere to go and we feed and let them live here for a little work. We have five left. They can leave any time they want to."

"Are the two with you slaves?"

"No they are free."

"Come on in the house, you can spend the night with us."

As soon as they were in the house Gene introduced Flo and told her to send the girl out to tell her mother and father to take care of the other three.

"I'll be happy for you to take your mother. She is the only white person buried out there."

The next morning Clay was awakened by the sounds of

picks and shovels digging in the earth. He quickly dressed and went downstairs to find the Pierces sitting at the table having a bountiful breakfast.

"Good morning," Flo said. "Pull up a chair. We tried to be quiet so we wouldn't awaken you. We knew you must be tired."

"May I be excused for a few minutes?" Clay asked. "I hear my boys outside starting to open the grave. I need to talk to them."

"Sure," Gene said, "but hurry, we'll try to keep it warm for you."

Clay went out back where they were already down over two feet. "Be careful with the pick when you get down a little further. She is buried four feet underground. Be careful," Clay said again as he headed back to the house.

In the kitchen Clay stopped to wash his hands, face, and comb his hair before returning to the dining room.

Gene had some questions for Clay but could see how anxious Clay was to get back outside. He did ask him if he had any trouble coming down from Missouri. He also warned him about some outlaws that were still roaming around. That was why he always carried the shotgun.

Clay thanked him for the warning and asked if he had any advice for him.

"I hope you are carrying a gun." Gene replied.

"Don't have a gun but would buy one if you can sell me one."

"I have an old sixteen gauge shotgun but only have three shells. It works good but I can't find shells for it around here."

"How much do you want for it?" Clay asked.

"I'll let you have it for twenty-nine dollars." Gene said.

"Don't have much extra money," Clay countered. "My boys are pretty good at throwing rocks, guess we'll have to rely on them."

"Suit yourself," Gene said obviously disappointed that Clay didn't take the gun.

Clay finished his meal and hurried outside to find that they already lifted the box. It was made of walnut lumber and was still in pretty good condition out of the grave. Clay looked at it then went for the truck so they could load it in the back.

When Clay left, Gene told Bill and John to hurry and refill the hole. Without a word they both picked up shovels and soon had the hole filled.

Clay backed the truck up close so they wouldn't have to carry it far. "Wish we had some canvas and rope to wrap it in," Clay commented.

"I have some," Gene said, "How much are you willing to pay for it?"

"I'll have to see it first," Clay said.

Gene left and was soon back with a large piece of good tarp and what looked like new rope.

Clay walked over to have a closer look before saying, "Tell you what I'll do. I'll give you twenty dollars for the tarp, gun, shells, and rope.

Gene gasped for air and threw up his hands saying. "Forgive him for stealing God. I'll take your twenty but only because I feel sorry for you."

As soon as Clay gave him the money, they wrapped the coffin and tied it in place in back of the trunk.

Don and Clay got in the front expecting Bill and John to get in the back but they refused and told Clay that they would rather walk.

Clay looked at them and could plainly see by the white in their eyes that they were scared. "Mother would love to have you escort her to Missouri."

"Mister Clay, I just can't sit by her in her condition. Not right now anyway."

"Pick up a bunch of them throwing size rocks and put them in the back," Clay said.

They both looked at Clay with confused expressions but did what he asked. Soon as they were deposited in the back Clay opened his door, got out and said, "Come on boys, get in. I'd be honored to sit by you. Scoot over Don."

Bill and John were quick to get in and share the front seat

even with the old 16 gauge shotgun.

Clay asked them if they had breakfast.

"Did we ever," John said. "It was the best I've had in a long time. Grits, grits, and more grits with eggs and hog jowl. They know both our parents and we left directions for them so they can find us."

They were only on the road a few miles when they had to stop for an old dead log across the road.

"This looks funny," Clay said. "Everyone stay in the cab and hide the gun." Clay got out to walk over to the log to see what was needed to get it moved or to find a way around it.

Three very rough looking men with long beards, big floppy black hats, and guns drawn stepped out from behind the trees. "What cha got in the truck?" one asked.

"I got my mother," Clay said.

The one closest to Clay thought he was being wise so he brought the butt of his gun around and caught Clay on the left side of the head knocking him down and out.

He then walked to the back of the truck to have a closer look. He motioned to his two buddies to come over and have a look.

"See what it is," he said.

They leaned their guns against the truck and cut the ropes. They then removed the canvas and used one of the shovels to pry the lid off feeling sure they would find more gold or silver than they had ever seen.

As soon as the lid popped up they both grabbed their noses and jumped out of the truck without saying a word.

The one with the gun lowered his gun and stepped forward to have a look and immediately wished he hadn't.

John jumped from the truck with the big sixteen gauge leveled at them while yelling. "You no good white trash, I think I'll kill all three of you."

All three fell to their knees begging for mercy.

Clay came to his knees and realized what was going on. "Hold it John, he yelled as he got to his feet. "Give me the gun. Let me do it." Clay was really mad and the three knew it. They thought for sure they were going to die. "Throw your billfolds over here," Clay said. "I want to know who I'm killing. Now stand up and turn your back."

"Get their guns John and throw them in the back of the truck."

Clay then told John and Bill to come to him. He whispered to them to get in the back of the truck and pick up the rocks and when he told them to run they would see how many rocks they could hit them with.

Clay then said, "You low-life bastards, I'm going to give you a chance. When I say go, see how fast you can run and I better never see you again."

Clay yelled, "Go" and John and Bill began pelting them with rocks. All three were hit and knocked down several times but they all finally made it out of sight and reach of the rocks.

Don finally got out of the pickup and told Clay and the boys he would put things back in order since he was the only one who didn't know Ethel.

Clay, John, and Bill walked into the woods to a big log where they sat not knowing if they wanted to laugh or cry. They first shed a few tears but then John said, "How many times did you hit them, Bill?"

"I had five good rocks and they all found their mark," Bill said.

"Wonder what they were thinking," Clay said, as he began laughing. "I'll bet they have a lot of bruises and probably some broken bones. You boys don't need a gun."

As they walked back to the truck they had their arms around each others shoulders laughing hard. This reminded them of when they were much younger. Clay had his right arm around John's neck and John had his arm around Bill's. Clay quickly stepped in front of John, bent over, and threw him over his back, putting him on the ground.

Clay ran to the truck faster than he had moved in a long time. He knew John would man-handle him if he caught him.

The rest of the way back to Thomasville Don was very quiet because he still did not know what Clay had in mind for him.

When they reached Thomasville, Don asked if he could stay there and look for Jane and Jean. He assured Clay he would make things right.

Clay looked at him with a uncertain expression but finally relented. He warned Don that he would send the sheriff after him if he couldn't find him.

Don got out of the pickup and thanked Clay as he walked away.

Bill and John went home with Clay where they opened a grave beside Buck and gently lowered Ethel to her final resting place.

After filling the grave, they came to the house to see Lucy and to find something to eat.

When they entered Lucy's room they were not ready for what they saw. She looked like a very old and frail woman.

Lucy recognized them and smiled broadly as she motioned for them to come to her.

She reached her arms to both of them and gave each a kiss on the forehead. "Did you help bring Mother home?" Lucy asked.

"Yes we did," John said. "She now rests beside Buck."

"God bless both of you," Lucy said in a very feeble voice. Even more feebly she uttered, "I'm ready to go now."

Ivy came to the door and said, "Clay told me all about the trip. I would love to have seen you rock them bastards. Come eat, I have something for you."

After they finished eating, Clay delivered them back to Thomasville. He gave them each a five dollar bill and thanked them over and over. He assured them he would check on them more often and come take them for a ride and let them listen to the radio.

~ SEVENTEEN ~

The next day, Clay went to town to see if the sheriff knew anything. Climbing the steps to the sheriff's office, he began to feel a little sorry for Don. When he opened the door, the sheriff loudly said, "Boy, am I glad to see you. You'll have to sign this complaint," he said, pointing to some papers on his desk. "He almost got away. Them two Indian women warned him. He drew his money out of the bank and Mr. Weaver suspected something and sent someone to inform me.

"I caught the three of them in a buggy about three miles west of here. They were definitely trying to make a getaway. I already have one in jail to hang, and I'm sure the judge will want him to hang too."

Clay's face flushed red, but he signed the papers without commenting.

"I had to let the women go. Didn't have anything to hold them for. He's in the jail below me. Want to see him?" the sheriff asked.

"No," Clay quickly answered as he started to leave. At the door, Clay turned around and asked, "How long do you think it will be?"

"The judge will be by next week, so it could be soon. We'll hang them from the old burr oak tree between the creeks."

Clay turned and walked out, really having second thoughts. "I know what he done was wrong, but it was nothing to die for. He is responsible for building my house. He brought me home from the army. What would I have done without him?" All the good things kept running through his mind.

Clay left the sheriff's office feeling terrible. He thought he would try to find Jane and Jean to see what their story was. He drove around to shantytown where he first found them.

There was no more shantytown. It was completely burned to the ground. Clay wondered where all the people went, but then he noticed a new house going up on the southwest corner of the block. Instead of starting his truck, he decided to go ask one of the workers.

When he came close, he recognized the preacher who also recognized him and immediately came to greet him.

"What happened?" Clay asked.

"The whole block burned. Doesn't it look better? I bought it, or rather, God gave it to me with my promise to clean it up. None of them went to church anyway," the preacher said in a sanctimonious way.

"Where did the people move to?" Clay asked.

"I think the two old Indian women you are looking for are between the creeks."

"You think Jane and Jean are between the creeks?" Clay asked.

"I heard someone say they were there, living in a teepee, but I really wouldn't know. I don't have much to do with their kind."

"I'll bet God doesn't love them either," Clay said as he turned and walked back to his truck.

Between the creeks and under the big burr oak tree where Don was supposed to hang, sure enough, was an Indian teepee. Clay pulled his truck off the road as close to the teepee as possible. He sounded his horn but no one came out. He opened the door and walked over to the teepee where he rattled the flap covering the opening. Still, there was no response. He smelled something, and looking up, saw smoke coming from the opening in the top. Clay pulled back the flap and stepped in. Jane and Jean were sitting cross-legged on the floor by a very small fire. They were the most pitiful creatures he ever saw. They glanced up at him, then each tried to hide their faces behind the other. No Mona Lisa smiles were showing today.

"I'm terribly sorry," Clay said as he sat on the floor across from them. "Do you want to come home with me?" he asked.

They both shook their heads no.

"Do you have something to eat?" he asked.

Again they shook their heads no.

Clay stood up and left, but was soon back with a good supply of food from the store. "Do you need anything else?" Clay asked.

Jane and Jean shook their heads no, but Jane said, "We don't have anything to cook in."

Again Clay left and returned with a kettle, a coffee pot, cups, and some coffee.

Jane said, "Thanks. Are you really going to let Don hang?"

Clay couldn't answer. He only turned and left.

Back at Spring Creek, Ivy and Lucy were both curious to know what Clay found out. After an explanation, they both agreed that Don didn't deserve to die.

"Think of all he has done for us," Ivy said. "What would we have done without him? I don't want to see him die."

Lucy looked up from where she sat by the fire and asked, "Please don't let them hang him, Clay. Don't send me to my grave with this on my mind. I certainly forgive him."

"I'll see what I can do," was Clay's only reply. He was still feeling sorry for Don but still mad about what he did to the family.

∾ EIGHTEEN ∾

*W*hile Clay was gone, Ivy dug up the rest of the buried money. She found it exactly where Lucy told her it was. She counted out over seven thousand dollars in gold and three hundred in silver. She put it all into fruit jars and hid it in the house. She replaced the box and brushed away her tracks. She really didn't know what she was going to do, but things were piling up in her mind. Her mother really needed her. She needed a man. Clay was lazy and listless. She didn't approve of what was happening to Don.

When Clay was finished with his explanation, Ivy said, "I want you to take me to Birch Tree."

"What for?" Clay asked.

"None of your business. If you won't take me, I'll take myself," she said as she got up and went to her bedroom for her coat and purse full of gold. When she came back through the library, she asked, "Are the keys in the truck?"

"You can't take the truck," Clay said emphatically.

"Where did you get the money for it? What makes you think all that money was yours?"

"Oh, shit," Clay said as he stood up and put on his coat. "Come on, I'll take you. I need to go to Birch Tree anyway."

Birch Tree was about fifteen miles north, but a new gravel road had just been constructed from Thomasville. It took them approximately forty-five minutes to reach the city limits. Dr. Davies' pharmacy and Drug Store was the first building they

Dr. Davies' drug store where Ivy had her first fountain drink.

saw. Ivy told Clay to pull around in front and stay in the pick-up.

"I need to go to the hardware store," Clay said. "But I'll be right back."

Ivy opened the front door of the building and walked in very proudly. She saw bar stools and a big marble counter with a huge mirror behind it. Dr. Davies was facing the mirror washing dishes when Ivy sat at one of the stools, parking her heavy purse on the counter.

Dr. Davies looked in the mirror and saw her reflection. He continued washing dishes but his face turned redder than his hands.

He again glanced up at Ivy but said nothing. Ivy then pulled a pistol from her pocket, pointed it at him, and said, "Unless you want breakfast in hell, you better talk to me."

Dr. Davies, with both hands shoulder high, turned to face her but didn't say anything.

"Are you going to marry me?" Ivy asked.

Dr. Davies still didn't answer.

Ivy opened her purse and exposed what looked to be thousands of dollars in gold. "Now what do you say?" she asked, seeing the doctor's mouth fall open.

"Put your pistol away so we can talk," the doctor said.

Ivy removed her finger from the trigger and slid the safety back on as she eased it back into her pocket. For the first time, she had a glimmer of hope, but it soon dashed away when the doctor said, "You can't believe the trouble I'm in. I couldn't marry you if I wanted to. There are two others with the same problem, if not worse. They don't have any money. I'll take care of the kid but I can't marry you," he said.

Let me fix you a cherry Coke, Dr. Davies offered. It is something new and very good.

Ivy relaxed and felt almost sorry for him as she asked, "Will you still come to see me?"

"Here you are," he said as he set the glass of Coke with a straw in front of her. "I'll be there tomorrow. Be sure not to make any other appointments."

Clay pulled up out front and Ivy went to the front door and motioned for him to come in. Ivy turned to Dr. Davies and said, "Fix Clay one like mine and put something stronger in it."

Dr. Davies mixed the drink, then reached under the counter and pulled a bottle of rum out, from which he poured a small amount in Clay's cherry Coke. Ivy leaned over with her straw and took a sip. She then handed her glass to Dr. Davies and said, "Fix me one like Clay's."

Clay wanted to confront the doctor but didn't know if he had the energy or inclination. He was really in a rut and didn't need any more problems. He just hoped that his rut didn't turn into a grave. So far, he could run back and forth, but didn't seem to be able to get out of it.

When they finished their drinks they headed back home not feeling any better. Back in the pickup, Ivy asked, "What is all that stuff in the back of the truck?"

"I may as well tell you. You'll find out anyway. That's copper tubing, barrels, and everything I need to start making whiskey. I even bought seven sacks of corn."

"Ain't there laws against that?" Ivy asked.

"Not if you are making it for your own use," Clay answered.

On the way home, Clay went back to the sheriff's office to

talk to him about Don. Clay asked if he could change his mind about pressing charges on Don.

"The hanging in supposed to be the day after tomorrow and the judge is already gone. I don't suppose we can get out of it."

"What about the other man?" Clay asked. "When is his hanging?"

The sheriff turned and looked at the calendar. "His ain't for two weeks. I don't even know him. He was a stranger in town. He deserves to die for what he done."

"What did he do?" Clay asked.

"Can't tell. The girl made us promise not to tell who her baby's daddy is."

Clay reached into his pocket and pulled out his coin purse where he always kept two twenty dollar gold pieces. "You don't suppose we could do some substituting, do you?" Don't they have their heads covered when you take them to the tree?" Clay asked.

"Sure do," the sheriff said, straightening up his chair and looking interested, especially in Clay's coin purse. "They are about the same size. No one but you and me will have to know."

"Good," Clay said, "I'll pay you after the hanging."

The morning of Don's hanging, everyone waited near the old burr oak tree, ready to see justice served. They already moved the wives' teepee back a few paces to make room. Clay hadn't even told Ivy about the switch, let alone his wives.

As soon as the sun started to burn the fog from between the rivers, the sheriff came from town riding behind the prisoner who had his hands tied behind him and his feet tied beneath the horse. A black sack was over the prisoner's head with a drawstring knotted at his neck. The noose was already over the limb and tied to the trunk of the tree.

The sheriff rode the horse directly under the noose and stopped him. "Well, this is it," the sheriff said. "Do you have a last word?" he asked as he placed the noose around the prisoner's neck. The prisoner turned his head from side to side and said, "Forgive me." He then tilted his head back and looked up and said, "You too, God."

Don's wives were sitting cross-legged on the ground pounding it and sobbing loudly. Ivy came over and sat behind them with an arm on each of their shoulders sobbing almost as loud.

The sheriff slid off the back of the horse and slapped him hard on the rump. The horse jumped from beneath the prisoner, breaking his neck instantly. Only a few kicks and a gurgling sound, then he hung still. The sheriff lowered him to the ground and told Jane and Jean to take him to their teepee.

Clay, Ivy, and the two wives picked him up, refusing offers of help and carried him inside the teepee. Once he was inside, Clay came back out and announced that the wives wanted no ceremony and they would care for him Indian style. No help wanted!

As soon as everyone was gone, they loaded the corpse into the back of Clay's truck with the two sobbing widows beside him and Ivy in the cab. They made their exit through Thomasville with no one jeering or making any derogatory remarks.

When they arrived at Spring Creek, Clay slovenly went to look for a shovel, all the time dreading the work involved in opening a grave. When he returned with a shovel, both Jane and Jean were shaking their heads no. "What is wrong?" Clay asked.

"We pulled the black bag off. It ain't Don. Where's Don?" Jane asked.

"I'll have to tell you later, but he's all right."

They both gave Clay their Mona Lisa smile and climbed down from the back of the truck and threw their arms around him. They thanked him with a nose rub.

"We'll still let the animals have his flesh," Jane said with Jean shaking her head in agreement. "I would rather become part of an eagle than a worm. You know our spirit only changes form. It can be neither created nor destroyed," Jane continued.

"We'll take him to the top of that hill." Clay said, pointing to the highest ground south of the house. "Where is Ivy?" he asked.

"She went to see about her mother. We don't need her. We'll help you," Jane said.

Clay went to the wood pile and picked up an ax and laid it in the back of the truck. "Do you want to ride up front?" he asked.

"We like to ride in the back," Jean said.

At the top of the hill, Clay selected a spot where there were four small trees about the right distance apart and backed the truck between them. With his ax, he cut them off while standing in the truck bed. He cut them about seven feet above the ground. He then trimmed up the tops, and with the use of some grapevines, he lashed the poles together making a lofty perch on which to lay the corpse. It took all three of them lifting and heaving to get the body on top.

Once on top, they used more grapevines to go around the poles and the body to make sure the body stayed where they wanted it.

"Looks like a good job to me," Jane said, brushing her hands together and wiping the sweat from her forehead before sitting down in the truck bed to rest. "I hope the eagles find him before the buzzards, even though he don't deserve it. Now tell us about Don. I can't wait any longer."

Clay told the whole story of how he was going to drop charges when the judge returned but he wouldn't be back in time to save him. The Mona Lisa smile appeared again on both their faces. "We want to go back to our teepee before someone robs us," Jane said. "We'll ride in the back of the truck. It's not too cold."

∼ NINETEEN ∼

Clay spent most of his time constructing and setting up equipment for his still. There was wood to gather and places to build to store the corn and the finished product. Ivy was getting larger every day with a baby that she didn't want. Lucy was about the same. She had some good days, but most of the time, she didn't feel well at all.

The still, after a few adjustments, was soon working fine. Clay was producing much more than he could drink and soon the word got around. Whiskey was left in a shed close to the still. There were all sizes of fruit jars—from a pint to a gallon. Everyone knew the price and left the money in a coffee can in the corner. This project became more of a job than Clay was willing to do. The barrels had to be continuously filled with corn and water, wood had to be collected every day, and jars had to be filled. He soon decided it just wasn't worth it. He would much rather listen to the radio.

The barn was falling in and the house needed a new roof. The water was coming all the way through into the studio, ruining most of his equipment. He finally boarded up the front porch and moved up there. It was about the only part of the house that didn't leak.

Once in a while, he would see some of his cattle and hogs in the woods. They were so wild that the only way to reap anything from them was to shoot them, then it was a chore to dress and cook them.

One day in Thomasville, Clay mentioned the wild cattle and hogs roaming in the woods around his place. An old German's ears perked up and he said, "I got a bunch of young boys who could catch them, I'll bet. What'll you give us to catch your stock?" the old man asked, sticking out his hand to shake and introduce himself. "My name is Claude Milner."

Clay grasped his hand and held it asking, "How about half of whatever you can sell them for?"

"It's a deal," Claude said, still shaking his hand. "We'll begin tomorrow."

The next day, Claude and his three sons headed on horseback for the woods close to Clay's house. At the end of the first day, they caught only one poor cow that no one would buy, let alone eat. They brought the cow by the house to show Clay what their day's work had gained them. Clay laughed when he saw the old cow with her hip bones and ribs showing through the skin.

"Turn her loose," Claude yelled to his boys. He was visibly embarrassed, but being the person he was, he wasn't about to give up.

The next day before sunrise, Claude was back in the woods with three hunting dogs and two of the meanest chow dogs in the area.

The sun was barely rising when the hunting dogs flushed a bunch of hogs. Claude and his sons hurried to the spot on horseback, while leading the two chows. What they saw when they rode up to where the dogs were baying wasn't expected. There were three big boars with tusks at least six inches long. The hunting dogs were in a circle around them, but the boars had their tails together and weren't about to run. The sows and some piglets were also in the center of the circle. Claude and his sons scattered about around the perimeter, but did not know how to attack.

"Turn the chows loose and sic them," Claude ordered.

The chows were lurching at their rope, wanting some of the action. The hounds were impressed with the chows' courage and rushed in to help.

The herd of hogs broke into splinter groups, trying to get away. The chows grabbed a boar by the hock. With their teeth fully implanted, they sat down, jerking the boar each time he tried to get away.

The Milner boys soon learned to get a rope on their head and another on a hind leg. The head rope was tied to the saddle horn and the leg rope kept the boar from charging the horse. They led and dragged them to the old Paty Barn where they built a big, strong, holding pen. By the end of the day, they had two boars, three sows, and some small pigs in the pen. The next day, they brought in ten more hogs and a decent looking yearling heifer.

That night, they went to town and found a buyer who was shipping a load to the market in St. Louis. When the buyer saw the hogs, he wasn't impressed, but he did offer them two dollars a head for the grown hogs and one dollar each for the pigs. The two days netted them thirty-two dollars after they paid Clay.

"Not bad wages," Claude said as he handed Clay his thirty-two dollars.

"When are you going to get some more?" Clay asked.

"When we can sell them. I'll check when there is another shipment," Claude said as he motioned his boys to mount up. "We'll be back tomorrow for the heifer. Maybe we can butcher her and peddle the meat in town," Claude said as he rode off.

Spring had finally arrived and everyone was ready for the warmer weather. What they weren't ready for were the spring rains and the leaky roof. Miss Lucy had her bed moved to the front porch since it was boarded up and the roof there didn't have many leaks. The roof above her bedroom leaked everywhere and the floor in the kitchen and dining room was sagging badly. Sometimes at night when everything was quiet, you could hear the termites and carpenter ants gnawing away.

Ivy was large and miserable. She wished she could leave and get rid of the baby, but she kept remembering that her mother didn't get rid of her, bedsides, sometimes, she found herself wishing that her mother would go on. She didn't know what to think of Clay. All he wanted to do was sit, drink, and listen to the radio. He even bought a battery operated radio for inside the house but kept it in a lard stand most of the time to keep it dry. She liked the music sometimes, but couldn't stand the baseball games. Clay wouldn't let her use it very much, he was afraid she would run the battery down.

It was the night of April 1 when Ivy's water broke and she started to have contractions. She yelled at Clay to get Dr. Davies and to hurry.

"It's three A.M.," Clay yelled back.

Ivy picked up the pistol that laid by her bed and fired two shots toward the ceiling above where Clay was sleeping. "Unless you want breakfast in hell, you better light a shuck." She heard his feet hit the floor. She then placed the pistol back on the floor under her bed.

The contractions were coming closer and closer together. She never had such pain. Lucy yelled, "Is there anything I can do?"

This made Ivy mad. She knew that her mother couldn't even walk let alone help her. Every time she tried to push, the pain was excruciating.

It seemed like Clay would never return. She was afraid to strain and afraid to try to hold it. She finally called her mother for advice.

Lucy said, "Don't try to hold it. If it comes out, wipe its face, clean its nose and mouth, and make it cry. They'll be here soon, I'm sure."

Ivy felt and could only feel something round which really scared her. "Mother, I think it's coming butt first. I don't feel any hands or feet," she yelled.

"Feel for a crack in the round thing," Lucy said, wishing that she was in Ivy's room.

"I don't feel any," Ivy answered.

"Hang on, Ivy, I'm coming," Lucy said as she rolled out of bed, trying to break her fall with one hand and one foot on the floor. It helped some but she still landed pretty hard. Lucy, unable to stand, began to crawl like a baby, but found it too strenuous. She then lay almost flat and slithered like a snake to Ivy's bedside where she pulled herself up and sat erect on the floor where she could see what was going on. She saw the crown almost out and told Ivy. "It's coming fine. Babies' hands don't come out first like calves and pigs do. Just keep pushing every time you feel the need. I'll watch for you."

"I just want it out," Ivy said. "Who cares how fine it is."

"Listen," Ivy said, "I think I hear them coming."

Sure enough, someone pulled up out front. The next thing Ivy heard was a knock on the door. Ivy couldn't imagine who would be knocking on their door this early in the morning. She knew Clay wouldn't knock.

Ivy and her mother looked at each other and Ivy yelled, "Come on in, we're busy."

Dr. Davies came in carrying his black bag and headed for the direction from which groans were coming. At the door, he stopped when he saw someone on the floor beside the bed.

"You took your time, didn't you?" Ivy said. "That's my mother. Help her back to bed if you don't mind."

Doc, from behind Lucy, stuck both hands under her arms and stood her up. "She can't walk," Ivy yelled, afraid he would turn her loose.

The doctor didn't answer, but brought her left arm around his neck and grasped it in front. With his right arm around her waist, he helped her walk back to her room.

When he returned, he leaned over and kissed Ivy on the cheek. For a moment, all her pain was gone, but it quickly returned when the doctor said, "Now let's see what's going on."

After a quick look and a feel to make sure that the cord wasn't around the baby's neck, he placed both hands on her knees and pushed up gently as he said, "Push down hard like you need to go bad."

Ivy did and the pain was worse. "Do it again," the doctor said as he eased his fingers under the head and gently lifted up. The head was almost out. Another push and he could see the shoulders and arms. With a gentle pull, it was out.

He wiped the baby and cleaned it's mouth and face. He then held it up by the heels and gave it three spanks on the buttocks before it gave a big gasp for air and began crying. He then tied two strings around the umbilical cord and with scissors, clopped between them.

"Well, you have a healthy baby boy," he said as he lay it on Ivy's breast.

"What do you mean what 'you' have?" Ivy said. "He's yours you know."

"I wish things were different," the doc said. "I told you I'd help take care of him and I will."

"Bullshit," Ivy said as she shoved the baby toward the doctor and turned on her side away from the doctor. The doctor began gathering up his belongings and began putting them back in his black bag. "You ain't going," Ivy said, hearing him move.

The baby was nuzzling on Ivy's back, trying to find some food. Dr. Davies picked the baby up and held it in front of him for a long time, really looking him over. Ivy, with her back turned, couldn't imagine what was going on. She turned back over so she could see. Dr. Davies lay the baby's mouth on Ivy's breast with his little finger on its mouth and quickly removed his finger, replacing it with a nipple. Dr. Davies then leaned over Ivy again and gave her a more passionate kiss on the lips and said, "Take good care of our son. I'll come to see you often."

"Clay went to Thomasville for some food but will be back soon. Have you thought of a name?" Dr. Davies asked.

"Oh, yes, I've thought of a lot of them, but none seem to fit." Hearing a noise, Ivy said, "Go see if that's Clay, and if it is, tell him to bring in some wood. We need a fire and Lucy hasn't been cared for yet."

Dr. Davies soon returned telling her that it was Clay and that he had to leave. He also said that a baby born at sunrise was a very good sign. She could expect great things of him.

"Tell Clay to bring the food in and build a fire before he takes you back to Birch Tree. Lucy needs to be cared for. Tell him to get his ass in gear. I could stand some help, too."

"I drove my own car so Clay won't need to take me back. Take good care of your son," Dr. Davies said. "He's a dandy," he added as he leaned over and gently kissed Ivy.

"Yeah, I know lots of great bastards," Ivy answered, turning her back to him again.

Ivy and her son, whom she called R.B. Amonette.

Clay came in and built a fire before he came to check on Ivy. She and the boy were fast asleep. He helped Lucy to the toilet, then to the kitchen where he had a large skillet with some fresh sausage in it. He had to get some fresh milk in town from Mr. Shirrell and when he said what was happening, Mrs. Shirrell offered to come help. Clay refused the offer for help but did accept some bread.

Using an egg turner, Clay broke the sausage into small bits. When they were brown, he added salt, pepper, and flour which he stirred for a few minutes before pouring in some milk.

The saliva had already started to flow in both his and Lucy's mouths before the gravy thickened. He laid three slices of bread on the stove next to the skillet to brown. He took three plates and placed a large piece of the toasted bread in the center and poured generous portions of sausage gravy on each. He sat one steaming plate in front of Lucy with a fork and a cup of milk. He carried another plate to Ivy and handed it to her. Clay didn't even bother to look at the baby.

"Take it to the table," she said. "I'm coming in there while Crappie is asleep."

Clay hesitantly did as she asked, and Ivy walked very gingerly along the wall to the table.

Picking up his plate from the warming closet, Clay dropped three more pieces of bread on the stove to brown. He finished eating his portion first and made some coffee while toasting more bread. "Does anyone want more?" he asked.

"I'll take a piece of toast," they both answered.

After handing them their toast, Clay tossed his toast into the gravy skillet along with another piece of untoasted bread.

"You could have saved some for lunch or dinner," Ivy said as Clay sopped the skillet clean.

When everyone finished eating Clay sneaked to Ivy's room to see his new nephew. He thought Crappie was a handsome young man and deserved a better name.

Back at the table Clay suggested they call him Robert or maybe R.B.

Ivy said, "Call him what you like. He won't be around long. I don't aim to let him tie me down. By the way what's happened to Don and his wenches?"

"I told him he could keep the money. He and his two witches decided to go to Oklahoma and live on a reservation with Jane and Jeans' kin. That's about all I know about them," Clay said as he licked his mouth to capture any more that might be stuck to his lips.

∿ TWENTY ∿

Spring finally gave way to summer and then to winter. Lucy was holding her own. The baby was growing fast. Dr. Davies was about the only one who came to see Ivy. The word about the baby got around.

Between Lucy, the baby, and her lazy-assed uncle Clay, Ivy didn't have much time for courting. Clay still listened to the ball games. The St. Louis Browns folded but there was a new team called the St. Louis Cardinals. Rusty Lewis, who used to pitch for the Browns, was no longer playing professional ball. Sometimes if the Thomasville town team had a really hard game, they would hire him to pitch and his brother Irvin to catch. They didn't lose any games with this combination, but other teams did a lot of complaining.

In the fall, when Clay wasn't listening to the ball games, he was sitting in the woods with his rifle, looking for some wild game or watching to see where the squirrels stored their hazelnuts, walnuts, or hickory nuts, so he could go get them.

The still had fallen on bad times and was no longer usable. The barn was falling in and the leaks in the house weren't getting better. The only thing improving was Crappie. He was growing fast. He wasn't just walking, but he was running everywhere. He loved Lucy and would crawl in bed with her if it was dry. Ivy never said why she called him "Crappie," but to her, it sounded appropriate.

He was only five years old when he crawled in bed with

Grandma Lucy and realized that something was wrong. She didn't feel warm and her arms were stiff when he tried to pull one around him.

He got out of bed and gently shook her and called, "Grandma, wake up." He had never seen a dead person, nor did he know what it meant to die.

He ran to his mother to tell her that Grandma wouldn't talk to him. Ivy waited for this to happen, but she hadn't prepared her son.

After a brief explanation, he seemed to understand, but when they dug the hole, put her in it, and covered her with dirt, he became hysterical, and shouted, "I won't be able to see her!"

That night, when Ivy went to bed, she couldn't find Crappie. She yelled for him and almost gave up when she decided to light a lantern and go look for him.

Outside, she heard a noise up the hill toward the cemetery. When she came close enough for the lantern to cast a light over the grave, she saw Crappie sitting on the ground with a shovel in his hand. When she moved closer, she discovered a big hole in the new grave. Ivy sat beside him, wanting to beat his behind, until she saw tears streaming down his cheeks.

"I want to tell her goodnight," he said, leaning his head on his mother.

Ivy picked up the shovel, and by the light of the lantern, refilled the hole.

"You ain't supposed to see people after they die," Ivy said, leading Crappie back to the house. After only a few steps, Crappie jerked loose and ran back to the grave. Ivy threw the shovel down and tried to catch him, but he made it to the grave first. Looking down at the grave, he said, "Good-bye, Grandma, I'm sorry you don't want to see me no more."

Back at the house, Crappie ran to Lucy's room and looked for her. He went from being hysterical to being completely withdrawn. Ivy thought he would soon get over it, but it only got worse. If Ivy insisted on his coming out of Lucy's room, he would go outside and sit where he could see her grave.

This went on for almost two years when Ivy told Dr. Davies that she couldn't stand it anymore. "I've got some kin in Leesville, Louisiana that might take him. I need rid of him and he needs to get away from here," Ivy suggested.

"I'll tell you what I'll do," Dr. Davies said. "I'll buy you and him a ticket on the train and give you money to live on while you find a place for him."

"I'll take the ticket but don't need your money as long as gold is any good. They will still cash them won't they!"

"Get your things together," Dr. Davies said. "You can go with me in the morning to catch the train for Leesville."

It didn't take long to pack. They wore almost everything they owned. Crappie only had one change of clothes and they were dirty. When Doc saw this, he said he would buy him some in Birch Tree.

The next morning, they all piled into the doctor's old Jeep among all the beer cans and empty whiskey bottles.

They left early the next morning, so they could drive through town before most people were up.

In Birch Tree, the doctor unlocked the front door to the pharmacy and sat Crappie at a stool at the fountain and made him a Coke. This was Crappie's first time away from the farm on Spring Creek. He never saw a town, let alone a train. He never tasted anything quite so good. He couldn't sit still. There were so many things to see. He wanted to be able to read. He didn't even know how old he was. Since Grandma Lucy died, no one even talked to him, let alone tried to teach him anything.

While he sat on the stool, the doc and Ivy went next door and bought him some clothes and a new pair of shoes. They then went across the street to the depot and got their tickets. They would have a layover in Springfield and again in Fort Smith. The train would leave at nine A.M. and would arrive in Leesville around eleven the next day. Dr. Davies said they would have to look around and maybe hire a taxi to take them to her relatives.

Back at the pharmacy, Dr. Davies said to Ivy, "You've got to give him a name. Crappie don't sound too good."

"Have any suggestions?" Ivy asked.

"How about Robert Buck Amonette?" the doc asked.

"Sounds good to me. Did you hear that, Crappie? Your new name will be Robert, so get used to it. That's what Clay wanted to call you when you were born."

Robert looked around, finally bringing his focus on Dr. Davies. "Thank you," he said. "Can I have your last name?" he asked.

"Amonette is good enough," his mother said. "We better get over to the depot. It's almost time."

When they heard the train coming, Robert ran over to the door to see what was making all the noise. Black smoke was billowing out of whatever was coming. When the train got closer, it applied the brakes and sounded the whistle. This was more than Robert could take. He ran back inside and buried his head in his mother's skirt.

When the train stopped and people started getting off, Robert couldn't believe his eyes but thought, "If they can ride it, I can too." He boldly took his mother's hand and boarded the train. Once they were inside, he liked it. When it lurched forward and picked up speed, Robert relaxed and really enjoyed watching out the window and constantly asked his mother, "What's that?"

Ivy never once answered any of his questions. She just kept on saying, "Shut-up, Crappie."

"My new name is Robert and I don't care if you don't like me. I'm going to find me a new grandma."

The rest of the way to Leesville, they didn't talk. Ivy acted like she had a lot on her mind but no one to talk to. She thought about making a new place for herself in Louisiana. She wished that she had brought the rest of the gold. She wondered what Clay would do when he discovered that it was gone. She wished that she had brought it all with her, then she would have no reason to go back.

On the train, Ivy noticed a young man who kept walking back and forth past her. She never made eye contact, but always looked away when she saw him coming. Curiosity finally got the best of her, so she looked up and smiled but he walked slowly on.

"Who was that?" Robert asked.

"Shut-up," was the only answer he got.

"I think he likes you," Robert replied while dodging a slap across the face.

It wasn't long before the man stopped by their seat. He tipped his hat and asked, "Where are you going, Lady?"

"I'm on my way to Leesville to deliver this young man," she said, indicating Robert.

"That's where I'm headed. Really don't want to go, but I guess I must."

Ivy scooted over and asked him if he would like to sit. Looking a little hesitant, Ivy patted the seat with her hand and said, "I have never been to Leesville and would really like to talk to someone who has."

"I've lived there all my life," was his reply. "My wife just died there and I went back to Fort Smith, Arkansas with her body to bury her with her folks. That's what she wanted. I really dread going back to that empty house."

Ivy's interest really picked up. "Do you know any Amonettes in Leesville?" she asked.

"Sure do. I guess I know most everyone in town."

"Do you know a man named Pete Amonette?"

"Sure do. Is that where you are taking the boy? They don't have any of their own."

"Does Pete have a leg off?" Ivy asked.

"Sure does. I hear he lost it in the Civil War. By the way, I'm Larry Parsons. Poor Pete and his wife never had any kids and they are too old now. I wonder if Pete lost more than his leg."

"I can assure you that he didn't," Ivy boldly spoke up. "I'm his daughter and this is his grandson. Could you show me where he lives?"

"Sure could. Does he know you are coming?" Larry asked, a little embarrassed. "I guess I could drive you over there. I left my car at the train depot."

"That would be great," Ivy said, scooting over closer and seeing his face flush again.

"You don't know where I could stay tonight?" Ivy asked.

His face really turned bright red and he didn't answer.

"You don't have a room, do you?" Ivy asked.

Larry began to try to say something but was staring at the boy.

Ivy noticed this and said, "Crappie, take a walk. Get!"

Robert got up and sauntered down the aisle, wondering what was going on. This was the first time he heard this and didn't dare to ask about his grandpa.

"How long was your wife sick?" Ivy asked, deciding that this man may be the one for her. She really began to look him over. He was tall and thin but had muscles. His hair was black and was not turning or receding. She scooted over closer, laying her hand on his leg, just above his knee.

"How old are you?" she asked. "Let me see," she said, leaning over and out to get a better look. "I'd judge you to be about twenty-eight," she offered.

"I'm thirty-two," he answered, not knowing what to do or say. He felt like jumping up and running, but another part of him wanted to stay.

Ivy removed her hand from his leg and gripped the muscle in the upper arm, pulling him toward her. Larry responded by leaning toward her.

"My name is Ivy. Ivy Amonette," she whispered. "I'm not saying where the name Ivy came from."

Robert returned and took a seat across from them. He really wanted to ask some questions, but from the way his mother looked at him and from where she had her foot, he decided that he better remain quiet or take another walk.

Looking back at Larry, Ivy asked, "How much further is it to Leesville?"

"Only a few miles. We should be there in less than an hour."

"Good," Ivy said. "I'll leave Robert before dark with his grandpa."

"How long are you staying?" Larry asked.

Looking up at Larry, she smiled and tried to flutter what little eyelashes she had and answered, "It depends."

At the depot, their luggage was soon in Larry's car. Ivy sat very close to Larry in the front seat and Robert sat in the back.

"Nice car," Ivy said, rubbing the seat where she should be sitting.

Pete Amonette's home was a few blocks away. It was after closing time at his gas station and Larry felt sure that he would be at home. Larry pulled to a stop on the street in front of the house. Ivy jumped out on her side and opened the back door. "Come on, Crappie, this is your new home."

Larry started to follow with Ivy's luggage when she suddenly turned to him and said, "Just stay with it in the car. I won't be long."

Still, with mixed emotions, Larry turned and walked back to the car. Ivy walked down the boardwalk to the front door and rapped hard. The house was made of red bricks and had a long front porch and big windows. It was above the average that she had seen in Leesville, and was in good repair. The lawn had many flowers and was well manicured.

A beautiful, smiling, middle-aged woman opened the door and asked, "May I help you?"

"Is Pete here?" Ivy asked.

"He just returned from work. He's in the bathroom cleaning up right now."

"I'm his daughter and this is his grandson," Ivy said, pulling Crappie from behind her to the front.

The lady who opened the door finally said, "I'm Opal," after she got her mouth to close. She just stood there, not knowing what to say.

Pete, yelling from the back of the house asked, "Who is it, Dear?"

"You better come and see," she answered.

"Just a minute. I'm almost ready," Pete answered.

Opal asked them to come in and have a seat. They sat on one side of the room and Opal sat on the opposite; neither said a word.

Pete didn't bother to put his leg on and used his crutches to come to the living room. He stopped ten feet from Ivy and Robert. With a blank expression, he asked, "Am I supposed to know you?"

"You have never seen us but you knew my mother well."

Pete's expression didn't change.

"My mother's name was Lucy Paty. You knew her at the hospital in Thomasville. This is your grandson, Robert Amonette."

Pete stood for some time, leaning on his crutches. Finally, a big smile appeared on his face and he said, "Come, give me a big hug. I've often wanted to know what happened to Lucy and the baby." Turning to Robert, he stuck out his hand and balanced on the crutch. Boy, am I glad to see you. We didn't have any kids, but we always wanted them."

Turning to look at Opal, he said, "Our prayers have been answered. We won't have to grow old alone. The tears were running down both Opal's and Pete's cheeks as they all were invited to the dining room where Opal set the table for the evening meal.

Ivy told about Buck and Clay before saying that Lucy had been in poor health before she died. Ivy also said that she was looking for a place for Robert.

Peter shouted, "Thank You again, God. He must stay here. I have a filling station that I really need some help with." He got up and walked around the table where he leaned over Robert and kissed him on top of his head. "I'll make a grease monkey out of you. We'll get along fine. Now let's eat."

"We'll have to stretch the pots," Opal said. "I wasn't expecting company. Who was that who brought you?"

"Larry...Larry, I can't remember his last name. We met him on the train. His wife died."

"Oh, we know Larry," Opal said. "Ask him to come in while I get another plate. We can stretch the pots once more."

After they finished eating, Larry tried to excuse himself but Ivy told him, "Just hold on a minute. I'm not quite ready."

Ivy told Pete that she would be around for a while and that

she would try to see him again soon. Turning to Opal, she said, "Thanks for stretching your pot. Come on, Larry," she said, offering him her hand.

Ivy didn't expect this kind of reception but really had no feelings for her father. She was only thinking of herself.

Larry, shaking his head, went out holding her hand. It wasn't far to Larry's house. Ivy sat close with her left hand on his shoulder and her right checking out the radio.

The house was a modest house near the downtown area. The next morning, Ivy woke up completely satisfied and already decided that she was definitely going after this man. At least this was her plan until Larry announced that he would have to go to work and pick up his kids at his sister's place. Ivy almost fell out of her seat when he mentioned kids. Her disappointed expression was obvious to Larry. Ivy finally asked, "How many do you have?"

"Two," Larry answered. "A girl, eight years old and a boy, five. I've got to find a closer baby-sitter. It's too far to drive to my sister's house every day."

"Well, I'm not going to be your baby-sitter. Why don't you see if your sister won't keep them for a while?" Ivy asked.

"She has two of her own, but I'll see. I don't know what she and her neighbors are going to say when they see you here. It hasn't been two weeks since my wife died."

"Who cares?" Ivy answered. "Tell them I'm your cousin here to help."

"They know all my cousins," Larry said as he began getting ready to go to work. As he went out the door, he turned to Ivy who was still sitting at the breakfast table with her head propped up with her hands, obviously in deep thought. "The train depot is only four blocks to your right if you need to get a ticket," Larry stated.

Ivy didn't even look up, but gestured him to go on. Ivy sat there for a long time, trying to decide what to do. Everything imaginable was going through her mind. Her biggest problem that she saw was the kids. She thought of every conceivable option, even murder. She wanted Larry but couldn't stand the idea of being tied down with kids. Everything else was what she dreamed of. A good husband, a roof that didn't leak, nice furnishings, and money to use as she pleased. She just wished she had brought the rest of the gold with her. It was almost noon when she decided to be domestic. She cleaned, rearranged, and prepared a good meal for Larry. She even found candles and selected one of Larry's dead wife's best dresses to wear. Her shoes were too tight, but Ivy soaked them in hot water and finally got them on.

When Larry came home from work, he hoped Ivy would be gone. He opened the front door, and much to his disappointment, Ivy was there waiting for him. She reached for a kiss which Larry gave unenthused. It wasn't until Ivy started to the table that he recognized the dress and shoes.

Ivy noticed his reddening eyes and thought the tears were from happiness. She picked up a napkin from the table and wiped his eyes and said, "Go clean up while I put dinner on the table."

Larry didn't want anything to eat; he didn't want to clean up. All he wanted was to be rid of this woman. Instead of going to the bathroom, he went to the bedroom and stretched out across the bed and tried to get his thoughts together. He thought, "How can I get rid of this woman?"

Ivy finished setting the table and went to look for Larry. When she opened the bedroom door and saw Larry, she said, "Come on, let's eat."

Larry didn't move. Ivy walked to the bed where she found Larry still in his work clothes. She stooped to untie and remove his shoes. Climbing on his bed, she unbuckled his overalls, then got off to where his feet were extended from the bed and grasped the pant legs and gave a hard tug, then another, until they came off.

Larry slowly got up and walked to the lavatory, barefooted and only dressed in underwear and a shirt, where he half-heartedly washed his hands and face before going to the table.

At the table, he still wasn't impressed, even though Ivy worked hard to try to please him.

After dinner was finished and everything was cleared away, Ivy was ready to go to bed but Larry wasn't very enthused. He wanted to see his children. He went to his room and came out with clean clothes on.

Ivy hurried to finish the dishes and thought Larry would be waiting for her in bed. When she saw him come out fully dressed, her feathers drooped.

With both hands on her hips, she asked, "Where do you think you are going?"

"I'm going to get the kids," he answered.

"Just a minute, I'm going with you," Ivy said as she draped the dish towel over the back of a chair.

"I don't think you should go," Larry said. "It's too soon."

"I'm going," Ivy answered walking hurriedly toward him. Larry quickly sat on the couch with his head in his hands while Ivy opened the door and yelled, "Come on."

Larry peeped from his hands toward Ivy and finally said, "I can't go with you in that outfit."

Ivy kicked off the shoes and muttered, "Them things are killing my feet anyway." She went to the bedroom where she put on her own clothes.

Larry still had to be encouraged when Ivy returned. She took him by the hand, pulled him from the couch, and almost dragged him toward the door.

It was a thirty mile drive to his sister's. Not a word was spoken the entire distance. Larry couldn't think of any explanation to offer his sister.

The children were still outside when they drove up in front of the house. Both children came running to greet their father but didn't even seem to notice Ivy. They took their father by the hand after hugs and kisses and led him to the house. At the house, Larry's sister met him at the door with a big smile that quickly vanished when she saw Ivy.

Ivy stepped forward with a outstretched hand and said, "My name is Ivy. I've been looking forward to meeting you. I'm helping Larry during his time of grief."

Larry's sister didn't offer a name but reluctantly did ask

Ivy to come in. "Have a seat while the children collect their things," she said. She then turned to Larry and asked him if he would come to the kitchen for a moment.

While they were in the kitchen the children returned to the living room with their belongings and sat glaring at Ivy.

Larry soon returned to the living room, obviously red-faced and upset.

"Come on, lets go," Larry announced in a loud voice while he walked toward the front door.

The children jumped up and ran to the car. They tossed the luggage into the back seat and climbed into the front beside their father. Ivy, seeing this, showed anger but opened the back door and got in. All the way home, not a word was said. The tension was thick enough to slice with a knife.

When they drove up in front of the house, the children grabbed their luggage and ran to their father's bedroom where they quickly got into their night clothes and crawled into Larry's bed. Larry came in, undressed, and crawled between them, holding one in each arm.

Ivy stood at the door in her night clothes, waiting to be invited in but no invitation came. After a few minutes, the boy raised up and said, "You ain't our mother."

Ivy turned and walked to another bedroom where she lay on the bed, plotting her strategy. She could manage Larry but how was she going to manage the kids? She finally went to sleep deciding what her attack would be.

The next morning, Larry got up and went to work, leaving Ivy and the children in bed. Ivy finally got up and went to the kitchen where she set the table before going for the kids. At the door, she announced, "Time to get up, kids."

Again, she heard from beneath the cover, "You ain't our mother."

Ivy walked over to the bed and yanked the covers off and said, "Get your asses out of bed, now!"

Both of the children were shocked and shied to the opposite side of the bed, very scared. "Breakfast will be ready in five minutes," Ivy announced as she stomped out of the room.

As soon as Ivy was out, both of the kids hurriedly got dressed and came to the table where Ivy prepared scrambled eggs, bacon, butter, and jelly.

The girl said, "I don't eat this. I want cereal and a banana."

Ivy walked around the table and stood beside her smiling. "Just smell how good it smells," Ivy said as she gently placed her hand on back of the girl's head and eased it forward. Once her face was over the plate, Ivy shoved it down hard and held it there until she began gasping for breath. When Ivy released her, she looked at the boy and asked sweetly, "Would you like some cereal?"

Ivy didn't even know their names and only called them "boy" and "girl." She repeated sternly, "Boy, I said, would you like some cereal?"

He answered by picking up his fork and quickly eating his food. The girl, between sobs, began eating.

Ivy turned to leave after she told them to clear the table and wash the dishes when they were finished. "Also, make your bed and unpack your luggage in your rooms."

They looked at each other, afraid to say anything. After they finished their assigned chores, they slipped out the back door and hid in a corner, hoping Ivy wouldn't find them, but it wasn't long until Ivy came around the corner, obviously mad.

"I hope you don't think you are finished for the day. You can help with the laundry, Boy." She grabbed him by the ear and freed him from the corner. She reached and grabbed the girl by the hair and said, "You can scrub the front porch and sweep the house." She held onto them and led them back into the house.

The children thought that their dad would never return from work. Before he returned, Ivy told them to go clean up while she prepared the evening meal. "When you are finished, go sit in the living room."

They were both tired, and had gone since breakfast with nothing to eat or drink. As soon as Ivy saw them sitting, she marched in and asked them to stand up. She looked at their ears and their hands. After looking at them, she said, "Now go to the table, and if you complain to your dad, just remember, I'll be here tomorrow. Also, you'll sleep in your own room tonight."

When Larry walked in, both kids ran to hug him, but were afraid to say anything. Ivy walked over with cooking utensils in her hands and stuck her cheek up to him which he reluctantly gave a small peck. Looking around, Larry liked what he saw. There were clean kids, a clean house, and dinner on the table. He began to wonder if Ivy would be all right.

The next day, after Larry left for work, Ivy began her rampage all over again. Each day was progressively getting worse. Ivy now slapped and kicked them for no apparent reason. She hoped that they would leave and that she would have Larry all to herself.

What happened wasn't expected by Ivy. They did run off, but they went to Larry's sister where they told the whole story, and showed the bruises they had and told how they got them. Larry's sister went directly to the police where they repeated what was happening.

The police went to Larry's house to see who was staying with him. Ivy didn't like what the police had to say. The officer said he would return after Larry got home from work.

As soon as the police pulled away, Ivy quickly grabbed her belongings, along with the gold, and headed for the train depot as fast as she could walk. At the depot, she looked out for the police. There was a train sitting on the track, almost ready to leave for Fort Smith and then to Springfield, where she could make connection to go on to Birch Tree.

She really wanted to go see her dad again, but didn't want to take the time or to chance it. She doubted that she would ever see Crappie or her dad again, but she really didn't care.

All the way to Birch Tree, she was scared that the police were following her. She couldn't wait to get to the safety of home and Spring Creek. When she arrived at Birch Tree, she hurried over to the pharmacy where she tried to look as pleasant as possible. She went in and parked herself at a stool at the fountain and waited for the doctor and a spiked Coke.

Dr. Davies was in the back of the store giving an old lady a shot in the hip. Ivy watched as the doctor selected a syringe from a glass enclosed case and proceeded to draw some fluid from a bottle. He then said, "Bend over, Aggie, and drop your panties." The doc lifted her dress and emptied the syringe trough the sharpest of his dull needles. He wiped the needle on his pant legs and returned it to the glass case. Aggie pulled up her underwear and the doctor lowered her dress and looked up to see Ivy seated at the fountain. He wiped his hands on his pants and walked behind the counter to the fountain where Ivy was sitting.

The first thing Ivy said to the doc was, "I got rid of him. When can you take me home?"

"I'll be ready to go in about an hour," Dr. Davies answered. "Put your things in my Jeep and look at the tires. I had a flat the other day."

Ivy finished the drink Doc fixed for her and went out the front door and around to the back to where Dr. Davies parked his Jeep. Ivy was only in the Jeep for a short time when Doc came around the building.

On the way to Spring Creek, Ivy asked him again if he would marry her. Dr. Davies again told her that he would have to think about it some more.

Ivy forgot how run down her home was. The west side of the house was practically falling away. The roof leaked everywhere. The front porch was boarded up and the yard fence fell down. The house was covered with vines and bushes. Green moss was growing everywhere. No doubt there were probably snakes, too. Copperheads love old, decaying buildings.

When Ivy saw this, she said, "Let's drive over to Paty Pond. I'm sure it couldn't be this bad. I wonder where Clay is," she said, looking around for his truck.

Dr. Davies didn't object to driving on. The thought of snakes scared him.

When they arrived at the pond, it was grown up also, but at least the bunkhouse wasn't falling down. They parked the Jeep close and followed the path to the bunkhouse. Inside, they found that it had been used recently. The beds looked clean and there was food in the shelves. It looked a lot better than Ivy's house.

Ivy and the doctor spent two days in and around the bunkhouse. They made love, ate, and walked through the woods, often just sitting and listening to the sounds of insects and animals.

When it was time to go, Doc dropped Ivy off at Spring Creek. He noticed that Clay was there but never got out of the Jeep to talk to him. He thought that Clay was one of the laziest, smart men that he had ever seen. Dr. Davies didn't tell Ivy, but he already decided that their relationship had to stop. He could see that it was going nowhere. He didn't even tell her good-bye when he drove away. He did wish that he had gotten his son's address, but on the other hand, he was glad to break all ties.

Clay walked over to where Ivy was sitting on a rock. He dreaded going into the house. "What happened to the gold?" Clay asked in an accusing manner.

"I took it and spent it," she lied.

She had emptied the original box but she had hidden two fruit jars full and still had a good amount in the leather purse she was carrying.

"I was going to use that to repair the house," Clay yelled.

"You used your money," Ivy stated. "The gold was mine, and if you don't like it, do something about it," she said as she got up and went inside. Once she was inside, she looked around and couldn't believe how fast the house had deteriorated. The floors were falling in. The once beautiful carpet was rotten and all the furniture was falling apart. It was too dangerous to go into the kitchen and dining area. The beautiful, old cookstove was rusted out, all except the nickel, chrome, and enamel. The only good thing about the house was that it was free of mice and rats. The cats were crossed with bobcats which made them very quick and strong. A mouse or rat didn't have a chance. Clay had one cat he called Max on a leash tied near his bed when he wasn't hunting with him. He would hunt diligently but would only return to Clay what he hadn't eaten. Rabbits didn't stand a chance. Some squirrels and quail escaped if they saw Max in time. After catching and eating two rabbits, Max wasn't interested in hunting anymore. Clay finally gave up on making Max a hunting cat, since he ate almost everything he caught.

Clay still had wild cattle and hogs running on the open range but it was too much effort to help with the roundup and he had no one to bring them home to. Once in a great while, he could get the Milners to catch some livestock for him. The bank account was almost gone now, and Ivy told him that the gold was gone too. His still was beyond repair and the old pickup needed tires. Between batteries for this radio, liquor, and a few groceries, Clay's money to spend wasn't much. He really needed to see a doctor. He was coughing more and more. It seemed that each morning it took longer to clear out his pipes. There were still many deer and turkey in the woods but it was a lot of trouble to care for them and to cook them after they were shot. Sometimes they would run down into a deep ravine where he would never attempt to retrieve them. His shoes were practically worn out as well as his winter coat.

Clay often wondered if life was worth the effort. He thought many times about sticking his gun to his head.

The summer gave way to winter and there was no place in the house to keep warm. All the covers in the house were piled on the beds but each time they had to get up, they were cold. Clay's cough was getting much worse. He had just about given up. In fact, he started to dig his grave. He had only enough breath to dig a little each day. He dug next to Bucks' grave. He used old boards to hold the dirt uphill from the grave so Ivy wouldn't see it and kick the dirt back in. It took him almost three weeks. All this was unknown to Ivy. He didn't want to leave her alone, but he wanted to make things as easy as possible.

It was early one sunny fall morning when Ivy was awakened by a gunshot close to the house. She rolled out of bed, picked up her pistol and went out the door. She looked around but saw nothing. Back in the house, Ivy went to Clay's room and pulled away the pile of covers but didn't find him. This really bothered her. She pulled on her shoes and a heavy coat. Walking toward Buck and Lucy's grave, she saw the mound of dirt uphill from Buck and couldn't imagine what was going on. Before she reached the pile of dirt she could see the hole at the base. She also saw Clay's rifle and a forked stick laying near it. When she reached the opening, she saw Clay's body crumpled at the bottom of the open hole. Ivy sat for a few moments at the edge of the grave with her head down but no tears would come. She hopped down into the grave, turned Clay over on his back, and straightened him out to face the morning sun.

When she tried to get out of the grave, she found it very difficult. She stepped on Clay's shoulder and grabbed one of the boards that was holding back the pile of dirt. The board gave away and dirt poured in knocking her backwards against the opposite side of the grave. With the dirt still sifting, she began climbing up until she was able to pull herself out. As soon as she recovered from her fright of being buried alive, she stood and walked around the grave and kicked more boards out, allowing more dirt to slide into the grave. After she kicked all the boards out and the dirt stopped sliding in, Ivy went to the house where she found a long-handled shovel she could use to finish filling the grave.

After Ivy finished filling the grave, she piled rocks on top. She then decided to walk up the hill to where they left Don's substitute for the birds. She, nor anyone else had been there since they left him on the scaffold. When she reached the spot, she discovered the scaffold still in place and sturdy, but not a bone was to be seen anywhere.

Ivy sat on a big clump of moss on the sunny side of a large, white pine tree. Her mind was running rampant. She was the only one left. All her relatives, except Crappie, were dead. She was getting old and she didn't have any friends anymore. The house was falling in and she was always cold in the winter. Even the southeast corner of the house where she slept started to leak and she was sure there would be more snakes in the house in the spring.

She would often build a fire outside using pitch pine. It burned easily and made the fire get hot. She placed large sandstone in the fire. She would use her long-handled shovel to place the rocks into a cream can which she would drag into the house and place in the middle of the rags where she slept. She would then get into a fetal position around the can which knocked off the chill for a long time.

Her eyesight really began to fail, so she carried her pistol either in her pocket or in her hand. At the slightest sound, she would point the gun and say, "Identify yourself unless you want a breakfast in hell."

One day, she heard a horse coming through the woods which always excited her. She loved company, but without hearing their voice, she couldn't recognize them.

This time she yelled, "Who are you?"

The horse pulled up close to where she stood, wearing Buck's old ground length Civil War army coat and her homemade shoes. She used tire tubes to make her shoes and had perfected the creation. She cut a long tongue which she pulled back over the top of her foot, then pulled flaps from each side up over it and wired them together with baling wire. The back was shaped similarly. These kept her feet dry, and with some of Buck and Clay's old socks, she stayed pretty warm.

The man on horseback said, "I have bought the place below you on Spring Creek. My name is Frank Rose. Looks like you need some help," Frank offered.

"Sure could use a man," Ivy answered. "The roof over my bed is leaking bad."

"Mind if I have a look?" Frank asked.

"Get down and come on in," Ivy said, Heading for what was no longer a door. The door had fallen off the hinges and was being used to walk on during wet weather.

Frank couldn't believe what he saw. Everything was in the last stage of deterioration. The only place to step on were the cross-timbers under the floor. The floor couldn't be walked on for fear of falling through.

Frank backed out the door and took a closer look at Ivy. She pulled her sock cap above her eyes, exposing part of her head which looked like her hair had been singed off.

"What happened to your hair, Lady?" Frank asked.

"I'll tell you," Ivy said, leaning back against part of the outside wall that looked barely strong enough to hold her. "I was walking through the house the other night with an old coal oil lamp when my foot went through the floor. I threw that lamp and broke it. The fire was all over me and everything else. I looked up and said, 'Lord, I have always believed in you but never needed you, now I need your help.' He must have heard me, for the fire went out immediately. Just like that," she said, snapping her finger and thumb.

Frank remembered seeing the broken lamp and some blackened things inside. "I'll be back tomorrow with some roofing and something to go on your floor," Frank said as he walked back to his horse.

"I'll pay you if you will take gold," Ivy said as he mounted up and rode away. He either didn't hear her or didn't believe what he heard.

That night, Ivy couldn't sleep, because she was thinking about her new neighbor. There were many things that she wanted to ask him but didn't think about at that moment. She didn't even tell him what her name was. If she had anything decent to put on, she would go to the spring in the morning and wash up, even if she had to break ice.

Sure enough, early the next morning, Frank was back with a team and wagon load of supplies. He had black tar paper for roofing and lots of wide boards to patch the floor. He had a hammer, saw, and nails all ready to go to work. In practically no time, he rolled out the roofing, lapping it over extra, and nailed it on top of the old, leaky roof. He carried in wide boards and nailed them to the old cross beams on top of the old floor. He made a path with new boards all the way through the library and into the slanted kitchen floor. He leveled and made a twenty-four inch wide path and even propped up the old, rusty kitchen stove to an almost level position. He realized that everything was very temporary, but it was an improvement over what she had. On the way out, he lifted the outside door from the mud and put it back on its hinges and nailed it in place.

Ivy explained how she heated rocks and put them into a can to warm her bed. Frank couldn't believe how anyone could live under such primitive conditions. "What do you eat?" Frank asked, looking around.

"Oh, that big can over there," she said, pointing to Clay's old lard stand that he used to keep his radio in. "It's full of walnuts and the one beside that one is full of hazelnuts and there is watercress in Spring Creek. Sometimes I find some snails." Ivy grinned as she said, "I don't get fat."

"Is there anything else I can do?" Frank asked as he carried his tools back to the wagon.

Ivy went to her hiding place and extracted a twenty-dollar gold piece which she handed to him. Frank looked shocked as he took it and bit it, making sure his eyes weren't failing him.

"Lady, you don't owe me this much," he said. "By the way, what is your name?"

"I'm Ivy Amonette. I'm the last of the family."

"Ivy, I'm going to Thomasville tomorrow. Would you like to come and get some groceries?"

"I'd like to go, but I guess I better stay here and guard the place," she said, pulling a pistol from her pocket and waving it around.

"I'll get you some groceries," Frank said. "And how would you like to have a dog? I have too many and need to get rid of some."

"Oh, that would be wonderful," Ivy answered. "How much money do you need for the dog and the groceries?"

"You gave me plenty. Do you have many of those?" he asked, holding up the twenty-dollar piece.

"All I need," Ivy answered.

Frank left but returned the next day with gobs of groceries.

He got practically everything the store had that was canned. He even brought some cheese, crackers, and hard bread. He brought some puffed rice cereal, and some canned milk, sugar and salt.

Ivy saw all of this but was more impressed with the cute little dog that was rubbing on her legs. Ivy sat down and the dog quickly jumped into her lap and began licking her in the face. "I think I'll call you Feisty Britches," she said as he jumped off her lap and took off after a little ground squirrel that was playing among the old logs and rocks just outside where the old fence used to be.

Ivy and her new dog, Feisty Britches.

Frank handed Ivy a can opener which he showed her how to use by opening a can of peaches. Ivy looked in amazement and smiled from ear to ear, exposing her toothless mouth as she ate a piece of peach. It had been a long time since she had tasted anything so good. She pulled out another slice and called Feisty Britches, holding it out to him. He quickly forgot the ground squirrel and came immediately to her and took the peach and licked her fingers before going back to look for the squirrel.

Frank looked at Ivy and said, "There were people at the store who asked about you and your family. They didn't know Clay was dead and that you are the only one left. Some of them were telling about the parties and dances that they used to come to down here. Some of the older ones were really curious about you." There must have been a newspaper reporter there, judging from all the questions he was asking her.

For the rest of the winter, Frank made it a point to ride over to see about Ivy. When he had extra food, he would bring Ivy over a plateful. At both Thanksgiving and Christmas, Frank brought enough food for several meals. Ivy never looked at it, but would say, "Set it somewhere. I'm not hungry now. Feisty Britches and I will eat it later." She was more interested in having someone to talk to.

Every time Frank would start to leave, Ivy would think of another question. She would even trot along side of the wagon until she got tired, still trying to talk to him.

When she discovered that he was building a new fireplace, she insisted on showing him some beautiful sandstone that would split like cordwood.

Frank was skeptical but found what she was saying to be true. It was only a short distance down the river to his farm, but it was too rough and muddy to bring his truck. He finally found a way to go toward Thomasville and circle back. He could haul many more stones on the truck. Every time Ivy heard him working, she hurried there to have someone to talk to. Feisty Britches was always with her and always stayed between her and her company. He was truly her companion and protector.

Frank brought a picture of a 1912 Ford that was the first car he ever saw in Thomasville. Andrew Jackson Williams owned it and these were his children.

∽ TWENTY-ONE ∽

*I*t was the middle of June when Ivy heard what sounded like thunder coming down the road from the woods. Cars pulled up in front of her dilapidated old house, almost scaring Ivy and Feisty Britches to death. She pulled her pistol from her pocket, but didn't know where to point it.

People piled out of the cars and swarmed the place like chickens over a newly discovered pile of cow manure.

The West Plains Daily Quill decided to give her front page coverage with many large pictures. She continued to wave the pistol, which made reporters a little nervous, but didn't stop them from making their way through the house, snapping pictures.

When she was asked to put the gun away, she stated, "Besides my dog, Feisty Britches, this is my best friend." The safety on her .32 caliber pistol was off and her finger was on the trigger as she continued to wave the pistol.

One of the men identified himself as the son of the man she had traded a cow to for the pistol. He asked Ivy is he could see and Ivy responded by handing him the gun.

The article on the front page of the West Plains Daily Quill began, "In a small valley, deep in the Mark Twain National Forest, is a pistol-packing, 80 year old Oregon County woman who today lives closer to nature and the bitter elements of winter than pioneer women a century and a half ago.

"She is Ivy Amonette, who has never seen TV, has never

One of Ivy's visitors that was allowed to handle her pistol. She told this man that she had traded his father a cow for this pistol many years ago.

had electricity, and has not traveled the six miles to Thomasville in the last eight years."

They called her "Thomasville Nature Woman." and said, "She and Feisty Britches live in a forest home."

They asked her what she ate. Ivy replied that she had about lost all interest and desire for food. She stated that she just ate when she felt like it, and just whatever she had at hand.

From that day on, for the rest of her life, things changed dramatically. From the first day the article appeared, there was a constant stream of traffic on the road to Spring Creek and Ivy Amonette's. They were like a bunch of vultures descending on a fresh carcass. Some came to see, but most came to pilfer. Everything inside and outside of the house disappeared. All the silverware, old glass vases, and her furniture that was barely holding together disappeared.

The stories she was told, could only have been dreamed of by a con artist. A lot of her things went to needy churches, or so she was told. No one brought anything to barter; they just came with their woeful stories and took everything in sight. They even took boards from the house for something to remember her by.

When they first started coming, Ivy enjoyed them, but it soon became evident why there were there. She would invite them to come in and sit with her in her parlor, which was then rocks on the ground. No one had time to talk, they just wanted to look around and see what they could carry away. The stream of traffic continued for months until there was nothing left.

Ivy finally just turned it over to the vultures. Each morning, she would walk behind the house to the woodchuck rock where she would sit and reminisce. She often thought of her male visitors and wondered why they never came to see her anymore. She had fond memories of the old Paty Pond roundups and of how much attention was paid to her. She thought of the hospital and the gray ladies her mother told about. She had long ago forgotten about Pete Amonette. She still dreamed that some day Dr. Davies would come and take her away from all her miseries there on Spring Creek. She seldom thought about Larry, but did wonder about Crappie. Days when the sun was bright and she felt well, she and Feisty Britches would sit there for hours.

One day, while sitting there, a wild boar came rooting through the woods, looking for acorns. Feisty Britches couldn't keep his mouth shut, and ran after him. Ivy was glad that she had the dog to distract the boar while she made her way back down the hill. She was afraid to shoot at him because this might make him charge her. She was also afraid that she might hit Feisty Britches, the way he bounced around and because she couldn't see very well.

Summer passed and fall already arrived. The valleys were white with frost each morning. Frank was still coming over to check on her fairly often. He often brought scrap and drift wood that he picked up along the road between their farms. Ivy told him about the big boar she saw, how long his tusks were, and how Feisty Britches kept him away from her. She also saw some wild hogs that she was sure were descendants

The big boar hog that Ivy called Rocket.

of the big boar she called Rocket and two of her cows she called Red Wing and Snow Fawn.

The original stock came from Westshire England and were called saddle backs. They were very popular when lard was used for all kinds of cooking. This was long before all the cooking oils of today that are made from nuts and seeds.

This hog weighed well over one thousand pounds. Before he went wild Ivy would ride on his back and let him carry her home when she would find him in the woods. She then became afraid to go near him. He had grown long tusks and gnashed his teeth releasing a lot of slobbers, both looking and sounding dangerous. He was so big and fat he could hardly move, let alone run.

Frank told her that he had seen several wild hogs along the river and even some unbranded, wild cattle.

"Wonder if any of the Milner boys are still around," Ivy asked. "They know how to catch them. When you go to town, ask around and tell that anyone is welcome to come catch them on halves. Now, you shoot one any time you need meat," Ivy stated.

"I sure would like to have a mess of fresh pork and some watercress," Ivy added. "Frisky Britches would, too."

After Frank announced about the wild hogs and cattle at the general store, all the young men decided to have a big hunt. They all decided on a day and rode up to Spring Creek, carrying ropes and were followed by their best dogs. The older Milners told them how to catch the hogs. It sounded like fun to them and was a good way to make a little extra money. They contacted a pig buyer to bring his low trailer in the late afternoon to haul their catches.

Ivy heard them outside and Feisty Britches clawed and barked at the door, wanting to get outside to sniff and greet all the new dogs. As soon as Ivy opened the door, Feisty Britches hurried out and began to mark his territory. He completely circled the house, wetting on every bush that he could. The visiting dogs completely ignored him as he made his rounds greeting each of them at both ends.

One of the young men went to Ivy's door to inform her of what was going on. She opened her door with her pistol in her hand and her finger on the trigger. Before he could explain, Ivy said, "Unless you want your next meal in hell, you had better speak up."

Shaking in his boots, the young man said with a quivering voice, "I, I'm one of the Milner boys who's going to hunt your stock today."

Ivy removed her finger from the trigger and returned the pistol to her pocket. "Well, good luck and be careful, them boars are mean. If it hadn't been for Feisty Britches, I probably wouldn't be here today. Take him with you if you want. He's smart."

"Thank you," the young man said as he went back to where the rest were waiting.

Ivy stumbled out of the house, lifted her dress, spread her legs, and relieved herself. She had long ago grown too weak to squat. When she had finished, she dropped her dress and waved good-bye to the would-be cowboys. She called Feisty Britches, but he didn't come. She was sure that he would like to go on the hunt.

Feebly, Ivy made her way down to Spring Creek to sit on

Ivy and one of her friends. There were several who stopped by to check on her in her latter days; however, no one offered to take her home with them, even though she would plead, "Don't let me die here." This man brought the trailer and was to buy the wild livestock that the Milner boys caught.

the big rock that had been warmed some by the morning sun. She could reach the water from the rock, which she used to splash on her face and hands. Sometimes she even brought a rag to wash her privates with. Bathing wasn't too important to her anymore and it seldom happened, even in the summer, when water was warmer.

It was mid-afternoon when the trailer pulled in, rattling worse than a train. There were two men in the truck that was pulling it. They got out and came over to where Ivy was sitting. Both introduced themselves, not knowing if Ivy would remember them. She did remember them from when they would buy cattle that had been rounded up each fall. They sat and talked for a long time, telling many stories. Ivy couldn't remember how well she had known them and didn't ask.

The man named Dude France asked if they could have their picture taken with her. "You ain't going to send a bunch of people over?" Ivy asked. "The last time I had my picture taken, lots of people came, wanting to see me. I don't want anymore of that," Ivy said.

"No one will see these pictures," Dude answered. "Bucky and I just want them to remember you by."

"I suppose that would be O.K.," Ivy said, feebly getting to her feet and pushing her cap above her eyes. She even lowered her chin away from her nose to show her mouth. The old army coat collar was turned up all around her neck to help hide her bald head, which she kept that way to avoid lice. She said, "The only good thing about winter is that it kills almost all the crawly things like ticks, chiggers, and lice. I guess I'm allergic to ticks. After a few days on me, they turn blue and fall off," she said with a soft chuckle.

Dude brought the camera and one at a time, they posed with her. "Clay used to take a lot of pictures," Ivy stated. "I didn't have my picture took for fifty years, 'til the men from the paper came. I sure hope they don't come back," she added.

Their conversation was interrupted by some yelling and barking coming from the creek. "What's coming?" Ivy asked, not able to see that far.

"Looks like they got something," Bucky said. "Boy, that's the biggest boar hog I've ever seen," he said, jumping up to run down closer for a better look.

Feisty Britches was there, running in to get a nip on his hock once in a while. They had him stretched out with one rope around his neck and another around his hind leg. Ivy hoped it was the one she saw up by the woodchuck rock. She would feel safer if he wasn't around.

Before the evening was over, they caught sixteen head of hogs and loaded them in the trailer. The Milner boys thought it was a great sport and asked if they could come back the next weekend.

"Let's get them while they are fat," Ivy answered. "By next spring, they'll be poor. All the acorns will be gone."

"We'll bring you your money next weekend," Bucky said as they pulled away with their load. He couldn't get over how big the one old boar was. "I'll bet he'll weigh over eight hundred pounds," he said to Dude.

"Maybe seven hundred fifty without all the worms and lice," Dude answered.

As soon as they were all gone, Feisty Britches came bouncing and squirming up to Ivy, acting like he was a real hero and got rid of all the ferocious animals himself.

The evening already began to turn cold, so Ivy thought she had better build up a fire to heat her rocks for the cream can. Each time she did this, she would wonder, "Will this be the last time that I will be able to do this?" Her wrists and ankles were swollen badly and every joint in her body ached when it became the least bit cold.

Three more times, the Milner boys caught hogs for her. Each time, they were harder to find, but Dude and Bucky would build a fire outside for her. They would shovel the rocks into the can and carry it into the house and to her bed.

Ivy and her last Easter Sunday

Frank still came by to check on her. She gave him all the money that she got for the hogs and he brought her the things she needed. The day he brought her a pair of fur-lined boots, some gloves, and a new sock hat, she thought that she could live forever. She was warm again when she got them on. She must have thanked him ten times. They meant more than all the food he ever brought. She had no idea that it was Christmas, and Frank didn't tell her until she asked.

"It isn't Christmas, is it?" she asked with tears forming and washing streaks down her face.

"Yes, it is, and I brought you something else," he said, reaching into his pocket and pulling out a sack of hard Christmas candy, which he handed to her.

Ivy looked at it, but couldn't tell what kind it was.

She selected a piece and stuck it into her mouth. "Peppermint," she exclaimed, "my favorite. There really is a God," she said reaching upward to say thank you.

The tears were finding it easier to make the trip down her face, now that they had cleared a path.

Frank threw some more chunks on the fire and said, "I had better go. I'll bring some more wood next time. Merry Christmas," he said. "And I hope you have a happy New Year."

"Come here before you go," Ivy said.

When Frank came closer, Ivy motioned him even closer. She reached for his neck and pulled his head over so she could kiss him on the cheek. "I'll never forget you," she said as she released him and stuck out her gnarled fist for him to take something.

Frank held out his hand, palm up, and Ivy dropped in it a twenty dollar gold piece. Frank looked shocked as he leaned over, looking for a clean place to kiss her. Finding none, he squeezed her and kissed the top of her new sock cap. He could hardly stand the thought of walking away and leaving Ivy here on Christmas Day, but she wouldn't fit in at his home.

Ivy was the happiest that she had been in several days. This day gave her the shot that she needed to go on.

The winter and Ivy both seemed to drag on. On Easter Sunday, Frank showed up with a pick-up load of wood, some bacon, eggs, bread, butter, and jelly. Frank even brought his wife, who had never seen Ivy, but suspected the worst every time Frank left for her house. She couldn't believe Frank was playing the good neighbor the way he said. She was shocked when she saw Ivy and treated Frank differently from then on.

Frank placed a piece of tin on stones and built a fire under it and invited Ivy to have a seat close by. He then placed some bacon on the tin to begin cooking. He handed Ivy a plate and a fork. He ran down to Spring Creek to fill the coffee pot, and after he added coffee, he placed it on the fire. He then broke six eggs on the tin close to the bacon so the grease would keep them from sticking. He wiped butter on the bread and placed it on the tin to toast. Ivy just sat there, enjoying the smell.

Frank's wife finally came over close enough for Ivy to notice her and said, "My name is Lilly. Frank told me about you, but I was always too busy to come with him," she lied.

Ivy peeped up from beneath her cap and said, "Glad you could come today. Will you have a seat in my parlor?" Ivy asked, gesturing toward a flat rock near the fire.

"Do you know what day this is?" Frank asked Ivy as he filled his plate with eggs, bacon, and toast with butter and some of Lilly's good blackberry jelly.

Ivy held the plate up close to her nose and smelled it before she began to eat. After a few bites, she answered, "It must be a day God sent. Who else could give me a day like this?"

Frank poured her a cup of boiled coffee and set it on a rock close to her. "It's Easter Sunday," he said as he filled Lilly's plate and coffee cup.

"I know," Ivy said. "It had to be one of God's special days. He sure is good to me," Ivy declared.

⌁ TWENTY-TWO ⌁

*I*t was the fourteenth of August when Frank found Ivy passed out on the ground under the big oak tree beside her house. He shook her, thinking that she was asleep, but got no response. Feisty Britches was lying beside her, and he had licked her face almost clean.

Frank found an empty can which he filled with the cool water in Spring Creek. He soaked his handkerchief and bathed her face. She slightly opened her eyes but was too weak to say anything. He propped her up to a sitting position and tried to give her a drink but she made no effort to swallow. He was afraid to pour water into her mouth even though it was open. Her arms were hanging at her sides, completely limp and her head was lying on her shoulder. Frank couldn't tell how long she had been here.

Frank laid her back on the ground. He got his pick-up truck and drove it as close as possible and lifted her to the front seat. He didn't realize how thin she was. She couldn't have even weighed ninety pounds. He thought she would probably die soon.

Once she was in the seat, Frank locked the passenger door and leaned her in the corner against it and headed for the nearest hospital—St. Francis Hospital in Mountain View. Highway ninety-nine and sixty were both paved roads now, so he made really good time. Every time he looked at her he was afraid that she had stopped breathing.

At St. Francis, he pulled to the emergency room at the back and began to frantically blow his horn. A man and a woman in white uniforms came running out. They quickly placed her on a gurney and rolled her inside. They stripped her and checked all her vital signs. From what they could determine, she was just weak and terribly dehydrated. They started an I.V. to give her some fluids. They began bathing her and removing ticks. She was covered with them. Many were already stretched to their limit and ready to fall off. It was two hours before Ivy opened her eyes and looked around. She was all dressed in a clean bathrobe and lying in a beautiful, clean bed. Frank was sitting in a chair on one side and a nurse was on the other. She looked at the nurse first and asked, "Am I in heaven?"

"No, you're at St. Francis," the nurse answered.

"Don't he help run heaven?" Ivy asked.

Frank stood and walked around to where Ivy could see him. As soon as Ivy saw him she asked, "Are you here, too?"

Frank began to explain to her how he found her and brought her to the hospital. Ivy began to understand. "Where is Feisty Britches?" she asked, looking on the floor around the room.

"He's out in the pick-up," Frank answered.

"Go bring him in," Ivy said. "He don't know where he is, either."

"Dogs ain't allowed in the hospital," the nurse told her.

"I want my best friend here with me. If you don't bring him in, I'll go to him," she said as she draped one leg through the bed rail and started to get up.

The nurse quickly grabbed her and eased her back down on her pillow. "Feisty Britches will stay with me until you are feeling better," Frank offered.

That didn't do much good, either. "I want my dog," Ivy said with all the strength she could muster.

"I'll bring him to your window so you can see him," Frank offered as he left the room.

When he held him up at the window, Ivy could hardly see well enough to recognize him but Feisty recognized her and began barking and pawing at the window.

Ivy began feeling under the cover and in her gown, like she was desperately searching for something.

"What are you looking for?" the nurse asked.

"I'll show you when I find it. Unless you want your next meal in hell, you better bring my dog to me."

The nurse, showing great concern, motioned for Frank to bring the dog in. The minute Feisty Britches smelled Ivy, he jumped on her bed and began licking her in the face and twisting excitedly. As soon as he was satisfied that she was all right, he jumped down and started marking the room as his territory.

The nurse rushed out the door, motioning Frank to follow. Outside, she frantically said, "Get the dog out. If one of the sisters sees this, I'll lose my job." She was wringing her hands, pulling her hair, and pacing back and forth asking Frank to do something.

Frank calmly went back into Ivy's room and tried to explain to her that this was no place for dogs. "If he ain't welcome, I won't stay either," Ivy said.

"You must stay a few days while you get to feeling better."

"Can they make me feel better?" Ivy asked.

"Sure can. You couldn't even move when I brought you in, and look at you already."

"Bring Feisty Britches here," she said, rising up in her bed. At her bed, she kissed him and told him to be good and stay with Frank and she would see him in a few days.

Frank turned and carried the dog back to his pickup and soon left for home.

Ivy pulled the I.V. from her arm and climbed out of bed. She was going down the hall when a nurse ran to catch up with her. "Where are you going?" she asked.

"I'm going outside to relieve myself," Ivy answered. "How long have I been here? It feels like wintertime. And how come I feel a breeze behind?"

"Oh, you can't go outside."

"I said, I have to relieve myself," Ivy responded.

"We do that inside," the nurse said, taking hold of her arm and trying to turn her back to her room.

"Whoever heard of crapping in your house when you can go outside? Do you have a slopjar? It is a little cool behind me."

"I guess you could call it that," the nurse said, guiding Ivy into the bathroom.

Ivy sat down on the stool and did several days' business. The nurse held her nose as she handed Ivy the tissue and told her to clean her bottom. She felt so much better now that she was clean both inside and out. The nurse helped her stand up, but really scared Ivy when she flushed the stool. Ivy almost jumped forward when she heard the noise and saw the water washing her deposit away. "Do that again," she said to the nurse.

The nurse showed her how to push the lever down and how the water rushed in. "Where's the spring?" Ivy asked. "I could sure use a good drink of cool water."

Ivy's stay in the hospital was certainly an experience for both her and the nurses. The social worker had a hard time filling out all the paperwork, getting her social security and her Medicare cards.

Ivy didn't like the food. She surely didn't like the gown and she slipped outside every chance she got. Nothing pleased her. It was too much of a change. She just wanted to go home.

The social worker made a trip to Thomasville and finally located her home. It only took one look for her to determine that she could not live in that old house. She went to the county court and had herself appointed Ivy's legal guardian. The first thing that she did was sell the farm and the second was to place Ivy in the nursing home at Birch Tree.

Ivy had been in the nursing home two days when she saw her first television. One of the attendants explained it to her and showed her how to operate it. She was watching it one day when an old man ambled over to the couch where she was sitting and plopped down beside her.

"I heard you were here, but someone had to point you out to me. I didn't recognize you. Even with my new glasses, I didn't."

"Who are you?" Ivy asked.

"Lord, I've slept with you many times," was his reply.

Ivy still didn't know. She leaned over and squinted her eyes. "Are you Dr. Davies?" she asked.

"Sure am," he answered, throwing his arms around her. Ivy grabbed him with both arms, hugging and kissing until they were both exhausted. They couldn't get enough of each other.

Everyone in the area was watching them in disgust. One of the attendants went to the charge nurse and asked, "How old are you when you quit having orgasms?"

The nurse jumped back, red faced, and began stammering. "Why do you ask such a question?"

"I think there are two on the couch in the lounge having one," he stated.

The charge nurse showed why she was called "Charge" as she sped forward to see what he was talking about. Sure enough, she would have to agree. She didn't know what to do. Ivy, Doc and everyone in the room seemed to be enjoying themselves.

Finally the nurse shook them and said, "You'll have to go to your rooms now."

As they started feebly down the hall, arm in arm, leaning on each other she heard Ivy say, "Your room or mine?"

∽ TWENTY-THREE ∽

The next day, Frank came to see Ivy to tell her about the farm. As soon as the word was out that Ivy was in a nursing home, people descended on her house with hammers, crow bars, chain saws, and even a bulldozer.

They took the house apart board by board and even stone by stone. Both fireplaces were torn down and the place was leveled. They were sure that they would find pots of gold, but if any was found, it was never disclosed.

After the demolition crew gave up, men with their metal detectors moved in. They also left empty-handed as far any anyone knew.

"Do you have any money hidden there?" Frank asked. "I heard that the government wants to return the farm to the national forest. They made a offer to buy."

Ivy grinned from ear to ear as she said, "I think that would be the thing to do. No one found it, eh? I knew I picked a good spot. I'll tell you what I'll do. I'll give you a hint if you'll use some of it to fix up the spring so people can get a drink there again. It fell apart before I left."

"I'll do it," Frank answered.

"Here's your hint. I returned the gold to where it was first discovered. Now go find it."

Frank left but in a few days, he returned, begging Ivy to give him another hint.

"No more hints," she said, "I hope it stays there until after I'm gone."

They were interrupted by a knock on the door.

"You'll have to excuse me," Ivy said as she headed for the door. "That's my dinner date," she told Frank as she walked by his chair. She opened the door with open arms. Doc entered and gave her a big squeeze and numerous mushy kisses on the face.

Ivy finally pulled back and introduced Frank and said, "We'll see you later unless you want to dine with us. It usually ain't very good," she added.

"I think I'll pass this time and get on home. Are you sure you don't want to give me another clue?" he asked.

"No," Ivy replied. "The first one should be enough. Come see us again," Ivy said.

In the dining room, everyone dined as far away from Ivy and Dr. Davies as possible. They couldn't stand the way they fed each other and cooed like a couple of love birds. The attendants just shook their heads with disgust and often commented that they had never seen anything like it.

"I really missed you last night," Ivy whispered into Doc's ear. "I wish we could be together all the time."

"All my other lady friends are dead and gone," Doc answered. "I don't suppose you would like to marry me, would you?"

Ivy straightened up and leaned back in her chair. "Would you mind repeating that for me? I'm not sure I heard you," Ivy said.

"I said, would you marry me?" This time, he said it loud enough for some of the others to hear. Those who heard began laughing and repeated what they heard to others. Soon, the entire room was snickering and making snide remarks.

"That is the first time any man ever asked me to marry him and the answer is Yes, Yes, Yes. When?"

"You set the date and make the plans. Whatever makes you happy."

Ivy pushed back from the table and stood up. She picked up her spoon and banged on her glass until she had everyone's attention. "I have something to say," she announced among the snickering. "Doc and I are going to get married and all of you are invited."

"When?" someone asked. "You better not wait too long," another said.

"I don't know yet," Ivy answered, "but you'll receive a formal invitation. We'll have a big cake and punch with something in it and the wedding will be followed by a dance. Wear your best and don't forget to bring presents," she said as she sat down. Getting up again she said, "I need to see the social worker soon. Are you here Miss Bennett?" Ivy yelled as loudly as she could.

Miss Bennett immediately came to Ivy's table and asked, "How may I help you, Your Highness?"

"Sit down and shut up," Ivy commanded. "Do you have a pencil and paper? I'm sure you couldn't remember all that I'm going to tell you."

Miss Bennett took a pad of paper from her pocket and a pen from the string around her neck and deposited them on the table in front of her.

"Tomorrow morning, I want you to drive me to Spring Creek. I need to make a withdrawal."

Miss Bennett said, "O.K., what's next?"

"When is the preacher here?"

"We can get you one any time you wish."

"Good," Ivy said. "We will need invitations. We need to get a big cake, punch with a kick, and favors for all who attend. I want the most beautiful bunch of flowers possible, and I want a new, white wedding gown. I don't want one of them rented ones that someone has already dribbled in. Have you got all that?" Ivy asked.

"I got it all," Miss Bennett answered. "What time do you want to go to Spring Creek?"

"Early," Ivy answered. "I'd like to see the sun rising over Spring Creek one more time. Maybe we can stop along the way and pick some wild flowers to put on the graves. I'm sure Buck, Clay, and Momma Lucy would like that. I'll also tell them about the wedding."

The next morning, before daylight, Miss Bennett knocked
on Ivy's door and found her up and ready to go. Before they
reached Spring Creek, Ivy instructed Miss Bennett to stop the
car. When the car was stopped, Ivy said, "Give me your hand."
Miss Bennett gave Ivy her hand as she pulled a piece of rope
from her pocket and tied it around her wrist and tied the other
one to the steering wheel. "You stay here," Ivy said as she
opened her door and slid out. "If you try to get away, I'll know
it. I'll be back in a few minutes," she said through the open
door. She then added, "Oh shit, we forgot to pick the flowers.
I'll tell them you forgot."

Ivy stopped first by the graves but only said, hello and
briefly told them about her coming wedding. "I'll stay longer
next time and bring you some flowers," she promised.

She then went to the big oak tree where Frank said he found
her and found her pistol. She picked it up and tried to wipe
some of the dirt off but decided she would need some soap and
water to get it all off. She stuck it in her pocket and went down
to the creek. She didn't take her shoes off afraid she wouldn't be
able to walk barefoot on the rocks anymore. She didn't lift her
dress either, she just waded out into the cold water. She looked
around as if she could see everything, then just stood listening.
All she could hear was the babbling of the stream cascading
over rocks. She finally found her turtle rock with her foot.
Stooping over she raised one side and felt under it. The gold
was still there. When she raised the rock the sun hit the gold
and glistened in the morning sun. She picked up a handful and
lowered the rock carefully back in place. She wanted to know
how much was left but didn't want to take time to count it. She
lifted her dress in front to make a dry pocket into which she
deposited the gold. She didn't know how many gold pieces she
had until she walked out of the water and sat on a big rock to
count. In the bright sunlight she could see that she had nine
twenty dollar gold pieces. She stuck them in her pocket on the
opposite side of her pistol and headed back to the car.

Back at the car, she crawled in and looked at Miss Bennett,
checking to see that she hadn't moved. "It's a good thing you

didn't try to get loose," Ivy said as she untied her. Miss Bennett rubbed her wrist to restore circulation before she turned the key and started the car.

Ivy pulled the pistol from her pocket and stuck it out the window and began pulling the trigger.

The car lurched forward before Miss Bennett suddenly applied the brakes. She was visibly frightened.

"You scared the shit out of me. Where did you get that gun? Give it to me," she scolded.

Ivy turned and pointed it at her with her finger on the trigger. "Where do you want it?" Ivy asked, looking dead serious.

Miss Bennett was shaking so hard that the car was moving.

"Just teasing," Ivy said laughing, "I just wanted to see if it still works." She stuck it out the window and pulled the trigger two more times, making a loud noise that echoed up and down Spring Creek.

Ivy slipped the safety on and stuck the pistol back in her pocket while she leaned over to Miss Bennett and whispered, "No one gets my gun and don't forget it. This pistol has been with me many years and it never let me down."

After sitting for a while Miss Bennett got her wits together. She started the car and nervously headed back to the Birch Tree Nursing Home. Ivy announced that she wanted to stop at the bank before returning to her cell. When they pulled up in front of the bank, Ivy opened the door and slid out leaving a puddle of water on the floor where her shoes and dress had drained. She also left a wet trail on the sidewalk as she walked.

Inside the bank she walked up to the first person she saw and held out the gold coins and asked, "What will you give me for these?"

Everyone in the bank gathered around to see what she had in her hand. The young man she first saw quickly said, "Come into my office so we can talk," and lead the way through an open door. "May I see what you have?" He asked holding out his hand. Introducing himself as Keith Bowden, Vice President of the bank.

Ivy handed him all that she had in her pocket.

Keith walked behind his desk and deposited the gold in front of him and asked Ivy to have a seat. He checked the coins and wrote down the date of each, along with the mint mark and condition of the coin. He then reached behind him for a book high on a shelf. After a few moments and some calculating he asked, "Do you have any more of these?"

"I could have," Ivy replied.

"I can give you about eight hundred dollars for these." Keith said.

Ivy's eyes widened as she said, "Give it to me."

Keith counted out the money into her hand and told her he would buy all she had.

Money in hand, Ivy headed for the car where Miss Bennett was anxiously waiting. When she got back in the car she turned to look back at the bank where everyone stood in the windows looking at her. She quickly pulled the pistol from her pocket and fanned it across the window. All faces went down like a row of dominoes.

"Now let's go by the barber shop so I can see if Bill can get a band together to play for a dance after the wedding." When Ivy emerged from the shop it was obvious what Bill had said. Ivy was smiling from ear to ear. "Doc told me Bill plays real good." Ivy said.

"Let's hurry back to the home. I can't wait to tell Doc what is going on."

"What a day!" Ivy yelled followed by, "Oh Hell! I forgot to order my dress. We'll do it tomorrow. What day do you think would be good one for the wedding. I won't want you giving any of the patients any of them quiet pills the day of the wedding."

Ivy pulled the money from her pocket and handed all but two hundred to Miss Bennett as they went through the front door. "I want you to spend it all on the wedding and if you do a good job I'll have some extra for you."

Miss Bennett couldn't believe the amount of money that Ivy handed her. Neither could she believe how alert she had become and the energy that Ivy was showing. It was as if she had found the fountain of youth.

Ivy leaned over to Miss Bennett and whispered while patting her pocket, "If you tell anyone about my friend, I'll do you in, understand? Now when did you say we could have the wedding?"

"I'll have to find out and let you know." Miss Bennett answered.

"Make it soon," Ivy replied. "I don't want to get an itchy finger."

Miss Bennett got things rolling. She contacted the baker and arranged for a cake to feed one hundred people. The wedding was to be two weeks from that Saturday. The cake, Bill's band, and the wedding dress were all taken care of.

The nursing home would convert the lobby into the area for the wedding, reception, and the dance. Even a bandstand was constructed in one corner. The home had agreed to give the largest bedroom with one queen-size bed, to Ivy and Doc.

The wedding was all you could hear. Everyone received a formal invitation and even the local papers were caught up in the excitement. All the ladies were talking about what they were going to wear and who they were going to sit by. Several of them discarded their wheelchairs, saying they would never be seen at a wedding in one. Some even discarded their canes.

Each day Ivy checked with Miss Bennett to make sure that everything was being taken care of.

When Miss Bennett asked what kind of punch Ivy wanted, she hung her head for a minute before replying. Finally Ivy said, "Get one of them old thirty gallon crock jars, fill it with apple cider to within about six inches of the top and finish filling it with vodka. It is real smooth and everyone will like it."

"Oh no Ivy, we can't have liquor in the nursing home." Miss Bennett said.

"Vodka ain't liquor or didn't you know? I also want you to go to the drug store and buy all the aphrodisiac they have and dump it in the crock. Don't forget who is paying the bill. And for goodness' sake don't make me get an itchy finger," Ivy said in no uncertain terms.

Ivy turned and walked down the hall mumbling to herself. "I can't wait to see some of them prissy old ladies lose control."

Everyone turned to look at Ivy when they heard her laughing to herself.

When Saturday finally arrived, everything was ready. The lobby was decorated with ferns and beautiful flowers. The seats and the bandstand were ready. The wedding ceremony was supposed to take place at six P.M., but by four-thirty they were all hurrying to get choice seats. No one showed up for the evening meal in the nursing home. They were all too excited. They were saving for punch and cake. Some of the old ladies still had their own wedding dress that they wore. Some had new dresses and hats. They all had on the best they owned.

When six o'clock came they were all in place. Bill played the wedding march on the mandolin. Tears were streaming down lots of cheeks. It was really beautiful.

The smallest old lady in the nursing home came sauntering down the hall with her basket of rose petals bowing first to one side then the other. By the time she reached the front of the room she had to wipe her eyes and give her nose a healthy blow.

Ivy and Dr. Davies came slowly down the hall acknowledging everyone with a slight bow and a kind word. "So glad you could come," Ivy was saying as she beamed.

The wedding ceremony was very short. The kiss, after the preacher said, "You may kiss the bride," lasted longer than the entire ceremony. Everyone applauded loudly for a very long time.

When the kiss finally ended, Ivy announced, "I finally got me one and he is a keeper. Now everyone line up for cake and punch. There is plenty, so don't be shy."

As they filed by, the guests wished Ivy and Doc well and left presents. Ivy served the cake while Doc poured the punch.

As soon as everyone was served and told to help themselves to seconds, the band began to play. They started with a waltz, then moved on to some more lively numbers. The band hadn't played long when the punch began to take effect.

People started to lose their interest in dancing. They wanted to sit on the couch with a drink and someone that they had never noticed before. It wasn't long before couples were heading down the hall with their arms around each other with ideas that they hadn't had for years. Some were kissing and some were being pinched and enjoying it.

Some people collapsed on the floor or on a couch in the lobby. Most of them had their arms around someone. It didn't seem to matter, as long as the body was warm.

The band stopped playing and carried their instruments out the door laughing hysterically.

Ivy and Dr. Davies didn't spend their wedding night in their queen-sized bed. They spent it in each other's arms, passed out on the floor in the lobby of the nursing home.

PYNES SERVICE STATION

"24 Hour Service"

LEESVILLE, LA. — 12-26-37

Mr. R. C. Paty Well old Boy has
Bin a Long time Sens I Wrought to
you. I am O. K. Work nights. and I
rust thought I Wold Say Hel. O. to see
if you ever thaught of Bob. as I think
Back. of you and I. Do. you Remember
when we ust to Role Rocks Down Hill
of Sundays. Say Clay. How's aunt
Luty. and How is frery. dont gess
I will Ever see any one of my folks
any moore. Clay Pleas tell one what
Pearls. adress is whire is george
in fact if you Dont mind and
till Pleas tell one whire is all of the folks
aunt Callie Living yet—
I wold Love to Set down
and talk to you for a Day.
yes a weak over

New **Goodrich** *Safety* **Silvertown** *with Life saver Golden Ply*

Clay tell Aunt Lucy Bob Still Loves
Her and if She is a Live I want you
to Please Hug her for me and Kiss one
for old Bob. tell I Very I Sed hel.o. to
Her Clay. if you Shuld Live to See
aunt Lucy Pass to the Grate Beyond
Peas Send one a Wire. if it Shold
Bee Phanged to me. You now She is
all the mother I have had for a
long time And. I Still Love Her
Bless Her old Hart.
wash you 3 - A Big new yere
ind asking you to Pleas ans this By
Return mail for I am still you
Cousin and Will all ways think
you near a Brother tan any one elce
to Bob. So good LucK with Love
R.B. Amonett Leesville, La,

A letter to Clay Paty from Ivy's son, Robert Amonette. Evidently he forgot that
Lucy died before he left and hadn't heard that Clay was dead.

⌒ Postscript ⌒

One cool June morning, many years after Ivy had passed away, I was sitting on my front porch, having my second cup of coffee, when I saw a continuous stream of vehicles going east toward Spring Creek, down the dusty rock road in front of my house. I ran into the house for my binoculars so I could get a better look at this motley array of vehicles. There were vehicles of every make and description with an abundance of Volkswagon buses painted every color of the rainbow.

A closer observation gave me goosebumps. I thought, *My God, Ivy's descendants are coming home.*

It was the Rainbows who were having a gathering on Ivy's old homestead. They came by the thousands as if they were drawn by a higher power.

I joined them almost every night as they gathered in a circle around a large fire where they listened to focalizers and partook of an evening meal brought to the circle from the many kitchens. After the evening meal, small roving bands played while the garbage was collected and properly disposed of.

Soon, hundreds of drums drowned out all other sounds. Their variety of size, all beat to the same heartbeat rhythm for miles up and down the fields bordering Spring Creek.

The dancing and celebration that followed was spontaneous. Everyone did their own dance and gave thanks in their own way. I could feel the spirit and hear it say, *Take care of what I have given you.* The large circle fire with sparks jumping toward a full moon overhead was a most impressive sight.